Studs Up!

Seven stories that are almost entirely nothing to do with football

David Lindsay

Rear Cover Photo: Seek A Geek Limited
Rear Cover Model: Samuel Mann

Studs Up!

www.facebook.com/davidlindsayauthor

ISBN-13: 978-1534726635 (CreateSpace-Assigned)

ISBN-10: 1534726632

Studs Up

Seven stories that are almost entirely nothing to do with football.

Manna From Hebden

'Football, eh? Bloody Hell.'

26th May 1999. Camp Nou, Barcelona. The first recorded words of Sir Alex Ferguson after Manchester United had won the Champions League, and therefore the Treble, by beating Bayern Munich with two injury time goals scored by two late substitutes.

Lorry drivers, eh? Bloody Hell.

This one – lorry too big for these small hillside roads – skidded, snaked and stuttered as it took the corner too quickly. It scraped the dry stone wall for what seemed like hours, and then toppled into one of Ollerington's fields, rolling three times before refusing a fourth and falling sullenly back to the soft earth. And then silence, like the birds had stopped singing, their breath drawn, wondering what might happen next. I looked across at Jethro, his mouth was wide open, the majority of a half-chewed Cornish pasty visible on his tongue. His real name isn't Jethro, mind. No; we call him that on account of the fact he's a big, gormless, useless bugger like the lad off the Clampetts. Everyone calls him that, even me – and I'm his dad. Not a bad centre-half, although mainly on account that he's too large to run around and he's very good at kicking tricky centre forwards.

We run a car repair garage at the bottom of the field, and we'd been having our lunch. I point this out because Jethro eating a pasty is no guarantee of the time of day. Or night, come to think of it. But that was why we were outside the workshop, and why we were able to run over to the lorry once it had stopped ploughing an extra trough through Ollerington's EU-subsidised potato crop. It's not every day you see an accident like that, no matter how hard you look, but you could have knocked me over with a featherweight boxer when we saw the driver clambering out of his cab, rubbing his head, but not a mark on him. Bloody Hell.

"You all right, son?" I shouted.

Now I'm not one to worry too much about where a man comes from. I'm not too keen on Southerners of course, all that Shandy drinking and not talking proper, but whether a person's black, white, yellow or red makes no difference to me. But this chap, well, I couldn't understand a bloody word. Sounded a bit like one of the Russians in the James Bond films, I suppose. Except he didn't speak English. Anyway, I'm beating around the applecart – me and Jethro pull him down from his cab and ask him if he's all right again. After he spouts a bit more nonsense-talk, this time with a bit of random pointing and gesticulating thrown in for good measure, we decide he's probably in shock and lead him back down to the workshop for a cup of strong tea. That'll fix him. Fixes anything, tea. He gets a bit excited again, but Jethro can be very persuasive when he snarls and shows his teeth.

"I'll give you some of that spray we use on the lads on Saturday if you like," I tell him. "Bloody brilliant that spray – fixes anything." He looks at me like I'm mad, but he hasn't seen the wonders I can do with a bit of spray and a magic sponge.

We get him back and sit him in the comfy chair. Five minutes later he's got a cup of hot, sweet tea in his hand and I've called Slim, the local plod. He's on the team as well – probably the fattest goalkeeper you'll ever see, but beggars can't have silk purses. Jethro's started calling the lorry driver 'Ivan', on account of his strange accent. Ivan's stopped his talking now and just seems to be sitting there, looking scared. Must be the shock setting in, or maybe he's thinking what his boss will say when he finds out he took a short cut. These things happen. I wouldn't like to negotiate with Ollerington for the release of his lorry though. Be easier to get Arsene Wenger to admit he saw a debatable incident.

"How's the diet going?" I shout as Slim gets out of his patrol car. He ignores the comment while Jethro smirks.

"So you've got the Russian Mafia here, have you?" he replies, all smug-like.

"I never said he were Mafia. And I don't know where he's from – just thought you should know there's a bloody big Artic somewhere it shouldn't be."

I nods up the hill and the policeman clocks the lorry for the first time. He won't be making detective anytime soon.

"Bloody Hell! Ollerington'll be having kittens when he sees that! Where's the driver? I'd better breath-test him."

I tell Slim he's in the back, sat in the comfy chair, drinking tea. "He'll be right enough there for a few minutes, and I can't smell any ale on him – I think he just lost it on the bend. Let's have a walk up to the lorry, see how much damage it's done to the Ollerington Potato Empire."

"Aye, all right," he says, looking doubtful. "We'll drive up to the top though – be easier."

Lazy sod. The three of us get into his car, brushing away several chocolate bar wrappers before we can sit down. "Energy," Slim points out to us. Energy to do what? Push in his clutch?

***

"Open it then."

"I'm not opening it," I say. "You said you heard noises – you open it."

Slim thought about it for a few moments. He must be the most cowardly policeman in Lancashire, that lad. And the fattest – 'Extra-Large was not enough' is what the lads
sing to him when they see him bulging out of his goalie shirt. We'd driven up to the top of the field and climbed down through the gap in the wall the lorry had made, walking round it several times, looking for markings: some clue as to where it came from or what it carried. Nothing.

After a few minutes, Jethro walks past us both and starts working on the locking mechanism. This isn't easy as the lorry is on its side, but he gets it open, and the stench of droppings hit us immediately.

"Pigs," I say, knowingly. Slim gives me a sideways look.

"Funny bloody pigs," says Jethro, peering into the darkness and holding a mucky rag to his nose, preferring a mix of Swarfega and Grade 20/40 to the overwhelming stench coming from inside.

"Blood and sand!" I gasp, as I peer into the gloom. "Better get the van up here, Jethro."

"Sod the van," says Slim. "Better get that bloody driver!" And he waddles off back to his car. I'd never seen him move like that before, and it took me a moment to realise he was running.

It was to be a day for unusual turn of events, all right.

***

It was early evening before we all got together in the clubhouse. Thrives on its football team, this town. Mingston United Football Club, North West Counties First Division – famous for taking Colchester United to a First Round FA Cup Replay and then being beaten nine-nil in the second game. That was when we were a Conference side; seems a long way off now as we struggle with relegation and crowds a quarter of what they were. Still, something happens and this is where we all gather, like a committee of village elders.

"We have to inform the police," says Gripper, the town's Plumber and the club captain.

"I am the police!" says Slim, looking hurt. You know, I'm sure that he was sweating, and I've never seen him do that. Not even in training.

"Yes, but the proper police."

I walk over to the window as a full-scale argument breaks out. Slim had always been a bit of a joke as far as police duties were concerned, but losing the lorry driver wasn't going to do him any favours with his sergeant. I suppose I felt a little guilty about that myself. It was me who told him he'd be all right left in the workshop, but how was I to know he was driving a container full of illegal immigrants? He was long gone by the time Slim had got back down, and no amount of searching had been able to find him. I look at the poor people sitting outside the clubhouse, enjoying the late August sun and some much needed fresh air, but clearly desperate and terrified, unsure what would happen to them next. They'd been cleaned, fed and given clothes to wear, but still they looked misplaced, haunted by horrors we could only guess at. We couldn't get a word of English out of them, not even where they'd come from. There were about thirty of them in all, every shape, size and age. Some of the older boys, kids in their late teens I guess, had started kicking a ball around, trying to get the little 'uns to join in. Traumatized they looked. Traumatized.

"We have to tell the authorities, let them take care of them," Gripper is saying, and my attention is drawn back into the room. "What can we do with them?"

"But the authorities will send them to a detention camp, or worse." This was Mavis talking now, bless her little heart. We'd been married thirty-two years and never a cross word. "We've plenty of room here. We've got houses that are boarded up and not used, and plenty of jobs on the farms – Olleridge has been crying out for labourers all year. Let 'em stay, just for a while, just 'til they sort themselves out." She wasn't winning them over. Slim was doing his best to back her up, but he had too much self-interest to be taken seriously. Gripper and the rest of them were having none of it.

The group were just about coming to an agreement to call Immigration when Robbie Moon (right-winger, fast little beggar, bit greedy) calls me back over to the window. "Look at that," he says, nodding appreciatively out towards the pitch.

Four of them refugees had taken the ball out to the centre-circle and were doing a good job of entertaining the youngsters with some quite remarkable ball juggling. From one to the other they kicked the ball; each performed a little routine then passed it on. Bloody good they were.

"Yeah, but that doesn't mean they can play football," says Robbie, who fancies himself a bit.

It was like they'd heard him. At that point, one of 'em sprints out to the wing – like Linford Christie, he was – two of the others run towards the goal. The man on the centre-spot has the ball, he flicks it up and lets it rest on the small of his back, flicks it again and fires a forty-yard pass out to the touchline, where his mate brings it down and is off in one swift movement. This fellah takes it on a few paces, then crosses it over to one of the other lads, who has positioned himself on the D, twenty-five yards from goal. I'd never seen anything like it: he swivels, and with his back to goal does this overhead-kick malarkey, connecting with the ball so sweetly that it shoots towards the top corner of the net for a certain goal.

Just as we were about to clap their efforts, the fourth fellah, who had been standing on the goal line, launches himself through the air, like a cat with a rocket up its backside he was, and just gets his fingertips to the ball, sending it the other side of the post. This all happened in seconds, and I can tell you, we were gobsmacked.

Gripper was the first to say anything. "Boss," he says to me. Everybody calls me that. "Isn't it the FA Cup qualifying round on Saturday?"

We all knew it was. We'd talked about nothing for weeks. If we could only have a half-decent cup run we might be able to get some more people in the ground, get some finances in, pay expenses to some players and then maybe get some better ones in to stay up. We all knew what Gripper was thinking too – it looked like Mingston United Football Club, MUFC for short, would be making a bold step into the International transfer market in the very near future.

**

I put the phone back in its cradle and stared for it for a while. It's peaceful in the office, and to be honest I just needed a minute to think. I mean, it's not every day a club like this plays in front of 4,000 people in the FA Cup First Round Proper. Outside is Bedlam. Bedlam. The fans, of course, with their singing and shouting and riotous behaviour, but there are photographers, television people with their make-up girls, boom operators and what-have-you and, worst of all, reporters. Most of those were a bit greasy and overweight, smelling of fags and booze – they remind me of Slackie, our left-back. One of them though – young lad, looks like that Harry Potter – he said he needs to speak to me urgently. Keen as ketchup he was, but I fired him off because I had to take a phone call from the Chairman of Burnley FC, giants of English football, and he wants to put in a transfer bid for our goalkeeper: a new set of nets and kit. I told him that it was a generous offer, but that I'd have to consult with the board, at which point he starts saying he could be tempted to part with some cash and I should have dinner with him at his golf club. Bloody Hell.

It's true what they say though: the calm before the avalanche. Anyway, I look up and there's three foreign looking blokes already in my office. Mustn't have noticed them come in with all the noise. One of them sits down, uninvited like, and says to me,

"We want those boys, and we want them now."

"Well, you'll have to take on the mighty Burnley." At this point, I'm not sure what's going on anymore. I needed some time to think and worry.

I'm not good at worrying, me, and especially not when it comes to those boys. They've made the town feel good about itself again. And not just because of the football, although the stuff they've been playing has been unbelievable – played twelve and won twelve since they signed up, we're halfway up the league and appearing on the telly in the FA Cup. But it's the families as well. Settled into the community from day one – kids are in school, adults working like Trojans. Olleridge is even trying to see if there are any extra EU grants he can put his hands on.

"If you do not co-operate I will ensure that you are tortured within an inch of your life. I will imprison your wife for the rest of her life, and I will set fire to your home while the rest of your family are sleeping."

"Bloody Hell! I'd heard football agents were getting tough these days, but this is ridiculous," I say. "I take it you're from Chelsea then?"

Three things happened all at once. The foreign chappies all produce a gun, three more blokes walk into the office, all of them carrying guns, and I begin to realize that they're probably not football agents.

One of the new blokes takes a seat, again uninvited, and just stares this other bloke in the eye. Eventually he says,

"We have a missing cargo and, incidentally, a missing tractor and trailer too. Our buyer is not very happy, and we are outstanding a large sum of money. We request the return of those items, and in return we may allow you to carry on living." His eyes never leave the bloke across from him; both of them have guns pointed at each other. His accent was just like the lorry drivers – Russian, Polish, Serbian and Montenegrin? I don't know.

Bloody Hell.

I can tell you, I was a bit worried.

The door opens again, and this time it's Jethro, eating his pre-match banana; or one of them. I'm just about to warn him away, but he walks into the office, followed by the rest of the team, all in their kit – kick off is in 15 minutes. Last one in is Gripper, the captain, and he's got the young reporter lad with him, Harry Potter.

Now this isn't a scene you see very often. I've got six foreign blokes in my tiny office, all of them pointing guns at each other like in that film, Reservoir Frogs, and lined up around the walls are thirteen Mingston United footballers, all togged up in red and white, knobbly knees and all.

No-one says anything for a minute. 'Come on you Mingers' and 'M-U-M-U-F-M-U-F-C-OK' drifts down from the terraces. Eyes are darting all around, seeing who will make the first move. Eventually Gripper coughs and speaks.

"They've gone," he says, and it took me a minute to realize the refugee boys weren't there. "They've all gone, the boys, the children the wives and the grandparents. Ollerington says you can have your lorry back though – minus a few parts he's used for his harvester."

Gripper edges closer into the room – no mean feat as the office resembles a tube train at rush hour. "This is Jay Schaffer," he says, nodding at Harry Potter. "He's a researcher for Amnesty International, and he recognised our boys as soon as he saw them." Looking scared half to death, Potter takes up the story.

"Four months ago Iran reached the Olympic Football Finals. Despite them basically being a youth team, their football was dazzling. The whole country was galvanised behind them, the streets filling with all-night celebrations following win after win. The government took all the credit, of course, and that's why they reacted so badly when they lost the final. Not just because they lost on penalties, but because they lost to Israel.

"When the team returned home they were arrested, and their families were abused, tortured. We think some of them are still in prison there, and we know some of them are dead. Then we heard a rumour that there'd been an escape, that four of the players had got away. I turned up to the match today just to watch, but when I saw them warming up I thought I'd better warn someone. You see if they go with the Russian Mafia over there, then they'll be sold into a life of crime and slavery, but if they go back to Iran with that lot, well … they'll be executed."

Potter edges back towards the door, as the foreign blokes' eyes bore into him.

"Now," says Gripper. "There's two things can happen. You lot can shoot some people and draw loads of attention – there's about a hundred and fifty coppers up there, by the way – or we can call it a draw and all walk away. Either way, the refugees have gone."

This time the length of the silence is unbearable. Everyone is just waiting for a gun to go off. Then the main Russian, cool as you like, puts his back in his pocket and smiles. Smiles, I tell you. "We'll find them," he says and they get up to go. The Iranian bloke does exactly the same, and they all file out past the players.

"Well come on then!" I shout, flabbergasted. "We've got a game to win, 'aven't we? And I don't want any fines for late kick-offs."

We didn't win, of course. Not without those boys. Although I thought 8-0 was a bit unfair, and I'm convinced that their fifth was offside. We didn't get much money out of it either. Jethro and Gripper had re-appropriated any cash we'd collected at the turnstiles to the refugees, and we had to buy a new team coach because they gave them that as well.

I was a bit down-hearted for a while after that, thinking of those boys. I mean, we didn't know if they'd got away, or what sort of life they'd be leading if they did. They deserved more. Then, about six months later, I got a post card from Paris. "Who do I know in Paris, Mavis?" She were no help, of course. The only thing it said on it was 'Sunday, Channel 5, 8.00pm ... thanks, Boss.'

"Mavis, what's Channel 5?" Again, no bloody help at all.

I found it in the end. Sat down with a stout and me feet up, and on comes the French Cup Final. Not a bad match either, Paris St German against Lille. Quite enjoyed it, but then a funny thing happened near the end. One of the Lille blokes, on the D, twenty-five yards from goal, swivels and, with his back to goal, does this overhead-kick malarkey, smacking the ball so sweetly that it shot into the top corner. I've seen that somewhere before, I thought. The bloke runs to the fans to celebrate his goal, and I know it's him, one of them refugees. He'd had some of that plasticine surgery, but it was him all right – he always used to do that same goal celebration for us, dancing with a corner flag.

Football, eh? Bloody Hell.

Sixty Thousand Muppets

"I'm not really sure you should be doing that."

"I'm sorry?"

"I said, 'I'm not really sure you should be doing that'."

"Oh." Dean considered her for a moment. She was tall, pretty and, unlike himself, sober. A small, angry dog yapped at her feet, straining against a short lead. How odd. Still: *I'm not really sure you should be doing that.*

"Do you know," he said eventually, "people have said that to me all of my life."

"And anyway you're doing it wrong."

He stopped what he was doing.

"That's amazing. That's the other thing people have said to me all my life. Almost all of them women as well, of course."

"It's just that, that's a mortice lock, and if you're going to get it to open you'll ideally need a thin metal pick and a small sprung metal tension wrench."

Dean looked at the piece of plastic between his fingers, then back at this woman. She was his age: late twenties or thereabouts. Like him, she wore an impressive array of designer labels. Unlike him, hers were not copies.

"How come you're such an expert on breaking and entering?"

"I read a lot," she said.

"I think I've killed this credit card now anyway," he mused.

"I've said that a few times in my life too."

Dean smiled a disconsolate, worn out smile. He appreciated her attempt at humour – but he'd failed to pick the lock, so he wasn't going to get in.

His alcohol fuelled plan had failed. He sat down on a small wall and fumed.

"Why were you trying to break into Roddi Rodregues' house anyway," she said. The dog, although still straining to bite him, had stopped yapping and was now merely growling in Dean's direction.

"How do you know whose house it is?"

"I live around here – everybody knows where the footballers live," she said, rather defensively he thought. "Anyway, it was me asking the questions."

Dean sighed. It was one of those rare moments when he wished he smoked, just so lighting up would give him time to think of a good story. In the end he realized he was probably too drunk to think up even a bad story.

"Do you like football?" he asked her.

The question seemed insulting to her.

"I have no opinion on the matter one way or another!" she said in an off-hand, Radio 4 kind of way.

"I like football," he continued, unperturbed. He was half-dreaming now. "I love football. I'm sorry – I know there are other things in life, but I just love it all. I love the pre-match build-up with my friends, the drinking, the banter, the songs. I love all of it. But most of all, I love the football."

"Good. We've established that you love football. Now, how does this tie in with you trying to break into one of my neighbour's house, exactly?"

"I was a footballer, you know?" He obviously wasn't going to be rushed. "At fifteen I was on schoolboy forms with United. I was good too – tipped to be the next big thing. It was all I lived for." He drifted off into his own memories.

"And?" She said, with all the patience of Jeremy Paxman. The dog raised the volume of its growl.

"Oh. I got a cruciate ligament injury. And this was before cruciate ligament injuries were fashionable."

He paused again. The dog barked angrily and he took this as a cue to continue.

"They couldn't fix it, not properly. I never played again. When I left school I took all my coaching badges – it took me ages because they kept failing me. I don't think they wanted someone so young with official coaching credentials, but I kept going and I got them. It didn't do me any good – unless you were a thirty-five year old ex-pro you just couldn't get a paying job. I gave up on the dream.

"For two years after that I couldn't even look at a football. I'd walk out of friends' houses if they had the match on. I hated it – I had nothing else you see.

"Then one day I was at a friend's birthday party – some pub in town. There was a match on the telly. Little by little I was drawn in. The skill, the passion, the excitement of it all came rushing back to me again – I couldn't take my eyes off the game."

He looked up, somewhat surprised to see she was still there.

"Alaves beat Barca, 3-2," he added, as if this was somehow important.

"Get on with the story, or my dog will bite you."

Dean looked down at the growling ball of white fluff and carried on. He was taking the threat seriously.

"So, for the last nine years I've followed United home and away. If we played in Southampton or Newcastle, it didn't matter. Northampton in the cup? No problem, I was there. Into Europe? Of course. World Club Championships in Tokyo and Brazil? There too. We've had some great times – ups and downs, obviously, but it's been like a rollercoaster ride from one game to the next.

"Until this season. This season we're playing like a bunch of women – no offence. Don't get me wrong, I know we don't have any divine right to be successful, and I accept that. It's just the way it's happening. It's the players: they seem to have no fight in them, no passion. They don't seem to care anymore. It could have been me out there, you know? And if it was I'd run myself into the ground for the club; blood, sweat and tears - every pass, every tackle, every shot."

"Very nice speech. Now, I'm just calling the police – would you just hang on there a minute, please?"

"So today we play Blackburn at Ewood. Should be a guaranteed three points, and we go one-nil up after ten minutes: Mick O'Shea, beauty!" He smiled momentarily. "Then it all went wrong. I don't mind so much the 3-1 defeat, it's just the attitude of the players. And the worst one? That Roberto Fernandes Anselmo Rodrigues: supposedly Portuguese Footballer of the Year, takes more dives than a seagull, rolls around on the floor like he's been shot, whinges, complains, sulks and eventually asks to get substituted with ten minutes to go."

"Isn't that what all footballers do?" She asked, pulling a mobile phone from her pocket.

"Yes, but they don't miss a penalty and three open goals on top of it. Not every week anyway. So after the match I'm too upset to go drinking with any of my friends."

"You have friends?"

"So I find this quiet, expensive bar on the Locks. After about an hour or two of disconsolate binging I hear all this laughing and shouting. I look up and there's Roddi Rodrigues and some overly-attractive blonde bint, sharing a joke with the owner as they get shown to their private booth. So I watch this for a while, and you know what? He's having a good time. There I am, somewhere in the pits of depression, there he is, like he doesn't have a care in the world, having just played like a complete tosser, and he's having a good time. I ask you! Well, I marched right up to him and I told him."

"What did you tell him?" She'd un-flipped the mobile phone, but hadn't yet dialled.

"I said to him, I said: 'Roddi, you were a disgrace today. I can play a bit, and you know what, anything you can do, I can do.'"

"So what did he say?"

"Oh he was very cool. He just said 'I'm sure you can,' and then carried on talking to his groupie. I went back to my bar stool and my depression, but after a while anger got the better of me and I went back up to him. 'Listen,' I said. "You're not so good. I can do anything that you can do.'

Again, dead cool, he just says, 'I believe you. I'm sure you're every bit as good as me.' Well, that just wound me up, so I told him again. 'No, you don't understand. I'm good. Anything you can do, I can do."

"I'm going to unleash Adolf here if you don't get to the point."

"Do know what he did then? He took out a roll of hundred pound notes, probably enough to pay off my mortgage. He licked his thumb and stripped off four of them. He looks me in the eye and says 'Can you do this?' Then he burns the notes on the candle in front of him and chucks them in his ice bucket."

She laughed despite herself. "Actually that's quite funny. What did you say?"

"What could I say? I just said, 'No, I can't.' Rodrigues just looks at me, like I'm some sort of Muppet and says, 'Well fuck off then.'"

The girl is laughing now. The dog has stopped snarling and is giving her a confused look.

"So then what happens?" she manages to say between giggles.

"I had this strange sense that I was flying, and then cool air rushed all around me. It was only when I hit the floor outside that I realised that I'd been thrown out by his bloody minder." Dean subconsciously rubbed his elbow, which had caught most of the fall.

She flipped shut the mobile phone and returned it to her jeans pocket.

"So," she decided to continue the story herself. "You came round here, to his house, to what? Burgle him? Beat him up? Burn a fiver? What?"

"None of those. My mate always records the game from the Norwegian channel, so that I can watch it all again. So I got a taxi round to his house and picked up the disk. My plan was to be waiting for Rodrigues when he came home, and make him watch though all his stupid mistakes whilst I told him what the fans, who pay his wages remember, really think of him."

"Brilliant!" she lied, in between belly-laughs. "And once you'd used your credit card against that big metal gate in broad twilight, how were you going to get through the state of the art security system, past the CCTV, and overpower a 180lb athlete to make him watch the game with you?"

"I haven't really thought this through, have I?" The day was going from bad to worse and back again.

"I won't call the police," she said, wiping a tear from her eye and trying to stop herself laughing again. "But get yourself home before someone else does. They call MI6 around here if they see a car more than two years old."

He looked up at her again, feeling like a foolish child. "Thanks," he said. He stood up from the wall and brushed his jeans where he imagined dust might be, but even the walls in Hale Barns are clean. "It's not right though, you know? I mean, I know you won't understand it, but thousands of people put their money and their whole lives into supporting that team. Grown men will have gone home in tears tonight, they'll be devastated. Some of them won't be able to speak to anyone for days, they'll spend tomorrow dreading going into work because of what their friends will say about their team. And there's Rodrigues, £100,000 a week and he couldn't care less. He's not just cheating the fans – our manager has done more for our club than anyone in its whole history: he's cheating him as well. It's just not right. Nice to meet you. I'll get out of your way."

He started to go. "Wait," she said. "You actually care about the manager as well?"

"Of course. He's a legend. He deserves better. We all do."

"And you think telling this Rodrigues what you think will make a difference?"

"It was a stupid plan. I'd have just got into trouble. Again."

"But if there was a way. Would you do it?"

This surprised him. "Er, yes." He offered, eventually.

"Okay. There's a café on the High Street, Marvin's. Meet me there at three o'clock tomorrow, and bring some masks."

"Masks?"

"Of course: Masks. If we're going to break into a famous footballer's home we'll need a disguise. See you then."

She turned and walked briskly away. The dog let out one last warning yelp then followed. Dean just stood there, a look of dazed bewilderment on his face.

"Oh yes – you: Raffles!" She'd stopped about twenty yards away. "All this football, you don't have a girlfriend, do you." It was a statement, not a question.

"Not one I can keep," he shrugged.

"Thought not. See you tomorrow."

**

He ordered a cappuccino and wondered why he'd bothered going. His recollection of the previous evening was sketchy to say the least, but he did remember that she was better looking than any other girl he'd met for a coffee at three o'clock on a Sunday afternoon before. He'd never had a problem getting a girlfriend, but they didn't generally ask him out. If that's what she'd done – he couldn't be too sure. He'd gone home after she'd left and fallen asleep in front of Match of the Day. He'd woken up at 3.00am, still clothed and in his chair. And after spilling the can of lager that was still in his hands, he'd stumbled into bed, desperate to sleep off his impending hangover.

It hadn't worked.

So here he was, in Marvin's Café, at the correct time, with two masks, and not at all sure that that was what she'd said. He rubbed his eyes and sipped some chocolate froth.

"Didn't you order for me?" She had turned up. Better still, she was as attractive as his shattered memory had suggested. She looked at his Asda shopping bag, sat clumsily next to the table, and put down her John Lewis equivalent next to it.

"Oh, err … what can I get you?"

"Mmm. You look a little more with it than last night, although not much. I'll have a double espresso, thank you."

He got the drink while she settled into her bistro style surroundings.
"I'm sorry, I was very drunk. I wouldn't normally have tried to break into Roddi Rodrigues' house."

She eyed him purposefully. He felt as if he was naked.

"Shame," she said. "Because I thought that was exactly what we should do today."

"Look, you'll have to excuse me." He placed his fingers on his temples and closed his eyes. "I'm still a little worse for wear, and I could have sworn you just said that we should break into Roddi Rodrigues's house."

"Yes, I did."

"In spite of what you said last night?"

"Yes."

"Despite my infantile planning."

"Yes, despite that."

"I see. How does that work then?"

"It's simple really." She threw the espresso down her throat in one gulp and eyed the waiter for another. "I can open the lock to his gate – don't ask how, it's not important. I have the code to his entry system, which will also disable the alarm, I've brought some duct tape to tie him up, and a copy of last night's Match of the Day to show him how unacceptable his performance was to you."

The espresso arrived.

"How do we overpower him?"

"Oh, apparently it's well known that he's a big girls blouse – he'll do as you say. Now, I've been thinking: it's not enough just to show him the error of his ways. It won't change anything. We'll have to torture him too."

Dean shifted uneasily, then smiled and looked round for a hidden camera.

"Listen, I'm serious," she continued. "I'm not talking about physical harm. Well not as such. But," she reached into her shopping bag and produced a large Monkfish, "I was thinking of slapping him around the head with this. Apparently he has a bit of a fish phobia."

She smiled and plonked the fish onto the table. The waiter raised an eyebrow, but said nothing.

"I see," said Dean. "And, incidentally, are you just visiting this planet, or do you intend to make it your home?"

"Every time he makes a mistake during the game, you slap him with the fish. It's like training a dog. In his next game he'll start associating making mistakes with being slapped by a fish, and try harder. I told you - simple. Now, did you bring the masks?"

"Come on – where's the camera?" Dean smiled and looked round, a telling expression on his face.

"It's completely up to you, of course. I'm just trying to help."
"You're serious aren't you?" said Dean. She smiled her response. She was serious.

"Hang on a second, how come you know his entry code and how come you know about his aversion to fish? He's from Portugal – they eat sardines for breakfast over there."

"Not Rodrigues. See." She produced a book from her shopping bag. "Page 182 of the United yearbook: 'Don't invite Roddi out for a fish supper – he hates anything that comes from the sea and would even run a mile from Nemo!' As for the entry code, I have a friend who works at the ground. I called her, she got it. Shall we go?"

"I still think this is a wind-up, but yeah, why not? We're about to get thrown out of here anyway. Bring your friend."

She popped the fish back into her bag, bolted her coffee and sauntered to the door. It was unusually sunny for summer in northern England, and Dean took off his jacket, resting it over his arm. They started the short walk to Rodrigues' house at a leisurely, almost lethargic pace.

"What's your name?" he said.

"Call me Chill."

"Okay." They walked a little further before he added, "Why?"

"Because I'm trying to establish it as my new nickname. I'm not sure whether I want it to be short for Chilled or Chilli. Maybe both."

"I see. I think. My name's Dean."

"That's a very good name. Definitely. At least for a member of the clergy, or a small forest. I bet your friends call you Deano, don't they?"

"I refuse to answer that. Anyway, how come, and assuming this is not a wind-up of course, but how come you're helping me do this?"

"I was bored. It seemed like a good idea. Something to liven up a Sunday afternoon in Hale Barns. Otherwise it would just be bedding plants and tea at the vicar's."

"We're going to get caught though, aren't we?"

"I would think so, yes. Ah! Here we are. Hold this, please." She passed him the shopping bag and took two slim metal objects out of her pocket. She was through the gate in thirty seconds.

"Twenty-five minutes I was trying to get in there last night."

"It was more like ten. I was watching you."

"You were watching me?!"

"Yes. That's how I knew you were harmless. Now, pass me a mask. You did bring the masks, didn't you?"

"Er, yes. I did get some."

"Well what are you waiting for?"

"It's just that, well, I didn't actually think you'd turn up, and I certainly didn't believe that we'd be going through with this. So I bought something that I thought I could use again."

"Dean, did you bring the masks or not?"

He produced two masks from his own shopping bag.

"Dean, and please accept my apologies for my lack of more suitable diction here, but what the fuck are those?"

"Well, this one's Animal, and this one's Gonzo."

She served him a look that would kill a Rhino at fifty paces.

"They're from The Muppets," Dean added helpfully.

"I know who they are. What I don't know is what sort of remedial amoeba would think to use Muppet masks to hide their identity during a serious crime. Would you rob Barclays Bank in one of those?"

"Well, to be honest, I wouldn't rob Barclays Bank."

She sighed and rolled her eyes to the sky. "Okay – give me Animal."

"What? I thought I'd have that one - a woman couldn't be Animal. Animal is aggressive and violent."

Chill smacked him square in the face and took the mask. She started off towards the house whilst Dean rubbed his chin and had second thoughts. After a few seconds he put on the Gonzo mask and followed her up the most neatly manicured garden path he had ever seen in his life. He caught up with her as she reached the door, reasonably confident that this is where the adventure would end, and more than reasonably surprised to see Chill confidently punch a six figure code into an electronic keypad.

The door clicked open. Chill turned to him and put a silencing finger to her lips or, more accurately, to Animal's lips. She pushed the door open a few inches and listened.

"Come on," she whispered, and disappeared through the front door.

Dean hesitated. Last night's bravery had worn off along with the courage-building qualities of 5.2% proof Belgium lager. But he couldn't leave her now. And this was his idea after all. He followed her on tip-toe.

A long, wooden floored hall amplified every shuffle of their entry, but noise from a distant television gave them some auditory cover. They moved towards the sound of a cowboy film: gunshots, ricochets and Red Indian whooping. A door, straight ahead, was ajar – the corner of the immense plasma screen visible through the gap. Chill peered into the room and entered quickly. She moved so fast that it was almost over by the time Dean got there. He took in the scene. Roddi Rodrigues, sat in the largest leather chair Dean had ever seen, which itself was positioned in the largest lounge he had ever seen, in front of the largest television he had ever seen, by his side a bottle of the largest … well, no; he'd seen plenty of bottles of Tequila that big, but still. Roddi had obviously dozed off in front of Bonanza after serving himself several helpings of Mexico's finest. This explained, at least in part, why Chill had managed to strap him to the chair using the duct tape so swiftly. A slither of silver also plastered his mouth shut.

"Check the rest of the house," she mumbled through her mask as she expertly bound his ankles with more tape.

Dean did as he was told, although he didn't have clue what he was checking for. There was no one else home, so he assumed his mission was over. By the time he'd got back to the lounge Chill had keyed up her recording of Match of the Day and had pressed 'Pause' just as United were about to kick off.

"Over to you," she said, and threw him the remote.

He dropped it, of course, and scrambled to pick it up. He was desperately trying to remember what, in his own mind, he'd rehearsed saying to Rodrigues when he'd got the chance to tell him where he was going wrong. But he froze. He was actually quite frightened.

Chill took up the challenge. It seemed she was enjoying this.

"Let me explain what is going to happen." She addressed Rodrigues, who was cowering into the corner of his immense chair, a look of panic and fear sat deep in his eyes. "My friend here, The Great Gonzo, is going to play you excerpts from your performance yesterday. At any point where you look like you're not trying, or if you miss a pass, tackle or shot that, and I believe I'm using the correct terminology here, my granny could have made, then I will slap you across the face with this."

She produced the Monkfish from the shopping bag. Rodrigues tried to scream behind the duct tape and closed his eyes.

"There will be extra slaps for diving, and you will receive a poke in the face with the fish's snout for every time you swear at the referee. And oh, I nearly forgot …"

Again she went to her shopping bag, this time producing an iPod. She put the earphones onto a shivering Rodrigues and continued her opening statement.

"In addition to the punishment by fish, you will also be subjected to aural humiliation."

She pressed a few buttons to make sure it was working. Rodrigues tried to scream again, which told her it was.

"Let me be frank, Mr Rodrigues. You are fortunate that what we are going to show you here is twelve minutes of edited highlights. Let me be very clear about this: if you ever put on a performance like this again in a United shirt, we will be back to go through the full ninety minutes, including injury time and slow motion replays. Understand?"

He nodded.

"Good. Let the trial begin." She looked at Dean, who took the cue and pressed 'Play'. Thirty seconds in, Rodrigues attempted a pathetically under-hit pass to his teammate, whom he immediately berated for not making it to the ball. Dean pressed pause.

"Shocking!" said Chill and simultaneously sent a Monkfish uppercut to Rodrigues's jaw whilst pressing 'Play' on the iPod. The footballer strained against his bonds, pulling and pushing to get free. He couldn't, and it had only just begun.

"You see, you're not hitting through the ball," said Dean, no doubt going back to his old coaching classes. He did a slow motion demonstration of how it should be done using a cushion. Rodrigues nodded his understanding and Dean, satisfied, pressed 'Play' again.

Thirteen minutes later they were out of the front door. Rodrigues had been left a gibbering wreck, but they'd loosened the tape, so that he'd be able to free himself within a few minutes.

"Just what was on that iPod?" said Dean.

Chill smiled beneath her mask. "I'll tell you later. We'd better split up now. Give me your mobile number – I'll call you tomorrow."

They closed the gate behind them, and walked away in different directions.

***

Back at his flat Dean hid the masks and flicked on SKY News. He didn't expect much and was therefore relatively shocked to see the ticker-banner running across the bottom of the screen proclaiming: 'United star in hostage drama.'

The anchor man looked serious as he asked the on-the-spot reporter for the latest update.

"And we can now go over to Andrew Butler, our on-the-spot reporter, for the latest update." he said seriously. "Andrew, we're getting some rather startling reports, can you give us any more information?"

"Yes, thank you John. I'm outside the house of Roddi Rodrigues, United's star centre-forward, where it … oh, and I believe we can now speak to Inspector George Moodie, the officer in charge of the investigation. Inspector Moodie, can you tell us what has happened here tonight?"

An ancient, rather dreary, sour looking man appeared on camera. He wore an alarmingly dull anorak, despite the relative warmth of the evening, and a tie that sported several variations of fast food. Moodie had one of those 'lived-in' faces; lived-in, probably, by a family of angry ferrets. His expression clearly stated that he had little time for 'media types', and his voice took on a timbre that screamed boredom and impatience.

"I can, yes. It would appear that Mister Roddi Rodrigues, a footballer with the local United side, was held hostage within the confines of his own home. The hostage takers, who were masked as the popular eighties Muppets 'Animal' and 'Gonzo', subjected Mister Rodrigues to a repeated attack of an amusing nature."

"I see, and can you give me the details of this attack?"

"No, of course not. We're keeping certain details from the public at the moment. But what we do seem to have here is some sort of kangaroo court."

"Don't tell me there was a kangaroo in there as well!" Joked Andrew, who fancied himself as a bit of a comedian.

"It's a saying, son. What I'm attempting to tell you is that the motive for the break-in and, shall we say, 'shenanigans' that followed, appears to be to let Mr Rodrigues know that his recent performances have not been up to scratch, and whilst this is currently a one off incident I would warn other members of the United team to be extra vigilant at this time. Perhaps take out extra security. Either that or get their finger out on a Saturday afternoon."

"Is there anything else you can add, Inspector Moodie?"

"Yes, of course there is, but it's late and I'm tired. Goodnight."

Andrew gave a knowing look to the camera and handed back to the studio.

"Thank you, Andrew. Well, extraordinary news there. We'll obviously keep you informed if there are any developments, but elsewhere this evening ..."

***

She didn't call him on Monday, as she had said she would. It was against company rules to keep his mobile on at work, but he told his Team Leader that there was a family illness and he may be needed urgently. It wasn't an outright lie, he reasoned with himself; after all, football was an illness in his family. All day long he quoted insurance and waited for his phone to beep. It did once, about 2.00pm, but when he answered it turned out to be a boy called Ranjit, who sounded about eleven, and who asked if Dean knew he was entitled to a free handset. It was going to be a long day.

The newspapers all carried reports of the attack on Rodrigues; most of them where actually sympathetic to The Muppets cause. Some of the quality papers carried columns decrying the appalling deterioration of our society, when rich sportsmen are not safe in the comfort of their own homes without veiled maniacs bursting in and commenting on their inability to run the offside trap from one of the channels. Where would it all end? With Wallace and Gromit storming into 11 Downing Street to lambaste the Chancellor on his naive tactical handling of the EEC rebate issue? Something, they theorized, had to be done!

This view was not shared by the popular press. Only in the football world could two masked intruders break into somebody's house, subject the occupant to a callous and vicious attack, leave them blubbering inanely, strapped to a chair, and actually be seen as the good guys. The Sun even proclaimed them national heroes, and only in a mildly jingoistic way:

United Star in Muppet Mayhem

… of course, we can hardly claim that Animal and Gonzo are a modern day Batman and Robin, fighting football crime on the mean and dirty streets of Cheshire. And, although some United supporters may disagree, we can hardly say that Rodrigues is The Joker either. However, whilst The Sun cannot condone the abuse of our Great British Law, it is about time that some of these foreign imports got what was coming to them. They are happy enough to take money out of the game, but it's about time they were told we wanted something back. Lazy footballers everywhere watch out! The Muppets may be after you next.

Tuesday was even longer. The mobile remained on his desk, but failed to ring. He realized he'd miss her if he didn't see her again, even though she was clearly mad and would certainly get him into trouble. She'd refused to give him her mobile number, claiming that it was brand new and she hadn't yet memorized it. Now, as Dean replayed their conversations backwards and forwards in his mind, that seemed particularly unlikely. She was bright and intelligent; mad as a wasp, yes, but not the sort of person who couldn't remember a mobile phone number. By Tuesday night he realized he'd been dumped and, as usual, dealt with it by getting drunk.

Wednesday morning was tough. He'd put himself down for the early shift, so that he could get away for the United game – an 8.00pm televised kick-off at home to a resurgent Everton. He switched his mobile phone to vibrate, put his Lucozade and Resolve next to his computer, and attached his telephone headset to his pounding head. "Good Morning," he lied, as a blip in his ear told him that somebody wanted a quotation. "Thank you for calling Cover-and-Go Insurance; you're through to Dean; how can I help you?"

He hated his job. It gave him just enough flexibility to get to his football matches and not quite enough money to pay for them all. He'd turned down successive promotions, knowing that with greater responsibility came less opportunity to get to Watford for a 7.30pm Tuesday night kick-off in the League Cup fourth round.

His mobile emitted a short, sharp ring somewhere during mid-morning: a 'Withheld Number'. Dean answered, intending to tell Ranjit just where he could stick his free handset. It was Chill.

"How does it feel to be a wanted criminal?" she said, clearly enjoying the situation.

"I hadn't really thought about it, Weren't you going to ring me Monday?" He immediately wished he hadn't said that. Too pushy.

"Been busy, sorry."

"Listen," he glanced over the acoustic panelling that surrounded his desk, checking that he wasn't being watched by anyone that mattered. "United are playing tonight. Why don't you come along; see how Rodrigues plays?"

"You think he'll play? I thought he might have been on the next flight to Lisbon."

"What, and risk his wages not being paid? Or a repeat visit by Animal and Gonzo? He'll play. If there's one thing I know about his boss, he won't stand for any cry-offs in his team. Why don't you come? I'll drive if you like."

"Hmm. No. Thanks for the offer, though. I've got to go, I'm at work, but listen, meet me for a drink tomorrow night?"

"Er, okay then. Why not?" Yes, yes, yes!

"Great. Mulligans in town at eight o'clock. Oh and Deano …?"

"Yes?"

"Bring the masks."

***

Something was different. He was used to the match atmosphere hitting him as he jumped off the tram, cool night air mixing the smells of hot dogs, burgers, fried onions and tobacco smoke, but he could taste the anticipation cutting through it all. The impressive stadium appeared in front of him as he turned a corner, its floodlights giving a halo effect in the half-light of the late summer evening. A two-man radio crew was interviewing a group of supporters, teasing out their semi-drunken views. Further down, a TV unit was looking for fans dressed in the most extreme regalia to interview. Anyone who looked remotely intelligent was passed over in favour of those sporting a red and white wig or a three sizes too small football shirt.

There was only one line of questioning.

There was only one topic of conversation.

Dean felt faintly displaced. His surroundings were so familiar, but there was something surreal about it all. It could have been because he, and Chill, had caused all this to happen. He was responsible for this ripple of anticipation flowing through the veins of all these people.

It could also have been – and he couldn't fail to notice as he got even closer to the ground – because every fourth or fifth person he walked past seemed to be wearing a Muppet mask.

Of course! At the bottom of the road the temporary trading stands stood with their T-shirts, their scarves and their … Muppet masks. They called them 'The Grafters': the people who within ten minutes of a match ending can have a T-shirt printed up with the score, the scorers and some amusing anecdote – usually casting sexual aspersions on a high profile member of the opposing team – on sale right outside the ground.

How do they do that? Naturally they would have had the foresight to buy up every Animal and Gonzo mask this side of Thailand.

He stopped to look at a man who was stood on the corner, a large holdall over his shoulder, two masks swinging in his hands.

"You want them, chief?" He merrily asked Dean. "Fiver each. They're my last ones – I can fuck off home then!" Business had been brisk.

"No thanks. I've already got one."

The street-trader shrugged, his smile never leaving his face. A man waving a ten pound note was already advancing towards him.

Across the road was the glut of people that always gathered outside the strip of off-licences, chippies and betting shops that had stood there for generations. Alongside, a querulous queue waited impatiently to get into a packed-to-the-rafters pub. Dean waited to cross the road, looking for his match day friends, his way blocked by a row of fluorescent policemen who were allowing a stream of traffic to edge through the crowds. After a minute, one of the policemen halted the cars and his colleagues stepped back to allow the supporters to cross. As they did, a song bellowed from the chip shop fans, stopping Dean in his tracks.

'It's time to start the music
It's time to light the lights
It's time to get things started on the Muppet Show tonight.'

A policeman enthusiastically encouraged him to cross the road by shoving him aggressively in the back. It had no effect; there was a second verse.

'So please don't steal my hubcaps
Or rob my house or car
It's time to beat the scousers at the Muppet Show tonight.'

"Oi! You been drinking, siiir?" The policemen enquired politely.

"I wish I had," replied Dean as he forced himself to cross the remainder of the road and thus avoid arrest. "At least it would have explained some of this."

The song was sung again, this time louder as more people picked up the lyrics. By the time Dean and his friends made their way to the ground a third verse had been added.

Dean got to his usual seat, just behind the goal in the East Stand, and took in the scene. Every row appeared to have at least one or two people wearing the masks. Animal and Gonzo seemed to peer at him from every angle, haunting him like Banquo's ghost. He half expected the linesmen to be wearing them.

The players ran out to a roar of approval, the match announcer reading through their names, allowing a pause for an 'hooray' or a 'boo' after each one. The biggest cheer of all was for Roddi Rodrigues, boosted by the sound of laughter coming from certain sections of the crowd. Rodrigues didn't appear to share the joke. During the warm-up the crowd sang for him to give them a wave, but he chose to ignore them, concentrating instead on some intense shuttle runs and painful looking stretches.

Everton looked good, their team reflecting their no-nonsense Scottish manager, who had put the team together with a minimal budget and a firm hand. They scored first – a sloppily defended set piece that would later give Hansen enough evidence to have the whole backline shot. By half time the away team had also hit the bar and forced two good saves from the keeper. In this, their third game of the season, United were already well on their way to their second defeat. Up front Rodrigues had definitely upped his work rate. He hadn't thrown himself to the floor once, he'd taken up some good positions and his passing was much more purposeful. On his own, though, it made little difference.

There was a muted response from the crowd as the players ran out for the second half. Three thousand away fans making more noise than the rest of the stadium. Ten minutes in Rodrigues tackled and won the ball on the halfway line; he feinted left and waltzed past two defenders; a burst of speed took him past one more and to the edge of the penalty area where he unleashed an unstoppable left-footed shot. Unstoppable, but just wide of the goal. He punched the air in frustration. Five minutes later he ran onto a misplaced backpass and rounded the keeper, only to see his shot cleared off the line. This time he banged the ground in anger before picking himself up and tracking back onside.

The crowd responded; they could see the determination and began to chant his name. Rodrigues looked around – it had been a long time.

Unfortunately, Everton hadn't read the script and decided to score. United's midfield dynamo, Ginger McCluney, had given the ball away thirty yards out. In truth, it had been some time since he had been called a dynamo, although he had been called many other less favourable things far more recently. McCluney lived on his past glories these days, and saw it as someone else's job to defend the penalty area. He watched with his arms on his hips as two Everton attackers made United's centre-backs look like incontinent Shire Horses.

With the notable exception of the away end, the crowd was silent. Two-nil down at home and playing like they were a relegation team, heads seemed to drop everywhere on the pitch. An air of gloom saturated the crowd.

And then it started. Who started it didn't really matter, but someone, somewhere in that vast collection of individuals started to chant:

'Sixty thousand Muppets,
Sixty thousand Muppets.'

Over and over again. One by one, they all joined in. Row by row, section by section, stand by stand until, it seemed, just about every home fan was singing.
'Sixty thousand Muppets.'

The irony was sweet; this was exactly what London fans often sang to them. Or to be more precise they sang 'Sixty Farsand Mappits,' but who are Northerners to give elocution lessons? The meaning was clear: if Rodrigues thought he was being hard done by with just two of them turning up, then the rest of the team had another 59,998 to deal with.

It may have had nothing to do with it. How much can a crowd affect a team's performance anyway? Mick Ruane – United's honest, down to earth left winger – began to shout encouragement at his team, waving his arms so that he looked like he was about to take off. Rodrigues too, completely out of character, was clapping his fellow players, begging for extra effort. A neat passing movement preceded a promising United attack. The keeper made the save, but the crowd responded to the change in pace. They dropped the Muppet chant and deafened themselves with the simple 'United, United, United!'. Fifteen minutes from time O'Shea cut in from the wing and hit the sweetest of chips beyond the despairing grasp of the Everton keeper and into the empty goal. Five minutes later a cross to the far post was met by a delighted

Roddi Rodrigues, who made no mistake with a header, bulleted into the top corner. Rodrigues, unable to contain his delight, was booked for his goal celebrations, which included a double-summersault, the removal of his shirt, and what can only be described as simulated sex with two different corner flags.

Had Everton not bagged an injury time winner, it would have been quite a good night.

Dean, and the rest of the crowd, slumped away sullenly.

***

24 hours later Dean was running up the three flights of stairs to his flat. Once again he'd thought twice about it, and once again he'd let Chill talk him into it. They were so nearly caught tonight, and his heart rate was still up near 200. He burst through the door, stashed the masks and flicked at the remote control. He sat on the arm of a chair, attempted to get his breathing back to normal, and went through all the news stations that his SKY package had to offer: nothing. He left SKY News talking about the legacy cost of the 2012 Olympics and went to get a drink from his kitchen, filling a pint glass with Vimto and water. Halfway through drinking it, the urgent sound of the newsreader reached his endorphin enraged brain.

"… another Muppet incident! Over to our man at the scene, Andrew Butler."

I knew we should have stayed in Mulligans, he thought.

"Thank you, John. Yes, I'm here again in Hale Barns where it appears that we have a similar incident to the now notorious Muppet Kidnapping. I'm joined again by the officer in charge, Inspector George Moodie. Inspector Moodie, can you confirm that these are the same perpetrators, or is this some sort of bizarre copycatting?"

"We're currently working under the assumption that it is the work of the same people. I can confirm that at or about 10.00pm this evening the property of a Mr Gerald 'Ginger' McCluney – known locally as 'The Ginger Whinger' and allegedly a central midfield player for United – was entered, apparently without force, and by persons unknown. Security cameras show that two individuals, again masked as Animal and Gonzo from the Muppets, walk straight through the occupants' front door, before confronting Mr McCluney, who is a somewhat paltry five foot six inches tall."

"Do you think that, like Roddi Rodrigues, Ginger McCluney was targeted because of his poor display against Everton?"

"Anybody who saw Mr McCluney play on Wednesday night would have had to come to that conclusion, yes."

"And I don't suppose you're prepared to tell the viewers the nature of the attack that took place."

"Actually I am."

"You are?"

"Yes. It has been pointed out to me by Mr McCluney, his coach, his family, his agent, his lawyer and no less than three Feng Shui consultants that revealing the facts of the attack will cause him, and Mr Rodrigues, considerable embarrassment. However, although that was of incredibly serious concern to myself, I have decided that it will aid the investigation by revealing the hostage-takers 'modus-operandi'."

"Fantastic!"

"Indeed. As with Mr Rodrigues on Sunday, Mr McCluney was tied to chair and made to watch re-runs of his own performance in last night's game. This included post-match analysis by a Mr Alan Hansen and a Mr Mark Lawrenson."

"Woeful!"

"Hmm. A Mr Lineker was also heard to say some rather discouraging and genuinely unfunny remarks. Anyway, it would appear that the victim is slapped across the face with a large Monkfish whenever he is seen to make, what I believe Mr Hansen refers to as 'a schoolboy error'. As you can appreciate, in the case of Mr Rodrigues and Mr McCluney, this resulted in some severe fish-slapping of a nature previously unheard of during my thirty-five years with the force."

"A Monkfish?" Andrew was a good journalist and was keen to check his facts. He was also failing to keep a straight face at this point.

"Yes. A particularly ugly one, it would seem - even by Monkfish standards. This is perhaps not the worst of it. During the assault, the victim is made to wear headphones connected to what I believe is called an M3P player. I'm afraid to have to tell you that in conjunction with the inappropriate use of fish, Mr Rodrigues was made to listen to West German soft rock ballads from the nineteen eighties."

"No!" At this point Andrew knew he was jeopardizing his future TV career, but could do nothing about the onslaught of raucous laughter.

"I'm afraid so," continued Moodie, oblivious, apparently, to any humour in the situation. "I'm told it included the work of a Mr Hasselhoff, but I wouldn't know about these things. It is here where there is a slight change of tack. It would appear that the music from these leather-clad, codpiece wearing, out of tune gimps had little effect on Mr McCluney. This is perhaps unsurprising, as Mr McCluney still sports a Chris Waddle style mullet haircut. In a cold-hearted and callous move, Animal and Gonzo played a version of 'I Like A Party With A Happy Atmosphere' sung, if that is the correct verb to use, by a Mr Russell Abbot."

"I'm sorry?"

"So am I, son. Don't forget, Mr Abbott is best known for donning a red, spikey wig, inappropriate kilt and strutting around the stage saying 'See you, Jimmy' in a scarcely believable Glaswegian accent."

"Shocking." Andrew was now restricted to one word interjections, having accepted that he'd lost his battle with his laughter.

"I'm afraid there's more."

Andrew was unable to get a word out at all now. There was more?

"It seems that following on from Mr Abbott's shameful rendition, the 3PM player was used to embarrass Mr McCluney even further; this time by playing him terrace chants which were rather disparaging to the player."

"Really?" Andrew fought to regain his composure. This was brilliant. "You mean like, 'He's fat, he's ginger – his girlfriend is a minger.'"

"That was one of them, yes."

At this point Andrew collapsed onto the floor, unable to continue. His deep belly-laughs could be heard off-camera, whilst Moodie stood there, looking unimpressed with this unexpected turn of events. The camera crew had no idea what to do, and for a few glorious seconds the screen was filled with a silent, morose police inspector, patiently waiting for the laughter to subside. It didn't.

Eventually the anchorman rescued the situation. "Well we, er ... we, er, appear to be having some technical difficulties with the feed at the moment, but we'll be back there as soon as the situation has resolved itself. Now, er, in business news ..."

***

Dean didn't sleep much that night. Every time he managed to doze off he dreamt of policemen in fluorescent vests with oversized truncheons, battering down his door and arresting him on the spot. He dreamt of judges, thumping enormous gavels and sending him to prison for life. He dreamt of prison warders punching him in the kidneys and spitting in his food. In his dreams all of them – policemen, judges and warders – wore the Muppet masks. And all of them were City fans.

Eventually night became morning, and Friday had become Saturday. That meant United at home to Chelsea, who had won all three of their opening games convincingly. He ate his Cheerios and uncharacteristically avoided watching any of the football shows on telly. At midday he put on his jacket, walked into town and just managed to squeeze onto a tram as its doors began to shut.

It was only then that he realized that his journey to the ground would not quite be the same as usual.

The tram was packed with Muppets. As supplies had been exhausted, Gonzo and Animal had been joined by their friends. Miss Piggy was offered a seat by a gallant Bald Eagle; Statler and Waldorf shared a joke at the expense of Rowlf; Beaker and the Swedish Chef drank cans of Stella and discussed today's probable line-up, and a proud Kermit the Frog held up his similarly attired son, whom he'd taught to sing 'Halfway Up The Stair Is The Stair Where I Sit'. Like Dean, not everybody was wearing a mask of course, but it was they who looked slightly out of place and just a little ridiculous. Dean noticed the smell before he'd realized what the further addition to the essential football supporters' match day attire had become: fish. People were carrying fish. To be fair, most were either stuffed, polystyrene or inflatable, and only the occasional militant fan had bothered to wander down to their local fish market and ask for their 'largest and ugliest Monkfish'. Those that had now considered themselves to be superior to their peers, and made sure their efforts took prominence despite the nasal consequences of a packed tram carriage on a warm afternoon. One man was using his Monkfish like a ventriloquists dummy, moving its jaw and pointing its eyes towards his group of friends.

"You know when that last Everton goal went in?" He made the fish say. "I was gutted!"

In the corner, two boys fought each other with bright orange Nemo fish, whilst a six and a half foot, 300 llb skin-headed beermonster used a large inflatable shark to gently prod a straight-faced bespectacled man, who had been desperately trying to avoid the whole episode by fastidiously reading his fanzine. A group of twenty-somethings, seemingly workmates, were using a packet of Kwik Save Boil-in-the-Bag Haddock to smack each other around the head. Each thwack of polythene on skin was accompanied by some scathing criticism on each other's job: 'That's for that wall you built last week. Call that straight?'

What he should have done was to get involved, Dean told himself. But he was gripped by an enormous paranoia. He had this unnerving feeling that everybody knew it was him, and that this whole charade had been orchestrated for his benefit. Maybe by the police to flush him out. Maybe by a particularly vicious, and inventive, former girlfriend – revenge for sneaking off to watch late night full re-runs of classic 1970s games on SKY Sports 3, perhaps.

He stepped off the tram and began the short walk to the ground. The street traders had branched out into red and white scarves depicting random Muppets and various slogans, such as 'Gonzo is a Red'. Glove puppets, mainly of Kermit, were also being sold, helped by the addition of a tiny red and white knitted scarf tied around the amphibian's neck. Peaked caps depicting a cross-eyed fish motif and the logo 'Win or Swim' were also selling well.

Dean stopped and did a slow 360 degree spin. He saw many strange things, but none of them seemed to be directed at him. He considered rushing unannounced into various buildings to see if he could see any evidence of a conspiracy. He felt like he was the main character in The Truman Show. His phone rang: Chill.

"Hey," he said. "Things are getting really weird down here."

"I know – I'm watching it on telly. They've just done a press conference with McCluney; he's resolved to pull out all the stops today. Says the team have got a wakeup call and they intend to put things right. That's down to you, you know."

"Don't blame me for all this, Chill. If you'd have left me alone I'd have probably got a night in the cells and a caution. Now my whole life is one big cabaret. I feel like I'm in The Twilight Zone."

"Ha ha! Okay, let's say it's a joint effort then. I really enjoyed it though. Better than most first dates anyway."

"That was a date?"

"Did you want it to be a date?"

"I certainly hoped so. Until I realized you were certifiable. Couldn't we just have gone to the pictures like most couples? You haven't even given me your mobile yet."

She laughed again. "Let's see how they play today. Then maybe we can get a DVD. What do fancy? 'A Fish Called Wanda'?"

"Stop it!"

"Shark's Tale? Finding Nemo?"

"I'm going! I can't hear you now anyway!"

"Okay – 'So Long, and Thanks for all the Fish'."

For the first time in many years Dean decided not to have a drink before the match. Things were weird enough. He bought a bottle of water and joined his mates, who were quite happy to ridicule him, both for not drinking and for not making the effort with a Muppet mask.

"Hang on," he said to one of them. "You're having a go at me for not being a fully grown man in a child's mask, and for not carrying an inflatable fish? Are you sure we've got this the right way round?"

The ground was worse. Whereas on Wednesday there had been pockets of Muppets here and there, today it seemed like there were just occasional pockets of non-Muppets. The teams ran out to tumultuous applause, vociferous cheers and the astonishing sight of thousands of various ocean-going creatures, which seemed to dance with scarf-wearing Kermit hand puppets.

To add to the surrealism, a determined and passionate United side beat Chelsea, the title favourites, 3-1.

After the game – just as he'd got to the bar, attempting to make up for not drinking earlier – Chill rang him again.

"Fancy a drink?" she said.

"I fancy more than one. Did you see us today? First to every ball, hard in the tackle, skilful, fast and exciting! Three-one!"

"Really? Oh, I got bored after five minutes and went shopping. Anyway, get yourself down to 'Below The Bar' – it's a cellar wine bar thingy on the High Street in Wilmslow. I've got a surprise for you. See you there, then."

She hung up without giving him chance to respond.

Dean had to think about this. On the one hand he could stay here and have a great time with his mates, drinking, singing and reliving all those great moments from today's game. On the other, he could go off with a mad woman, whose idea of a surprise was probably torturing Ant and Dec by getting them to say something above the intellect of a five year old.

On the other hand, which he knew meant he would have to have three hands, but he felt that just about anything was possible after today; she was as fit as a butcher's dog and he already knew he was falling for her.

He took out his mobile and dialled Dolphin Taxis.

Thirty minutes later Dean opened the taxi door in front of 'Below The Bar'. His first thought was that it looked expensive, and his second thought was that he was still two weeks away from payday. He paid the driver, feeling compelled to leave a small tip – after all, they'd bonded in that taxi-driver-passenger-never-see-you-again type of way. The battered Mondeo pulled away leaving him momentarily alone, wondering which of his credit cards could stand the biggest hit. Working in a call centre and following United the length and breadth of the country didn't make a sound financial equation. He shrugged his shoulders and walked towards the entrance.

"Oi, Gonzo!"

Dean span round and was relieved to see Chill smiling at him from a parked car: a BMW 630 ci Sports Convertible – steel grey, with the top down. Oh good, he thought, expensive tastes.

"Jump in – we've got work to do!"

He did think twice about jumping in, but not for long. Good looking girl in a sports car? He had no choice.

"What do you mean 'work'?"

"Put this on," she said, passing him a Gonzo mask. "We ride one last time, partner."

"You're kidding, right? I mean, this is some sort of joke, isn't it?"

The mischievous grin told him it wasn't.

"But we beat Chelsea 3-1. We were brilliant. Every last man played like their lives depended on it. Even the taxi driver said so."

"Good. One more then, just to keep them on their toes. Let's send a real message out."

"Look, Chill, I think a lot of you, I really do, but don't you realize how lucky we've been not to get caught already?"

She smiled again; a wicked, teasing smirk. "I'll make it worth your while," she said, as she squeezed his thigh.

Dean sunk back into soft leather, closed his eyes and wished he was stronger.

It didn't take them long. Another part of the Cheshire countryside, another footballer's mansion. In another clear breach of the Data Protection Act, Chill entered a five digit code into the side-gate's entry system and they heard the clunk of a lock opening for them.

"Which one lives here, then?" Dean's voice betrayed his deep trepidation.

"This one? Oh, this one's the manager's."

He stopped in his tracks.

"Oh no. No. No, no, no, no, no!"

"No?"

"Yes. No. No way. Those players? Fine, they deserved it, but The Boss? No chance. He's given more to this club than almost anybody else in its history. As far as I'm concerned he can do no wrong. He picked us up from the depths and made us into the most successful team in English history. We've won cup after cup, trophy after trophy, broken every record and played the most exciting football ever seen along the way. And because of a few over-pampered players you want to slap him with a fish? No way – I'm not having it. There's a line, and you've just stepped over it."

It was unfortunate that it was as he was turning to walk away that four policemen rushed towards him. Two of them held his arms whilst a third whipped off the mask in dramatic fashion – they'd drawn lots for the privilege earlier in the evening. One of the policemen sighed heavily.

"Ha! I told you it wouldn't be one of the Gallagher brothers. That's ten pounds you owe me!" said another.

Dean looked up, a rabbit caught in headlights, and was unnerved to see the face of Inspector George Moodie staring quizzically back at him. Moodie had become fairly well known over the past week, thanks to the Muppet capers, and had already turned down the chance to appear in Celebrity Big Brother.

"Hmm," he mused. "You actually look more like Gonzo with the mask off. Anyway, let's get him inside."

"Inside?" Dean panicked. "Aren't you going to take me to the station?"

"Absolutely. But all in good time. I think you owe The Boss an explanation first."

Everyone called him 'The Boss'. Even ex-players, superstars in their own right, who had gone on to successfully manage other clubs, still called him 'The Boss': a mark of respect for the Scot who had done so much for English football. This man had shaped Dean's life; charged his football emotions from deepest despair to unrestrained joy. He had built successive teams that Dean had followed near and far, through thick and thin, and almost to personal financial ruin. And now Dean was finally going to get to meet him. How often had he gone to bed at night, dreaming of what he would say if he ever got the chance of talking to him? Thousands, probably, but he'd never once thought his opening line might be, 'Very pleased to meet you. Sorry about smacking your players in the face with a Monkfish whilst dressed as Gonzo, and do you think you could ask these policemen to loosen the handcuffs?"

Moodie motioned them towards the house and Dean, buffeted by the policemen, knew he had no choice. Chill, who'd taken off her own mask, also made her way towards the imposing front door, looking every bit as calm as the night she'd casually interrupted his inept breaking and entering attempts. Chill. The name definitely suited her, thought Dean: she was as cool as they come. She was as guilty as he was – more so really, as she was the one who'd managed to get all the security codes for the players' entry systems.

The door closed behind them and Dean looked up to see the imposing figure of The Boss. Although now well into his sixties, his large impressive frame, thunderous beetroot face and savage, rapier eyes made for an ominous sight. Dean knew now why unwitting journalists who had asked him an ill-phrased or poorly timed question would wither with just one glance. Some of them never recovered. His stony-faced expression was unreadable, and Dean looked around nervously for any cups and saucers that were within throwing distance. How could any player not be scared witless into playing better when faced with this in the dressing room? If it were him, there's no way he'd go back in at half-time if he'd had a bad game. He'd rather stay outside and discuss flower arranging with the St Johns Ambulance woman.

"Operation 'Pigs in Space' has been successful, Boss," said Moodie. "These are the two responsible. There's no fish on them this time, and they don't have one of those LP3 players either."

One of the uniformed policemen sniggered, but it sounded alien in the charged atmosphere of the Boss's hallway; he coughed an apology and bowed his head in shame.

After what seemed like a ten minutes of injury time, the Scot rubbed his chin and said,

"Aye. You'd better come with me, laddie. I want to have a few words with you before I let the policemen beat you up. You too, young lady – follow me."

They all followed him into a large drawing room. Leather Chesterfields sat arranged around a smouldering log fire. He closed the door behind them and turned a key to lock them inside. Dean gulped audibly.

"Sit," said The Boss, as if addressing a disobedient dog, and everybody did. He addressed Dean.

"I heard what you said in the garden about me – that was very kind of you. However, that does not excuse the way you've insulted both myself and English football. What on earth made you think that you could exchange my years of experience, my incredible coaching skills and my extensive footballing knowledge, regarded by many to be unparalleled, for a fish and some tuneless Germanic rock epics?"

Dean knew it was a rhetorical question. He shuffled uncomfortably, aware all eyes were on him.

"Still," said The Boss, his eyes seemingly a little misty. "It seems to have worked." He walked over to a large wing-backed armchair, poured himself an outrageously large whisky from a decanter that sat next to it, drained the glass and sat down heavily, relaxing into its deep, welcoming leather upholstery. "I'm glad I agreed to go through with it now with my daughter, here." He waved the glass towards Chill and smiled like only a father can.

"W-w-w-?" Was all that Dean could get out.

"Oh, aye – I admit when she came to me that night and told me about the idea she'd got after she'd met you, I thought she was barking. Nearly called in the men in white coats, I can tell you. No question about that. But, well, I'd tried everything else. There comes a time, I suppose, when even though you're saying and doing the right things, the players have seen and heard it all before: they become immune. In the end I thought, why not? I knew what they needed was a good kick in the arse. Shaking out of their comfort zone."

"Chill is your daughter?"

"Who? Oh, you mean Claire. Yes, she is." He smiled at her again, but her eyes were fixed on Dean. "Thing is, it went better than I could have hoped. The players started getting in early for training and putting everything into it, but I expected that. What I didn't expect was that they'd listened to your ideas as well. Rodrigues's running off the ball improved ten-fold overnight, the lazy bastard. McCluney started to think about his defensive responsibilities and not just run about like a headless ginger chicken." He paused for a second. "Can you be headless and ginger? Anyway, that doesn't matter. What does is that you turned my team around, son, and I'm very grateful."

Dean looked around at the assorted policemen. There was no surprise on their faces.

"Oh don't worry about them," said the Scot. "They're all United fans too."

"Hand-picked," interrupted Moodie.

"So, I'm prepared to make you an offer." He refilled the whisky glass, this time taking just a considered sip before continuing. "Nothing about what has happened goes outside of these four walls, and I give you a job on my coaching staff."

"W-w-w-." Said Dean, rather predictably.

"You'll be on probation, of course, and you'll have to start at the bottom. I'll put ten grand on your current salary and you'll be on a win bonus, same as everyone else. What do you think?"

"I'd do the job for nothing."

"Really? You need an agent, son." He finished the glass, rose and shook Moodie's hand. "Thanks for the way you've handled this, George."

"Anything for the cause."

"You'll be my guest in the box on Saturday?"

"No, best not. Just get the three points and I'll be happy."

"Aye, well, thanks again the lot of you."

The other policemen smiled, their place in history assured. They'd say nothing of course, loyalty to a football club is deeper than any other, but perhaps one day, many years from now, when they take their grandchildren to their first United match, they could tell them how the club was once saved by Animal, Gonzo and their part in 'Operation: Pigs in Space'.

Chill winked at Dean. "Come on Gonzo – I promised you a drink."

Then The Bubble Burst

Henry leaned over from the back seat and tapped his grandson on the shoulder.

"Turn this rubbish off! Call this music? Bloody kids today …"

Sammy winced, then smiled at his girlfriend, Kylie, who was sat patiently in the passenger seat, enduring the car's slow progress. She reached across and changed the station, raising her eyebrows at the old man to see if the sports station she'd switched to would meet with his approval. He grunted sullenly and she took this as a positive sign.

"Well what a match we have in store today …" bleated a random ex-pro. "Thirteen years since the Merseyside Marauders have been back in the country's top flight, and the first time they've played their old rivals, the Manchester Tornadoes, since that Holland and Barrett Cup Game in 2033. The www.buyyourtrainees.com City of Liverpool Stadium is guaranteed to be a full house, with all 9,000 tickets reported to have been sold …"

"Pah!" commented Henry.

Sammy flicked the Auto-Driver switch on and turned to face him.

"What's the matter with you?" He said. "I thought you'd enjoy going to a football match, especially this one – I was lucky to get tickets."

"I stopped going when they sold Old Trafford for housing development in 2020." Henry talked in roughly the same way that a machine gun does. "I swore I'd never go again, not after they put City and United together anyway. The Manchester Tornadoes? I ask you! When was the last time you saw a tornado in Manchester? Should have called them the Manchester Drizzle …"

"Then why did you bother to come?"

Henry repeated his sullen grunt and scowled for effect. "I'm seventy-eight. I might not get another chance. One last time, just to see if there's anything I recognise from the game I used to love."

Sammy laughed and turned back to face the traffic as it edged painfully slowly towards Liverpool Docks. "Seventy-eight! You've got another twenty or thirty years in front of you yet, granddad. And I don't know what you mean – football's a great game."

"Football was a great game, son. Did that numpty say a capacity 9,000 crowd? We used to get nearly ten times that in the old days. That's when it was a game: passion, excitement … fun!"

"Fun? Oh yeah, I heard all about the fun in Social History classes at school. Didn't that fun involve obscene chanting and mindless violence? Some fun!"

"There wasn't too much violence after the Eighties. That was when I was in my twenties, and to be honest the music was so bad at that time it would have caused anybody to want to fight. Actually the football was bloody rubbish then as well, but at least you could go to the match and stand with your mates, have a good drink and sing about Scousers having no jobs, Brummies speaking funny or people from Norwich practising incest on a regular basis …"

"Did they practise incest on a regular basis?" Kylie chipped in, apparently without irony.

"'Course they bloody didn't! And Scousers didn't all live in council houses, eat from bins and steal hubcaps … not all of them … but that didn't matter. We were having fun!"

"Calm down granddad," Sammy admonished. "You know it's not correct to use the term 'Scousers' anymore; and stop swearing. Please."

"Swearing? I wasn't swearing."

"If you come out with the 'B' word in the ground they'll have you thrown out, you know. And what about the racism? I heard they used to boo black players when they touched the ball. How could you go to the games, being black yourself?

"Racism?" offered Kylie before Henry could reply. "Wasn't that at the same time as slavery?"

Bless. Lovely looking girl; but not the brightest.

"People didn't have the same perception of differences they do now, love." Henry's tone was conciliatory, speaking to her as if she were eight, not eighteen. "I know it seems odd now, but even twenty years ago people would be frightened by anyone different than themselves and then look to blame them for their problems." He turned back to Sammy and resumed his argument.

"It was the seventies that, son. I didn't really start going until the end of that particular decade, but you're right: it did happen. I'm not defending it, but it was more about putting off the opposition rather than anything else. I mean, we'd call a player gay, a rapist, a drunk, a child-molester, fat, ugly, disabled … all of the above …anything if it put him off his game."

"That's terrible! And not very sporting, either."

"Sporting? It was bloody football! Of course it wasn't sporting!"

"Well you just clap politely if Merseyside score today, and please stop swearing."

Henry sat back in his seat and 'huffed'. Outside, the East Lancs Road was at virtual gridlock, but on the radio the match pundits were in full throttle.

"Well, you can almost taste the atmosphere here, David, and with over an hour to go before kick-off. The Tofu Burger Vans are lining the streets, and the fans are making their way to the ground, enjoying their Smoothies and Health Shakes."

Henry saw a chance to re-ignite the conversation.

"Errm … did you bring anything to drink with you, Sammy boy? Only I'd kill for a lager."

"Granddad!" The Auto-Driver went back on as he swung round to reproach him. "You know it's an imprisonable offence to bring alcohol anywhere near a football ground. You've not got anything on you, have you? I promised Grandma I'd look after you!"

"Ooh, chill out, wild child," mocked Henry. "Don't you worry, son. I remember The Football and Alcohol Act of 2018. Beginning of the end, that was. They'd stopped us standing in the early nineties – that were bad enough. Then drink not allowed within two miles of the ground and breath tests at the turnstiles. And that was followed by The Objectionable Singing and Chanting Act of 2020. People were getting Life Bans and a £3,000 fine for singing 'You fat bastard'. In the end no one sang at all, and not too much later no one went at all. Are we nearly there yet?"

"Not far off – I told you we'd make it in two hours. Manchester to Liverpool's not that bad."

"I could walk quicker."

"Carry on like that and you'll get the chance."

"Ooh, look at that," said Kylie in genuine wonderment. "A pub that's showing the match. Not seen that before."

Henry looked out of the window, ignoring the pub, unsure if he was still talking to Sammy or just to himself now.

"Then the bubble burst," he said in tones usually reserved for the reverie of a lost love one. "Boom to bust in less than a decade. With gates down by sixty or seventy per cent the clubs couldn't cope. TV didn't want to pay huge sums to screen games with no crowd and no atmosphere. And all the corporate ticket holders – The Prawn Sandwich Brigade we called them, I can't remember why – they just buggered off to find the next big thing. Competitive Ice Dancing I think it was. Just about all the clubs went bust. They said football had survived, I know that. The biggest clubs all joining together, selling their stadiums and moving to newer, smaller ones. One professional league: The Simon Cowell Premiership. Then all the rule changes, trying to make it more exciting … re-branding the franchise …"

Sammy pulled into a car parking space. "Solar panels to re-charge. Doors 1, 2 and 4 open." Three of the car's doors opened gently, their sensor's causing them to stop just short of the vehicles on either side. The three of them got out and breathed in the air.

"Used to be burgers, onions, exhaust fumes and cigarette smoke," lamented Henry.

"Well thank goodness it isn't. Doors lock. Alarm on. Football is a far more pleasant affair altogether these days."

"Oh, I'm sure football is. Still, you don't think that it's strange that suicide rates are 300% higher than they were thirty-odd years ago? And that murder and violent crime are up similarly?"

"I remember this argument, granddad. It's nonsense. You can't convince me that the demise of football as a mass spectator sport has anything to do with those things. It's just the way of the world, these days."

Sammy, Henry and Kylie walked towards the stadium, joining an orderly and pleasant queue of face-painted adults and children.

"I think they're linked totally," Henry continued. "Think about it. Football was an excuse for violence, not a reason for it. With the game's demise it just moved somewhere else, just as the police had gotten good at controlling it. But in my view once you took all the passion out of the game, your average working man just had nowhere to vent his spleen."

"Bent his what?" Kylie was trying to keep up with the conversation, but it was losing her fast.

"It just means that on a Saturday afternoon – if you were lucky – you could meet your mates, have a few drinks and a dodgy pie, go and stand at the match and sing and shout to your heart out for ninety minutes. Hurl abuse at the ref, the linesmen, the opposition, their fans, even your own players. You'd laugh out loud at the funny things people did and said, and your team could take you from the highest high to the lowest low and back again. It didn't matter how bad your job was, how ugly your wife was, how much money you hadn't got, you could just get it all off your chest for that ninety minutes. Get it all out of your system."

"What's a linesman, Henry?" He admired her perseverance.

"I think you call them touch judges these days, Kyles. But my point is, without that outlet, frustration can just build up in a person, and I think that's what's happened with society. It's just not enough to clap politely when the other team scores; you need to be able to swear and shout and threaten to punch the bastards."

"Granddad! Language!" Sammy said in that way where you want to shout, but need to whisper. One or two children looked up at Henry, followed by one or two disapproving parents who looked down at him. "Please – you promised you'd be on your best behaviour."

Henry held his hands up in mock surrender. "Sorry, sorry, Brown Owl. I'll be as good as gold now, Scout's Honour."

They each went through Entrance 26, as directed on their tickets. Their retinas were scanned to confirm that they were bona fide, and Kylie and Sammy walked in. As Henry made to join them, he was approached by a large gentleman in a smart blue blazer.

"A quick word if I may, sir," he said, leading Henry gently but firmly by the elbow to a small recess.

"What's the matter?" He looked for Kylie and his grandson, but they were busy buying Programmes and Raffle Tickets.

"I've just had an alert on my Palm Top as you came in through the doors, sir. It's just routine – you wouldn't have got in here if it was anything serious. Let me see. Ah yes, you have a conviction from an incident nearly 25 years ago ..."

"What?! The only time I've ever been in trouble was for urinating in a public place."

"That's right, sir."

"Are you taking the ..."

"Sir?"

"But twenty-five years ago?" Henry spelt it out, pronouncing each word separately in case he'd misunderstood.

"It says here it was at a football match. Any offence that was related to a football match stays on your record for thirty years. Don't worry though, it was spent after ten; it's just company policy that we pull anyone who has your type of record for a little chat. Now, I'm not going to have any trouble with you today, am I sir?"

"Now listen, mate ..." Henry stopped himself, his judgement aided by the sight of a worried Sammy and Kylie walking over to see what the matter was. He didn't want to upset their day. "No," he continued. "No trouble at all."

"Good, but please bear in mind that the CCTV suite will be monitoring you specifically today, sir. Enjoy the match."

He walked away just as the other two joined him. "Wanted to sell me some hubcaps," Henry said, dismissively. "Now, who fancies a nice Tofu Kebab? Mmmm."

Henry was still trying to explain what hubcaps were to Kylie long after they'd sat down. Giving up on it, he leant over to Sammy and whispered, "Well, the seats are comfy and there's nobody pissing in my pocket, but other than that it looks like a football ground."

He received a warning punch to his ribs, but it was good-natured and Henry took the trouble to laugh. Sammy smiled back and Henry thought maybe he should get rid of the chip on his shoulder and try to enjoy himself.

The teams ran out to enthusiastic applause and congregated in the centre-circle where they all hugged and patted each other's' bottoms. Henry decided to let this pass without comment.

The three referees checked with each other, nodded to the four touch judges, and the match was started by blowing a whistle. Henry seemed pleased with this traditional touch. For a minute or two the game looked for all intents and purposes the same as he remembered it, the ball being passed along the backline, Merseyside looking for a way of penetrating the Manchester defence. Then he realised something.

"Why isn't anybody tackling?" He asked Sammy.

"Tackling was banned years ago. Too dangerous – it would be a straight red card."

"Don't you mean tackling from behind, or two-footed tackles, or tackling where the other player goes four feet up in the air and comes down with a broken leg?"

"Ssshhhh!!" A man from the row behind them interrupted the conversation.

Sammy smiled at his granddad and shook his head to answer instead, putting his finger over his lips to encourage him to keep his thoughts to himself. After twenty minutes the teams returned to their dressing rooms and the crowd, who had been silence personified, broken only by the occasional ripple of respectful applause, began chatting amiably. It reminded Henry of an Intermission at a Theatre.

"Was that it?" He asked his grandson.

"That was just the first quarter, granddad. What did you think?"

"Well, it wasn't very exciting, was it? I mean, no shots on goal, no mazy runs, no forty-yard passes, no corners even."

"The players are encouraged to keep possession. Because there's no tackling it means that if you don't give the ball away, you can't be scored against. It's become a very strategic game. But don't worry; as the tension builds up it'll get very exciting, you'll see."

The second quarter was remarkably similar to the first, with neither side willing to venture much beyond the halfway line. Henry consoled himself with the fact that at least there still was a halfway line. Then, towards the end of the third quarter one of the Merseyside midfielders intercepted a stray pass and charged towards goal. The crowd drew in their collective breath, but Henry had spotted a Manchester defender running across to intercept him. "Go on, son," he said, quietly to himself. As the midfielder reached the 18-yard box the defender drew alongside, attempting to shepherd him away from goal, allowing his team mates to get back and cover. The defender succeeded in this but, his scoring chances diminishing, the midfielder threw himself on the floor in the most blatant show of diving Henry had seen since Didier Drogba in 2006. Once on the ground, the player rolled around as if shot.

"At least some things haven't changed," chuckled Henry, ignoring a further 'Shush' from behind. "Where do think the sniper is hiding?"

The nearest referee blew his whistle and ran towards the still prostrate player, reaching to his pocket for a card. "I should think so," said Henry. "What the bloody …?"

The referee did produce a card. In fact he produced ten, fumbled around and found one emblazoned with the number '7' which he held up to the crowd in a show of flamboyant over-acting not seen since President Peter Kay's last acceptance speech. The crowd applauded, but the show was not over: the other two referees and all four touch judges all held up cards, numbers ranging from '6' to '8', again to the contained delight of those watching.

"What's going on?" Henry asked.

"They're marking his diving out of ten. Look." Sammy pointed to one of the scoreboards that was simultaneously showing a slow-motion replay of the dive and a combined score of '6.857'.

"Is that good?"

"Oh, yes ... he's been averaging less than six all season. He'll be pleased with that."

"But ... those points don't count for anything ... do they?" The word 'incredulous' may have been invented for Henry at this moment.

"Only in the event of a draw, which to be fair there are a lot of these days ... and they count towards the Player of the Season Award as well, of course."

The game started with a free pass to Manchester, and Henry was struck by a melancholy that seemed to sit on his shoulders, weighing him further down into this seat. His head bowed, his eyes sought sanctuary in the sight of his shoes, preferring them to the sight on the pitch. Then, a tap on his shoulder. He looked up to see three security personnel, all similarly blue blazer-ed .

"Sir," said the first. "We've had reports of persistent talking during a period of play that was not considered to be one of momentary high excitement. Additionally, the use of a word inappropriate to the 2021 Impolite Language Act. Please take this as a warning. If there are any other complaints I will have to remove you from the ground, simultaneously issuing you with a lifetime ban. Do you understand?"

Henry ignored the Blazer and turned to Sammy. "I'll see you back at the car, son. I'd like to have a walk to clear my head before we head home." He turned back to the Security Guard, who was beginning to get flustered, unused as he was to being ignored by anyone. "Don't worry, Officer Dibble. I'll come quietly. Please don't use the dogs on me again."

Two minutes later Henry, having been escorted out of the ground, found himself sitting on a bench in Car Park B, feeling totally depressed at the state of what they now called football. He must have nodded off, as he was suddenly aware of wakening. He felt dizzy, the colours of the world seemed paler somehow, objects seemed to expand and contract before his eyes, before settling, the colour returning to high definition. Bloody medication he was on, probably.

A jogger jogged past.

A minute later the same jogger jogged past in the opposite direction.

A minute after that the same jogger, a man of similar age to Henry, jogged past again. And stopped.

"'Scuse me, son."

It was pronounced 'san', marking the man out to be from the London area. Henry looked up and readied himself. Football grounds were the one place you could almost guarantee being violence-free these days, but old habits die hard. The jogger took off the earphones he was wearing, and Henry was surprised to hear a few bars of an old Stiff Little Fingers song ... punk rock was 'heavily discouraged' by the authorities.

"Sorry, mate" continued the jogger. "I couldn't help noticing you being thrown out of the ground there. Mind if I sit down?"

The man looked decent enough, but Henry was still cautious. Warily, he motioned for him to take a seat.

"Not what it used to be, football." The jogger stretched and touched his toes as he spoke. "Nah, it used to be my life, but this stuff? It's like a cross between Chess and a Pantomime."

"Isn't there a law against saying things like that?" Henry ventured.

"Nah, I don't think so," the man laughed. "At least not yet. There may as well be though – there's a law against just about everything else involving football. What were you thrown out for?"

"I wasn't thrown out!"

The jogger raised his eyebrows, half in surprise, half in doubt.

"I wasn't!" Henry looked around. There were a few high-visibility policemen wandering around, but nobody close. "I would have been though. There's no way I could have lasted through the rest of that match without going off into a swearing frenzy – at the very least. Now I'm just sad that I'll never see the game again. Not the game I remember anyway."

"Oh, you never know. Don't you think there'll come a time when real football makes a comeback? It's been banned before, you know? Oh yes. In the Middle Ages King Edward the Third realised none of the villagers had been doing their archery practise, so he banned it. He shouldn't have worried, really … if he'd have sent the likes of Billy Bremner, Ron Harris, Terry Butcher and Bryan Robson in against the French we would have had The Hundred Years War won by lunchtime."

Henry laughed. He was enjoying himself now. "Well you know your football mate, and your history. And I hope you're right, I really do. I'd love to see football, real football, back to what it used to be. I can't see it happening, though. Not in my lifetime."

"Why not? You must be about the same age as me? Late seventies?"

"Give or take."

"So, like I said, who knows what might happen, even in the next few years. Average life expectancy for a bloke is 108 now. You never know."

Henry took another furtive look around, although he wasn't worried about policemen this time. Was he really going to tell a stranger what he couldn't even tell his own wife?

"I've not got long. The doctor told me last month. I know they reckon they can cure anything these days, but not this. I've got days … weeks at best."

"Bloody Hell. Sorry to hear that."

"So you see, I don't want to swim with dolphins or climb Everest. I've already seen The Great Wall of China and the Empire State Building, and although it seems just about everybody you meet these days has been to the moon, all I really wanted was to see a football match. Well, if that was it, I'm probably better off dead."

The jogger studied him for a few moments. There was no pity in his eyes, just analysis. Eventually he seemed to make up his mind about something.

"Listen," he said. "I'm not jogging out here for the good of my health." He stopped and took a surreptitious glance in each direction. "I'm part of a movement, a resistance if you like. My job is to recruit people who are disaffected by the sports franchises of today, eventually to build enough opposition to be able to form our own political party maybe. The party will have one policy: to return football to its rightful place as the most passionate, emotive and exciting sport on the planet. This country invented the game once; now it's time to re-invent it."

The jogger himself was tense, excited by his own words. Henry certainly believed he was genuine.

"That's great, mate." he said. "I wish you the best of luck, but like I say, I've got a month at the most ..."

"I know, and that's why I'm taking a chance. Normally we would have you followed for weeks before approaching you. We have people who can check out your employment, your bank records, everything to make sure you're not KFC."
"Wasn't fast food banned in the twenties?"

"Yeah, not KFC – KFC. It's an MI6 undercover operation; it stands for Keep Football Contained. Anyway, the point is, if you're really sure about this, there's a game tonight ... well now, in fact," he said, glancing at his watch.

Henry wasn't totally convinced. But then, what did he have to lose?

"The name's Henry," he said, offering his hand and standing to go at the same time.

"Stuart," said the jogger. "Although most people still call me 'Psycho'."

Psycho's car was expensive, but could only go as fast as the traffic would allow. Henry had called Sammy on his mobile and had convinced him he'd taken a lift home with an old friend he'd bumped into. He consoled himself that this was at least tenuously true. They stopped to pick up two of Psycho's friends – guys about Sammy's age, both wearing dark jackets despite the warm autumn sun. And both wore those retro baseball caps – Henry hadn't seen those in years. They introduced themselves to him as Scholesy and Peanut, handing him a can of lager before opening their own.

"Whoa! This is strong stuff, lads," he said, studying the label for proof that it was just beer. "It's more than the maximum 3% proof, that's for sure."

"Scholesy smuggles it in from Latvia," Peanut beamed. "We got interested in football when we were studying 20th Century Social History for our degrees. We like to be as traditional as possible when we go to these matches."

He rubbed his chin and thought for a second. "Don't worry though," he added, a malevolent grin matching the mischief in his eyes. "We won't be asking you to join in any scrapping."

Scholesy joined in Peanut's joke, laughing along with him before patting Henry on the back and telling him to ignore his friend.

After an hour the car pulled into a lay-by and they waited, passing the time with another can of contraband lager. Psycho contented himself with a glucose drink, his obvious apprehension only breaking when his phone rang.

"It's on!" He announced to his passengers. "'Big Fat Ron Stadium' – let's go."

They drove off into the vast Skelmersdale Forest, planted over twenty years ago in an effort to negate carbon pollution. The car went deeper into the dense woodland, trees brushing both sides of the vehicle, and Henry began to get worried. He replayed the events over in his head: here he was, in a forest, miles from anywhere, with a man who claimed to be an ex-footballer, but who was now part of a secret resistance movement; joined by two replica hooligans who were happy to see him drunk. This was not the best decision he'd made in his life, but again: what did he have to lose?

Before long they joined a row of red brake lights, stopping and starting on the narrow tracks, but pushing deeper into the woods. A minute later Henry turned and saw at least six or seven cars behind them. Eventually the cars in front were forced to stop.

"This is as far as we drive, Henry. It's about a mile walk from here. You all right?"

Henry nodded. He felt safer now as he watched people front and back clambering from their cars. Some were dressed in similar attire to Peanut and Scholsey, but there were also families here and there, and several people of his own age.

"Only I've got to go," continued Psycho. "I'm running the line today, but these two will take good care of you."

"No problem," said Scholsey, handing Henry another can. "As long as you behave yourself."

They followed a thin crowd, walking along the line of stationary cars. Here and there, as the forest tracks converged, they were joined by others, until the road widened and became thick with people. A buzz of excitement and expectancy filled the air, and Henry felt fuelled by it, adding to the euphoria he was beginning to draw from the over-strength beer.

And then singing. Here and there were pockets of people singing. Some produced scarves, others banners, rattles and old fashioned football shirts. Henry felt less like a man dying and more like a man living. The forest opened up: a vast plain of around a square acre, marked out, goalposts and nets, and with embankments covering three sides. And on these embankments were more people. Some had clearly been there for hours and were busy clearing away picnics and making room for those that were now joining them.

"There must be two or three thousand here," said Henry.

"We usually get over three," confirmed Peanut. "Any more and our pitches won't be big enough. By that time though, there'll be enough of us for the revolution to begin. There's well over two-hundred thousand people on our database. There's games like this all over the country, an established league. We're nearly ready to start it all again, Henry. And this time it won't be run for the benefit of Coke or Nike; this time it's going to stay the people's game."

Henry made his way onto one of the embankments behind the goal. "Who's playing?" He said to a woman he found himself stood next to. She looked him in the eye – they were the deepest and most wonderful eyes Henry had ever seen in his life. She put her hand around Henry's forearm and squeezed him gently.

"Blackburn Rovers against Preston North End, love."

"Those clubs went out of business over twenty years ago."

"Aye, love," she smiled. "But this isn't business anymore. This is football."

The match kicked off to a cheer from the crowd, and singing, chanting rippled spontaneously from different parts, almost incessantly. Henry hadn't heard noise like that for years. He finished his can and was instantly replenished by the insistent Scholesy. On the pitch the action was furious – Henry had seen more skilful players in his time, but few more passionate. A crunching tackle right in front of him was greeted by a barrage of abuse from those around him.

"C'mon, Lino!" shouted a man behind him. "You're not taking penalties now – get your flag up!"

People laughed. The resultant free-kick was headed in and everyone around him jumped up and down as if electrocuted by rapture. Those behind the other goal remained static, glum. And now the singing was louder: cutting, cynical, comical, compulsive and contagious. The match re-started, its pace increased, its fervour multiplied.

Henry felt lifted, as if in some dream-state. He knew the alcohol was helping, but it was more than that. He felt young again, the aches and pains of his advancing years disappeared, replaced by a vigour he'd not felt for years. He closed his eyes and drank in the noise, the atmosphere. He tried to imagine the pitch in front of him, but with stands and terraces instead of grass embankments, with fifty or sixty thousand people instead of three or four. He opened his eyes and they were there: the stadium, the crowds … floodlights, TV cameras, electronic scoreboards.

Bloody good lager this, he thought.

Another goal! The crowd surged and jumped again – grown men hugging each other with unconfined joy. Then singing, impossibly louder than before: the elation of a two-goal lead lifting the atmosphere to impossible heights.

Henry laughed, shaking his head. "You know," he said to the woman. "I'm in absolute heaven …"

"You are, love, yes. It's wonderful, isn't it?"

Something in her voice. Something … angelic.

Henry looked for Peanut and Scholsey. They were gone. But the eyes of those around him met his, sheer love in all of them. One man grabbed him, "Two-nil … two-nil…" he shouted before hugging him. "C'mon, boys!"

Released, Henry turned his attention back to the pitch. The stadium was still there, still in all its glory. The crowd swayed and sang as one. He belonged here. He understood ecstasy.

He understood everything.

He'd made it.

Heaven.

Piffy On A Rock Bun

Author's Note (G Sharp Wild)

If you look up the word 'jib' in a dictionary, you will no doubt be left with the impression that it's a sailing term, or possibly an old fashioned word for a knife. You might hear the term 'I like the cut of his jib', and be none the wiser. What you probably won't find, not even in an urban dictionary, is the meaning it has to a select group of football supporters. Let me explain.

Sometimes in Manchester we steal things. We don't mean any harm by it. Okay, I'm not talking about street muggings, burglary or those riots in 2011 – they were just idiots and the vast majority of the town told them that they were. Well, they probably told them they were 'skanks', or some such colourful idiom, but you get my point. Manchester, and its conjoined twin Salford, is the land of the jib. There is nothing sweeter than getting for free via the process of some creative mischief something that you are supposed to pay for. When the combined forces of London's football hooligans termed themselves the 'Inter City Firm' because they travelled to their respective battles on the intercity train, they would no doubt have been passed by Manchester's 'Inter City Jibbers', whose mission it was to get to away games without paying the fare. Or the ticket into the game. Or even the half time pie, if at all possible. And they are very proud whenever a successful jib is performed – everyone is told about it. And quite right too.

So this story is a successful jib. I read the script of a play by John K. Hall called 'Abide With Me'. I've never met John, but it's a wonderful story, set in West Midlands around the 1968 FA Cup final – the first game of football to be shown live on colour television in the UK. Actor, writer, musician, director, friend and Northerner Ian D. Fleming re-wrote the script into a screenplay, with the working title 'Glory, Glory' and the ambition of having it commissioned for television. However, once I put the idea into his head that any story that is even loosely connected to a football game in 1968 had to involve George Best, Manchester music and the European Cup final, he struggled to think beyond it. I saw the beginning of the first draft of Ian's screenplay but then, as these things often do, other projects took over and it was forgotten.

I was kicking around ideas for this book and couldn't get the story out of my own mind. It needed to be written – Saint Georgie Best came to me in a dream and told me. So, with apologies to John K. Hall, West

Bromwich Albion and Ian D Fleming (I could never afford a middle initial), and whilst the end result is very different from the original, this is a bit of a jib. And I needed to tell you about it.

Piffy On A Rock Bun; A colloquial term used in and around the Manchester area of England; meaning to be kept hanging around or waiting unnecessarily.

ST ANN'S ROMAN CATHOLIC CHURCH
STRETFORD - MANCHESTER
15th May, 1968

Father Fergal O'Leary pressed his fingers to his temples and fought with his conscience. These were trying times for the Catholic Church: if it wasn't birth control, free love and rock and roll, it was LSD, excessive profanity and long hair. It was, as he often told himself, enough to try the patience of a Saint. The choir in front of him had sung beautifully, angelically, but now, as young Michael practiced his solo rendition of 'Abide With Me', the choice of hymn only served to remind him of a higher place: The Santiago Bernabau Stadium, in fact, where, at this very moment, the town's young football team were playing in front of 125,000 people against the Spanish Colossus Real Madrid for a place in the European Cup Final.

And here he was, caught in the recurring nightmare of Declan Hughes's wedding rehearsal – the fourth this month already. One-nil up from the home leg, a late arrival had whispered they were 3-1 down at half time over there.

3-1 down. 3-2 on aggregate.

He prayed silently for the virtue of patience, bit his lower lip and smiled paternally at little Michael as the ginger haired eight year old started on the second verse. The young boy beamed and returned the priest's smile, corrupting his cherub-like face with a gap-toothed grin. Proud of his moment in the limelight, he held his framed picture of Jesus a little higher towards heaven, as Mrs Hughes had impressed on him to do so. Father O'Leary smiled again. Was this a sign? What a sin, he told himself, to be thinking about football when the Lord's flock needed his help. He gazed soulfully at the picture just as, almost miraculously, a stray ray of sunshine found its way through the grime of the stained glass window and lit up the Holy image.

"Hang on," he mumbled, as he lifted his spectacles and squinted his sixty year old eyes at the frame. "That's not a picture of our Lord Jesus Christ – that's Georgie Best! It is a sign!" He checked his wristwatch from the corner of his eye, looked up to the heavens, crossed himself quickly and started down the altar steps, determined to wrap up proceedings so that he could at least sneak into the vestry and check the score on the wireless.

"Now Missus Hughes, Missus Hughes," he protested in his strong, Galway brogue, "I really think that young Michael has it off to a T now, don't you think? I really must insist ..."

The buxom, brassy, beehived-beauty that was collectively known as Mrs Marjorie Hughes continued to over-conduct Michael's solo; the child's voice wobbled slightly as he deliberated on whom he was most terrified of – the divine Holy Father, representative of the Lord here on earth, or the fourteen stone of home peroxide and foundation cream that was Mrs Marjorie Hughes. He continued to sing. She was not a women easily dissuaded from her own mind, and she began to motion the priest back up the altar steps, like a farmer shooing geese.
"No, no ... not just yet Father Fergal ... Oooh, that's lovely Michael ... yes ... yes ... 'When other helpers fail; and comforts flee...' good ... good ... and fortissimo, bellisimo..."

The groom to be, Declan Hughes, stifled a giggle as he recognised the fear in Father O'Leary's eyes – how many times had his mother shooed him upstairs like that at home? Far too many – and he was twenty-four, for goodness sake! The stifled giggle became a stifled groan as his fiancée, the long-suffering Róisín Malone, rabbit-punched him in the ribs. This was not a wise move on Róisín's part: Declan had come straight from work and was still dressed in his mechanic's overalls – she looked in horror at her meticulously bathed, highly pampered hand, which was now covered in several layers of engine oil, axle grease and, for some reason, raspberry jam.

Declan stifled another giggle as Róisín wiped the residue on the red and white scarf he had tied to his wrist.

She looked to the skies and prayed for strength, then back at Declan and prayed for a miracle. She loved him, of course. Or at least she loved the idea of him. She loved his height and slim build, intense eyes, his good looks and mischievous grin. What she didn't love was his schoolyard jokes and general sense of instability and immaturity. She certainly didn't like this terrible addiction to football that he seemed to live for. Would marriage change him? Is it right to want him to change? She loved him, and wasn't that enough?

He wasn't always in his overalls, covered in oil, she consoled herself. Very much into his music, he invested heavily in sharp suits, nifty shoes and shiny ties. Róisín, whose name was often shortened to Rosh and then further, given her tendency to want to better herself, to the nickname of Posh, loved nothing better than to dress herself up and go out on the town, dancing with him. She hated that nickname though. Just because she tended to pronounce her 'haitches' and was trying to be more than just a secretary at Louis Edwards' meat factory didn't mean she thought herself better than anyone.

Declan, meanwhile, was playing with his welding goggles and wondered why churches were so draughty. And so behind the times too, man. I mean, if he had to get married – and it seemed he had – why couldn't he have The Beatles singing 'All You Need Is Love' instead of half a dozen tone-deaf bin lids squeaking three-hundred year old hymns?

Michael started verse three. Two old women, neighbours of the Hughes', but there primarily for entertainment and to keep their heating bills down, sit at the back and listen intently.

"Lovely singing voice, that young lad of the Hucknell's," said one, Ethel.

"Beg pardon?" said the other.

"I said, 'Lovely singing voice, that young Michael Hucknell'."

"Oh, lovely, yes. Never do anything with it though."

"Oh no, lovely voice, but he was beaten with the ugly stick that lad …"

"Tha's reet. And those missing teeth … his mouth looks like Ordsall Cemetery on a rainy day."

"And ginger of course. Don't forget ginger."

"Oh no, of course not, Jeanie. Ginger. Lovely singing voice though."

"Oh aye – lovely singing voice."

They are silenced by a disapproving glance from Mrs Hughes.

Terrence McAllister is the Best Man. This is purely an honorary title for the sole purpose of Declan and Róisín's wedding, and not to be confused with any of his actual characteristics. He wears the same brand of overalls as Declan (which themselves are covered in the same brand of engine oil, axle grease and, of course, raspberry jam); the same brand of welding goggles hang loosely around his neck; the same kind of red and white scarf sits uncertainly on his knees. He differs from Declan partially because of his short, brylcreamed hair, and also because he is currently confined to a wheelchair, a plaster-casted leg extends out in front of him, a similar one incapacitates his arm. Terry's capacity for incapacitating himself is legendary.

He also has a finger to his ear, his attention far, far away from the little church in Stretford. He is mumbling to himself, unaware that, in the echoing chambers of St Ann's, he is beginning to attract attention.

"Go on ... go on, son. C'mon ... yes ... that's it, Johnny lad ... c'moooooon..."

Michael beams again, believing he is the subject of Terry's encouragement. Towards the rear of the church the two old ladies purse their lips in judgement; one of them has now noticed the ear-piece that Terry is doing his best to hide.

Impressed, she turns to her friend, "Security's going a bit far for this wedding, isn't it?"

"Oh, to the manor born, that one! Pompous cow."

Mrs Hughes, still trying to conduct little Michael with one hand and shoo Father Fergal with the other, casts the old women a second withering look. They smile back in unified two-facedness. Michael becomes distracted and goes off key. Mrs Hughes bats around at him, fussing and cussing.

"Neigh, lad. Neigh ... 'What but thy grace can foil the tempter's power' she screeches ... Oh, you'll get it reet on't day, I say, you'll get it reet on t' day! Better bloody 'ad," she admonishes. Failing to notice Father O'Leary's reaction to her swearing, she continues to direct proceedings, manhandling the poor choirboy into position.

"Anyway ... then you step down here ... down here ... bring the picture with you. That's it. Over to here ... by our Declan and Róisín; that's it, turn round and face t' other way ... that's it ... and Father Fergal will take the picture and offer a blessing to ..."

The careworn clergyman glances contritely towards the open church doors, where an impatient funeral party are crowded around a coffin draped in sky-blue and white City scarves. In the open coffin, the deceased is wearing his own beloved scarf, neatly folded around his neck one last time. His Maine Road season ticket has been placed lovingly in his suit top pocket, and he holds a football rattle in his corpse-crossed hands. The mourners too wear similar coloured scarves over dark suits.

"Now Missus Hughes, I'm sure we've got it after five run throughs. The Church does have other functions to attend to," he offers.

Mrs Hughes dismisses him with a wave, "Aye. Well. Humph! Shouldn't they be down St Peter's anyway, Father Fergal?"

"Missus Hughes …"

"Oh, Marjorie, please Father … Marjorie."

"We really need to be getting on. We'll have it dark before I can get to Mr Gallagher and his family …"

"They can wait." She false-smiles over to them and catches sight of Terry.

"And I hope you'll be ready wi' them rings on t' day Terrence McAllister … I say… hey! Cloth ears!"

But Terry is still captivated elsewhere; his mind's eye is in another country, his focus on another kind of religion. In this world of his own, he fails to realize that the eyes and ears of the whole church are on him.

"Go on … Go on! …" he says.

He stops abruptly: silence. The wedding rehearsal and the funeral party lean as one towards him. Nothing in the church stirs. Seconds pass, but feel like millennia, until at last the silence is broken.

"YEEEEEEEEEESSSS!! Yeeeesss!!! Aaaarrrghhh!" Terry's exuberance tips his wheel chair backwards. He lands in a heap and Declan dashes over to help him, while Róisín can only shake her head and turn away reproachfully.

"Me leg! Me radio!" cries Terry: now both are broken. "Flamin' Nora!"

Father O'Leary picks the wheelchair up as Declan, accompanied by some pitiful moaning and griping from Terry and some angry 'huffing' from Róisín, struggles to help him back into his seat.

"Ah … Ow … cheers, Decs, much obliged … ah! … much obliged, Father F," whimpers Terrence.

"I've told 'im Mrs Hughes, I've told 'im," complains Róisín … if he's got no other mates, get his brother to do it … but oh no … you'd have thought it natural to ask your twin brother anyway!" she rolls her eyes again and turns her back on the operation to get Terry back into his chair: arms folded, lip curled.

Several pews behind, Declan's twin brother, Aiden, looks up. He too is dressed in the same overalls as Declan and Terry – 'Chester Road Motor Repairs' stitched above the top pocket. Although an identical twin, they are very easily differentiated – Aiden hangs out with the Rockers, not the Mods. His hair is longer, lanker and, next to the immaculately coiffured head of Declan, he also sports a rough beard. He is here under sufferance. He hasn't got on with Declan for some time and although this marriage has been talked about since the early 1950s, this is the first time anyone has mentioned even the possibility of him being the Best Man. He considers what his speech might be '… Good evening, well Róisín is a beautiful, intelligent, humorous woman, which is why I can't believe she's marrying such a self-centred, arrogant idiot like Declan. Enjoy your night.' At least it would be short.

"I know Róisín love, I know. Is it really a good idea to have a best man that can't walk, our Declan? No offence Terrence, love."

"Ah'll be reet, Mrs H … reet as rain … promise."

Father O'Leary looks over his glasses, and raises his eyebrows with a question to Terry.

"Errr … uhummm … Bill Foulkes. 3-3. We're through. We're going to Wembley," he says, a little fearful of Róisín's reaction.

Father O'Leary gives a quick clench fisted 'Yes!' as the mourners at the door look across questioningly.

"Bill Foulkes. 3-3." Repeats the priest in explanation, rather more smugly than his faith would normally allow. He crosses himself before putting his hands together in a moment of silent thanks.

The Gallagher family's mood darkens further. One of them places a consoling hand on the corner of the coffin and peers in – just to make sure that granddad wasn't turning already: Manchester United, it seemed, had just become the first English club to reach the final of the European Cup.

ELTON STREET, STRETFORD
18th May 1968

High above the little terraced street, pigeons and crows sit on chimney pots and gaze in wonder at the strange bustle of activity taking place below. Neighbours put aside petty quarrels and help each other hang red and white bunting from lamp post to lamp post. Every child from three to thirteen is involved in a game of street football, eighteen-a-side. All of them are Georgie Best. Husbands are painting their doors and window frames red, annoying their wives who are trying to scrub their front steps.

In a street full of activity, the Hughes' house – actually two red-brick two up, two-downs, knocked together to accommodate their extended family – is the focus of particular commotion: a window cleaner scrubs the front panes furiously, clear that his work will be inspected closer than usual; another workman climbs an adjacent ladder, clasping a brand new aerial as he does so and, arousing the most attention, a white van is unloading outside the front door. While Róisín appears with two mugs of tea, Mrs Hughes directs proceedings, supervising as two delivery men huff and puff to carry a brand new colour television into her parlour.

"Careful now lads, careful. Precious cargo that. Precious cargo."

Next door, the two old ladies, Ethel and Jeannie, stop donkey stoning their doorsteps in choreographed unison and shrivel their faces in judgement.

"State of her. Cat with the pigging cream," says one.

"Beg pardon?" says the other.

The two delivery men huff and puff …

"Come on Reggie, come on, put yer back into it."

This is a worrying time for Mrs Hughes, "Oooh … slow down a bit there lads, slow down … careful! Hey, is there a village missing an idiot somewhere? Easy … easy … Oi! Break that and you'll be fettling it yourself, yer twonk!"

She nods towards the old ladies, taking a tea from Róisín.
Ethel and Jeanie get on with their work, ill at ease with the pace of the modern world.

To add to the confusion, a milk float trundles to a halt by the front of the delivery van and Gobind Livroop Ripudaman Sahib steps down. He grabs a half full milk crate and walks towards Mrs Hughes.

"It's here then Marjie. Eeee by 'eck. Colour bloody telly in Elton Street … who'dav thought it then?"

The two old ladies stop their chores a second time.

"Look at 'er. Again!"

"No shame …"

"Blokes …"

"Shocking!"

"… fellas …"

"… day in, day out …"

"… buzzin' round …"

"Like flies round …"

"… a lavvy?"

"Hmmph!"

With a beaming smile, Gobind loads Mrs Hughes down with his crate. "For my special lady," he says, coyly.

She lifts it, pushing her ample chest up and accentuating her large cleavage.

"You'll not sweeten me that easily..."

But Gobind, unperturbed, lifts his turban to reveal a carton of fresh orange juice, flirtatiously offering it her, as if it was the biggest bouquet in Beswick.

"Talk about currying favour!" says one of the old women.

"Ooooh ... I don't go for curry me. Plays havoc ... y' know? With ..." she looks round furtively and mouths "Me grapes."

Mrs Hughes is enjoying the game with Gobind and laughs saucily, "You'd better fetch them inside, m'dear. I'm a bit loaded down."

Gobind's eyes widen in appreciation of her assets and they go inside. Róisín smiles and shakes her head; she takes a sip of tea and follows them.

The activity in Mrs Hughes' living room reflects the pandemonium outside: a decorator and his apprentice, Barry and Paul, are just clearing up, the room having been newly papered; they chuckle to each other, rolling their eyes at the bold red and white stripes that Mrs Hughes has chosen for the wall. The television delivery men are installing the television, Reggie stretching his back, puffing and blowing; Mr Hughes – who, grey-bearded with unkempt long hair, has an uncanny resemblance to an older George Best – slobs in his armchair, a cigarette dangling from his lips, its inch-long wilting ash teetering under its own weight. It falls, landing on his stained vest as he discards the cellophane wrapper of a new packet and pulls out a fresh smoke.

Mrs Hughes, Gobind and Róisín bustle in, adding to the melee. Trapped underneath Mr Hughes' slippered foot is an Embassy cigarette coupon, and Róisín rescues it, stuffing it into a toffee jar. Along the mantelpiece stands a line of similar jars, each with their own individually handwritten label: electric blanket, eiderdown, towels, and toaster. Reggie turns to his delivery boy, Ronnie, and, after they share a moment of apprehension akin to the launch of the Apollo Space Missions, he flicks a switch and the television makes a pinging noise as its tubes begin to warm.

Mrs Hughes stares in wonderment, "Fan-tastic! Fan - bloody - tastic!"

Gobind and Róisín gawp as TV snow and rolling bars dance cheekily across the screen.

"Eeeee ... first colour telly in this part of Stretford, eh...?" says Gobind, genuinely impressed.

"First colour telly in Manchester more like... ne' mind Stretford." Retorts the hostess. Gobind smiles – this isn't true, but he's not going to be the one to put Mrs Hughes right.

The decorator's apprentice, Paul, is busy replacing ornaments on the enormous mantelpiece, and unceremoniously plonks a picture of the Pope in the middle, causing the frantic Mrs Hughes to run over and re-position it.

"Oooh ... careful, chuck, careful." She moves Paul IV and takes another picture from his namesake, placing this one carefully in the centre of the mantelpiece – pride of place. Stepping back to admire the framed painting of George Best, she momentarily forgets about the new television.

"Now that's what I call a Busby babe. I'd show him a move or two ... the little red devil. Sets me a-mind o' you when you still had yer looks," she says, throwing Mr Hughes a pitiful glance. "Spit of him ... he was. Now look at him." She shakes her head wearily, but is jolted from her reverie by a ghost-like image that flickers onto the television. "Hey! There! There! 'Ang about. That was it!"

Reggie is twiddling at the back of the television. The picture rolls then settles gradually on a local news item: BBC Football Preview – in full colour! An interview with Matt Busby at the United training ground has just finished. Star players from the team are training in the background, George Best playing keepie-up on his head.

"Well, I'll go t'foot of our stairs! I've never seen him in colour. Our Georgie ... El Beatle."

Reggie changes the channel to ITV. It's black and white.

"Hey I were … hang on what's that? Hey, it best not be broke, young man?"

"S'ITV, love. Nowt wrong with my televisions."

"ITV? I. T. black an' blummin' white more like. I haven't paid good money for black and blummin' white!!"

Reggie sighs; the customer is always right. However, "Only BBC's got colour for now, love, and even then not everything's in colour … not yet."

"Only BBC! Not ALL in colour! Never told me that in your bleeding shop did you?!"

They're distracted by the TV voice-over:

"Ten years after the Munich Disaster and Busby's new Babes take on the might of Benfica in the European Cup Final …and we've got the best view, live from Wembley … right here on ITV."

"Aye. In colour … in colour … right? Róisín, Róisín chuck us that Radio Times, chuck."

Mrs Hughes anxiously rifles through the magazine as the rest of the room hold their breath. Gobind, Róisín, Reggie and his delivery boy, the decorator and his apprentice all look at each other nervously. Reggie makes small movements towards the door. Outside, George the window cleaner, who has been wiping the same spot for the last fifteen minutes, gawps in, his shammy now static in his hand. Even Mr Hughes, who has just secretly added a measure of Irish Whiskey to his tea, leans forward, minutely, pushing the half-bottle back under his armchair cushion. Eventually the silence of the moment is broken, excessively, by Mrs Hughes, who has now found the information she was looking for.

"Whaaaaaat?! I don't be-bloody-lieve it! No … no … Nooooooooooooooooooooooooooooooooooo!"

At the other end of the street, oblivious to the drama at home, Declan kangaroo-rides on a wreck of a newly-acquired, backfiring Vespa scooter. He's struggling to stay in control, but manages to stop by knocking it into the back of the delivery van, lurching to a noisy halt. Feeling super-cool, he looks around proudly, steps off and faffs about pulling the scooter up onto its stand.

A little kid, snot escaping copiously from both nostrils, stops next to him on his tricycle. He looks at Declan then down at the scooter, steam pouring from its engine. He shakes his head, rolls his eyes to the sky, and pedals off. Declan, proud as punch, pats the seat. There's a creaking sound and the scooter stand collapses, toppling the machine sideways into the road. Hauling the scooter back up, he wheels it onto the pavement and leans it against wall by the Hughes' front door, taking a brown paper parcel tied with string from the rusty carrier as he does so.

He can hear his mother's ranting inside before he even opens the door, and when he does so he finds his way is suddenly blocked as Ronnie and Reggie sneak out of the house, nervously nodding to Declan on their way to the van. Declan watches them go, turns again to step inside, but is pinned to the architrave as Gobind dashes by, hotly followed by the decorators, Barry and Paul, still nervously chuckling through their fright and flight. Only Gobind spares him a few breathless words as he starts his milk van.

"Alright Decs? Hey … to think, eh? Colour telly on Elton Street. The future's racin' up on us … racin' right up on us. See yer later, gater."

Just then Mrs Hughes appears, chasing after Reggie with a rolled up TV Times; Gobind Livroop Ripudaman Sahib puts his foot to the floor and leans forward in his cab, willing the heavily laden milk float to speed his getaway.

"And what am I meant to tell everyone eh? Are you tryin' t' mek me a laughin' stock? Not in bloody colour!! I'll give you some bloody colour, lad. I say … I'll give you some colour! C' mere, y' little shitbag!"

Declan watches them go, before turning a third time to go inside, but is blocked yet again, this time by Róisín.

"Oh. Hiya, Posh … errrr …. Rosh," he says, airily, and goes to kiss her on the cheek. She pulls away.

"Don't you call me Rosh! Or Posh! You know I hate that. And where the hell 'av you been Declan Hughes? Meet at ours, you said. Half four, you said. I get off work early. I get meself dolled up, and then … what's that?!" She stares at the scooter, looking like someone has just added dog muck to her fruit salad.

"It's mine … well … errr … it's ours, love."

The scooter creaks again and falls over. Róisín storms back inside without another word.

Mrs Hughes has chased the TV men into their van and is bashing at their window with the TV Times.

"Open that bloody door, I say! Come back … I say … come back 'ere … you!"

The van speeds off – Mrs Hughes gives a short chase, then throws the TV Times after it. The old ladies, still donkey stoning in unison, watch from the corner of their eyes.

"What's wrong with her face?"

"Like a bulldog lickin' piss off a kettle."

"Common."

"As muck."

"And twice as loud."

Mrs Hughes retrieves her TV Times and composes herself, pushing a loosened clump of her beehive back into place, and assembling her bosom into an orderly presentation.

"Ethel. Jeanie."

The old ladies smile emphatically and give her a little unified wave:

"Marjie." They say together. "Bit o' bother?"

Mrs Hughes straightens her pinafore before answering.

"Nowt that can't be sorted, ladies. Nowt that can't be sorted."

Mr Hughes has enjoyed his few minutes of peace and quiet since his Beloved emptied the room quicker than an extra collection at Mass, but his idyll is crushed as Declan enters the parlour, hounded by Róisín.

"You've got responsibilities now, Declan Hughes You should show some maturity," she says.

"Awright, Dad?" manages Declan in between her verbal attacks, and is rewarded with an almost inaudible grunt. He takes this as a sign that his father is in a good mood and drops his brown paper parcel onto the enormous sideboard. A small Woolies bag, which was held beneath the string of Declan's parcel, catches Róisín's eye, and she picks it up without being deflected from her current line of interrogation.

"Well, I'm tellin' y' … you can take it right back to Terry … I'm not … we're not being seen on one o' them things!" She sighs in disgust as she realises the bag contains a record; she starts to prise open the parcel, but doesn't miss a beat of her berating.

"Death traps they are. And if you think for two minutes that when we're married you can just swan in and out as you please …"

Declan is currently aghast by the change the decorators have made to the room and has completely tuned Róisín out. She doesn't seem to notice. Mr Hughes slurps his mug of tea and takes a short puff of his cigarette, also oblivious.

"… well, you've got another think coming. And another thing …"

Beyond the dazzle of the red and white wallpaper, Declan finally sees the new television.

"He-heeyyy!! It's come then." he says, jumping onto the settee just as Top of the Pops is starting. "Eeeee … champion!"

He taps his feet to the beat of the first tune as Róisín continues on the theme of rust poisoning.
Then, from nowhere, he says, "I've always wondered about that."

"Eh?"

"Well, what you just said a minute ago," he says, still gawping at the television, "how you can have another 'think' coming. I mean d' y' know you're gonnar 'av a 'think' coming … or does it just … y'know … come …?"

He gets up from his seat, walks over to the television and turns up the volume, "What d' you think?"

Róisín puts his ramblings down to pre-wedding nerves, and anyway she's now opened his parcel.

"And what's these?"

"Jeans…"

"I can see they're jeans. You and that bloomin' Terry were meant t've been getting yer suits sorted. We're meant to be saving, Declan Hughes, not frittering away good money on … Oooh, 'ang on … bell-bottoms … are they f' me? What a nice thought!"
A despondent Mrs Hughes traipses in, and immediately fires a warning shot at Declan.

"Hey, you! Fingers! Fingers!" she says, pulling him unceremoniously out of the way. Producing a yellow dust cloth from her pinafore she scowls at her son and dusts the television lovingly. Declan flops back onto the settee, trying his best to see round his mum, air drumming along with The Who, who are the star turn on Top of the Pops.

"Yer mek a better door than a window, mam!"

Mrs Hughes ignores him. She's cleaning the screen, looking at the picture in dramatic disgust.

"Well, this rubbish is in colour! They've got it wrong … they must have … it must be in colour, eh Róisín? Did you know about this, our Declan?"

But he's in mid drum roll now, lost in 'Magic Bus'. Róisín meanwhile is testing the size of the jeans against her legs, and is somewhat puzzled at their excessive size.

"Oi! Keith Loon!" tries Mrs Hughes again. She gives up and changes channels. A black and white advert shows two bikini clad women throwing a beach ball between them. Mr Hughes almost imperceptibly raises an eyebrow. She turns it over again and finds BBC2.

"Ffffhhuuhh. See. Colour there." She flicks it back again to Top of the Pops.

"And this is Beeb One …"

Declan leans forward, keen to see who the next band is, while Róisín takes a seat next to him with the jeans. Mrs Hughes turns it over again: ITV; another ad in black and white. Mr Hughes' eyes flicker in anticipation, but the young ladies have been replaced by some men in white lab coats holding a large tub of washing powder in an extremely serious manner.

"Mam!! I was watching that!"

"Bloody fruitcakes, the lot of 'em."

"But I've never seen 'em in colour!"

Róisín holds up the jeans and says, "Y' do know I'm a size 10, don't yer?"

"And if come Wednesday night, we can't see t'Mighty Reds in piggin' colour … well … who's going to come t'wedding reception?"

"Eh?" says Declan.

"Th' match, of course. It's the same day as yer bloody wedding, and I was thinking that we could have the reception here and have the match on … in colour. That way we save a few bob on booking upstairs at the Dog and Partridge and we can afford that new dress for your bride to be." She smiles and winks at Róisín who returns the smile and, admiring the jeans again, nuzzles Declan and gives him a little peck.

"Bugger! I've 'ad all the tickets written up now …" adds, Mrs Hughes, for whom things are not proceeding to plan today.
He looks at them both as if they may well have a screw loose and gets up, taking the jeans from Róisín and picking up his record to take with him. He stops and considers the new wallpaper again.

"What made you go for red and white stripes, mam?" he asks. He knows the answer, and wonders if he should be the one to reveal this latest revelation. It's the opportunity to have a good laugh that made him ask though.

"Eh? Why do you think? Whole road's done up in red and white – United are through to the final and this house is going to show its support better than any other."

"Yeah, fair enough, mam. Only … you do know they'll be playing in blue on Wednesday night?" It's all Declan can do to stop falling about laughing.

"You what? Blue. Stop winding me up, buggerlugs. Yer can't kid a kidder."

"S'true, mam – they're playing in blue. See – it's in the paper." He points to the back of the Saturday's Pink, which is being conveniently held up by Mr Hughes as he re-reads the dog racing form for the umpteenth time.

"Whaaa??!! They're all out to get me, they are, all out to get me! First they're not showing it in colour, and then, whilst the wallpaper paste isn't even dry, they tell me they're playing in blue! Blue! That's City's colours … I blame that Louis Edwards, I do. Never trusted him since he sold that dodgy meat into St Mary's Primary in 1953. Probably on a bung for it."

"Nah, mam. Both United and Benfica play in red normally, so they're both wearing their second kits. And it's a deep blue, none of that sky blue nonsense like them from down the road. Mind you, Benfica's second kit is white with red trim, so it looks like you'll be supporting them on Wednesday night."

Declan can't hold back his laughing now, as he starts to leave the room, leaving his mother, whose anger is clearly visible in her face and has turned an appropriate mixture of red and blue, to look for someone to blame for this latest setback. It is just as he reaches the living room door that his mam's earlier words hit him; the smile drops from his face, which turns and immediate deathly white.

"The wedding. It's the same day as the match." he stammers, and his legs wobble.

"Are you feelin' all reet, petal?" says Róisín, most concerned at the possibility that he may be ill for the wedding. "Yer not comin' down with summat are yer?"

"It's the same ... day ... as ... the ... bloody 'ell?" he says again as he unsteadily reaches the door – his footsteps are soon heard taking the stairs two at a time.

Róisín huffs and folds her arms, but she softens as Mrs Hughes nods for her to go after him. She goes; her own footsteps quieter and more considered as she negotiates the narrow, steep steps.

Shaking her head at love's young dream, the house-proud Mrs Hughes stoops to tidy up the brown paper and take Gobind's milk and orange juice to the pantry. Still seething about the colour television and the, now, inappropriate wallpaper, she feels she has another think coming.

Upstairs, a Dansette stylus is lovingly placed in the groove of Declan's new 45 and, following a crackle, a hiss and a pop, his new record kicks in.
It doesn't quite drown out Róisín's commentary.

"... and if you thought it were a bad idea, then you should've said when y' Mam come up with it," she is saying as she draws the bedroom curtains to the daylight outside.

"I mean, Old Ma Morrissey from next door fair choked on her Battenberg she did ... jumped at the idea ... got her purse out there and then. I mean ... 'ave y' seen the price of that dress I like in Kendal's?"

"Rosh ... errr, Róisín: what are you on about?" Declan has picked up his acoustic guitar and is noodling about, trying to find the chords to his new record.

"Yer mam. She came up with this idea of having the reception here and charging people to come to it."

"What? Whoever would pay to come to a wedding reception? Never heard the like in my life."

"That's what I said at first, but she's clever, yer mam." She pauses to look at Declan, wondering why it hadn't been inherited. "And once that team of yours got through to the final she thought that if folks could go to the reception and see the game in colour, they'd pay for the privilege. Would have worked as well. Not now she's found out it's not in colour though. Bought the colour telly and got the room decorated too." She goes to the window and, forcing the curtains just an inch open, stares out glumly, realizing that, like Mrs Hughes' day, her wedding isn't quite going to plan either.

Declan's bedroom is not without its own collection of George Best photographs, some of them showing the footballer in his fab suits and his Beatle hair alongside those of him on the pitch. They are ill at ease against his racing car wallpaper. This room hasn't been decorated for some years and although the model aeroplanes have gone, replaced by cufflinks, aftershave and the assorted paraphernalia of a young Manchester mover, it is pretty much the same bedroom he has shared with his twin brother Aiden for the last twenty-six years. Aiden's side of the room has altered even less. It is neater, tidier, and his bed is made. The titles on the books underneath this bed may have changed over time, but their presence has been constant.

Róisín sits on Declan's unkempt bed, moving aside, with some difficulty, the enormous and heavy eiderdown, then patting the space next to her. She doesn't stop for breath, but her tone mellows.

"Ooooh … Declan it's like a fairy tale. She's only tryin' to 'elp, yer know. Yer Mam just wants us to have the best, dun't she? I've looked at that dress every weekend since I was nine. It's a special day Declan … me dream come true. "

Declan, meanwhile, has worked out the chords and is improvising some little lead lines and licks, in his head he is imagining himself playing to an audience of thousands. Róisín pats the bed next to her again.

"Don't you want t' sit down, Declan?"

Declan's attention span leaves his make-believe audience as he remembers his new Levi's. He finishes on a Pete Townsend windmill, then switches the guitar for his new bell-bottoms in one swift move. He holds them up against his legs and moves back to the mirror. Looking past the pictures of fashionable barber shop hairstyles he has sellotaped to the frame, he holds the jeans to his waist and pouts.
"Declan? I'm talkin' to you."

The mirror doesn't do the jeans full justice and, unable to see the length, Declan has to jump onto the bed next to Róisín to model them to himself.

"Alright, eh? Georgie Best wears these. Look …"

He points at one of the pictures on his wall collage: George looks back, beaming his approval. Róisín is less impressed.

"Yer not coming out wi' me in girls' pants," she states flatly.

Twisting to attempt another look in the mirror, Declan says, "Saw him in 'em down Market Street last week. They might be a bit slack on t' backside yet, mind."

She snatches them from him and pulls him down to sit next to her.

"Declan? You do want t' get married, don't you?"

For a second he looks like a rabbit caught in a car's headlights. He turns away, stretching to turn the music up a notch, buying time. She tugs him back down again.

"I mean … you do love me, don't you?"

"Eeerrr … yeah. 'Course. It's obvious, int it?"

He retrieves his guitar and begins to strum, pensively. He does make that guitar sound nice, thinks Róisín, but there are more important things to talk about.

"No, Declan Hughes … it's not obvious." She notes the fear in Declan's eyes and decides on a change of tone. "Look, Snugglebuns. I need to know. I mean, I know we've only been engaged for …" She pauses to count on her fingers, the mental arithmetic causing lines to form on her forehead. "… ten years now … but … well … I sometimes wonder. I mean, y' do fancy me, don't you Declan?

The record sticks. Declan gulps and taps the record player with his elbow. It plays on, but Róisín takes the guitar from him.

"Y … yeah … yeah … course I do."

"Kiss me then."

"But? Me Mam and Dad … are only …"

"Yer Mam's mekkin t' tea. Oooh … Declan. In the words of the great Elvis Presley … it's now, or …" She smothers him in a desperate kiss. "… never!"

The record sticks again. He's trying to get out of the clinch, reaching to fix it.

"Ohhhh … Declan," continues Róisín, optimistically mistaking his lunge for the Dansette as a move of passion. She's got him pushed back onto the bed … he's trying to get away without looking like he is.

"Róisíiiiin … Róisíiiiin?" Declan fears asphyxiation; Róisín is oblivious.

"You'll have moved on at t'garage … maybe a supervisor … as long as they don't make you re-sit your exams … again … and we can save up a bit and … hey y' could go for a job on t' Docks … summat wi' a bit of outdoor life … y'd like that wouldn't yer? … And there's them nice new flats … y' know … them towers going up t'other side of the ship canal over in Salford?

As if things couldn't get any worse, Declan now notices that she's creasing his new jeans. He struggles to reach round her for them … thrilled, she spins and throws herself on top of him.

"Róisíiiiin … Rosh! Posh! Ohhhhwww!"

He is winded. Perhaps fatally.

But Róisín remains focused: she mistakes his desperate pleas for passionate groans and grabs his hand to put it on her boob. The move helps him find a last reserve of strength and, in panic, he finally wrestles himself away. Jumping up, he busies himself in sorting out his jeans and getting the stuck record to play on.

Róisín sighs, but she is used to this behaviour from Declan by now. She straightens her cardigan and ensures her boobs are in their rightful place.

"Y' know … if I didn't know better Declan Hughes I'd think you didn't want me. If we're gonna have babies it'd be best to at least practise. We get married in less than two weeks and we don't want to get to our wedding night and find out we don't know what to do … or we don't fit or summat."

Declan freezes as the inner terror of the word 'babies' registers.

"Bay ... b ...?"

"Y' not th'only one who reads fancy magazines, y' know. I've read up on what we can do to get a girl and what we do to get a boy ..." She's back into her stride now, stoppable by neither man nor beast.

"But ... but ..." says Declan, inaudibly beneath Róisín.

"And if we need a break in 'avin' 'em, well we can ... y' know?

"But ... I ... we ... y'... you ..."

"Well y' know warra mean?" Her eyes glaze and she smiles. She's lost in a memory, but her narration continues. "Eee ... I remember that first time I saw you ... cuttin' a dash on t' youth club dance floor ... I thought ... 'Ooooh ... he's got rhythm he has ...'"

"But ... but ... I'm only 28 and you're ..."

"Precisely! Me Mam'd 'ad our Peter, our Mary, our Joseph, our Jimmy, our Maggie, our Dirk, our John and was expecting our Ruth by t' time she were my age."

At last, she pauses for breath. Declan's mouth gawps open and closed like a lame goldfish.

"I mean, I don't wanna to be left on t' shelf, childless ... like our Bernice, when I'm thirty!
Declan can't find his voice. The record sticks again.

"Well?"

Declan's not so much lost for words as, well, just lost. Finally he states the case for the defence.

"But shouldn't we be saving ourselves until we're married?"

"Eurgghh!!! I've had it wi' you Declan Hughes!" Róisín grabs the Jeans and throws them at the player. The stylus skids off the record. "Or rather I haven't!"

"Róisín!!" Finally, he finds his vocal chords. In panic, he rushes to save his record while Róisín, grabbing her coat, stomps towards the door.

"If you decide you want me, you'll know where you can find me!"

She leaves, but pops back almost immediately.

"And if tha'd hafe a brain tha'd be an ape, Declan Hughes!"

She slams the door, leaving Declan to a customary gawp.

A short time later an insistent P-lip! P-llliiippp! P-lip! of a faulty tap echoes around the steamy shadows of the Hughes's bathroom. Declan, barely recovered from his earlier emotional trauma, lies up to his neck in soapless water, flicking the pages of his favourite football magazine: Jimmy Hill's Football Weekly. He pauses as he lands on a snap of a smiling George in white jeans, pink blouson and defining black belt. Declan is used to the sharp suits of the mod era, but he can feel a style change coming on.

The tap drips and drips and drips.

Declan ignores it and thinks of his new look. His Levi's seem even cooler under water, hugging his wiry legs. And his hair, drowned under a full tub of hair conditioner, will look fabulous when blow dried. He twists his mouth into a naff approximation of Bestie's smile and feels his teeth with his finger.

An egg timer rings. Declan stops it and begins to carefully attend to his hair, rinsing out the heavy product with water from a plastic shower head, attached to the bath's taps. He looks guiltily at the bottle of empty Woolworth's Hair Conditioner, perched on the side of the bath, and hopes that his mam won't miss it for a day or two.

The door handle rattles.

He continues to rinse, thinking that perhaps half the bottle would have been sufficient.

A loud knock on the bathroom door interrupts his thoughts, making him jump and causing him to nudge his magazine into the water.

A more insistent knock.

"Alright! Alright! Five minutes!"

"I'm touching cloth here, Decs. Get a move on or you'll be clearing up the mess!" Declan's twin brother, Aiden, growls from the other side of the door.

Declan picks up the now sodden magazine. "Flamin' Nora!"

The magazine drips, but as he turns his attention to the job of drying it out, something catches his eye from within the glossy pages. There is a lifestyle piece on Bobby and Jackie Charlton, and as a photograph of the two brothers beam back from the drenched page, a plan starts to form somewhere under his overly-pampered mop.

Singing along to the Small Faces' Tin Soldier, Declan has blow-dried his hair in a rough approximation of Steve Marriott's, and has finished talc-ing and perfuming his body by the time Aiden, his own more basic toiletry functions fully attended to, joins him in the bedroom. Aiden carefully puts his over-worn leather jacket on the back of a chair. Next, he takes off his new Brothel Creepers and puts them underneath; somewhat surprised that Declan has not taken the opportunity to ridicule them. He sets himself down onto the narrow bed. From the corner of his eye he is unnerved to notice Declan watching him closely. Feigning disinterest, he reaches for a half read book that sits on his bedside table, brushing his long, greasy hair from his eyes as he does so.

"And you can turn this shite off as well," barks Aiden, looking derisively at the Dansette. He is surprised when Declan complies, but other than a quizzical look he says nothing, preferring to concentrate on his copy of 'To Kill A Mockingbird'. After a long silence, during which Declan has failed to make comment on Aiden's reading material, taste in music, shoes, clothes, hair, and avoidance of aftershave or any other deodorizing chemicals, he finally gives up and places the book carefully back on the cabinet.

"Okay, what's wrong?"

"What do you mean?"

"Look, you're never this quiet – you even turned your puffy music off without starting World War Three. Something's up."

"I need to ask you something," says Declan.

"I've told you – get your own drugs. You couldn't handle the stuff I score." Aiden doesn't take drugs, but prefers not to let Declan add that to his usual arsenal of put-downs.

"No, no, it's not that."

The silence returns.

"Well?"

"Well, what are you doing on Wednesday night?"

"Eh? Ahm staying in, brushing mi ferrets. What do you think? I'm going to your wedding, aren't I?"
"Yes! Yes, you are. Of course you are. You do like Róisín, don't you?"

Aiden is caught off guard. They've never discussed girls before, despite sharing both the same bedroom for over twenty years and the same womb for nine months before that, and he's worried that Declan has noticed his furtive glances in Róisín's direction – particularly at her arse.

"Errr … yeah, she's choice, why?"

"I need a favour. A big, big favour."

Five minutes later Declan, dressed in a button-down shirt, Beatle Boots and tailored, black three-buttoned suit, leaves the bedroom, slamming the door behind him. His proposition to Aiden has not gone down well and he retreats to the Dog and Partridge to meet Terry, hoping that alcohol brings on another think. He leaves the bell-bottoms drip-drying over the bath, feeling he needs something more 'blouson' to wear with them. And besides, he doubts the drinking dens of Stretford are quite ready for his change of style just yet.

Terry is already there when he completes the short walk from his house and enters the tap room. There is a full pint next to his half-finished one, and he pushes it in Declan's direction when the moping groom-to-be collapses into a chair next to him. He looks at the pint sulkily, but doesn't touch it.

"Got something that will put a smile on your face." Terry reaches into his pocket and carefully puts an envelope on the small round table in front of him, moving beer mats away first and ensuring there are no spills anywhere near it. He looks at it with some pride.

"Go on then, Decs, open it. You know you want to."

Declan looks reproachfully at the envelope and takes a sip of his beer to delay the inevitable. He knows what it is, and he knows the predicament it will put him in. He takes a further drink, a large gulp this time, and snatches the envelope, tearing it open in one move.

"Careful!" cries Terry.

Calming himself a little, Declan takes the small paper card from the envelope and puts it back on the table, this time sitting on top of the envelope to protect it from the stickiness of the table top.

"And don't go flashing it around," whispers Terry, conspiratorially. "There's people in this pub who'd kill for one of those. And look happy, will you? It's your Wedding Present."

Declan looks at the piece of art in front of him – a vision written on the gloss of green and grey paper.

EMPIRE STADIUM WEMBLEY

A knot rises in his throat as he reads on.

Association Football
EUROPEAN CHAMPION CLUBS' CUP FINAL TIE

Turnstile, Entrance, Standing Enclosure – the words start to blur as the knot in his throat threatens to suffocate him.

"Well say something then," says Terry, taking the huff and draining his pint in protest to Declan's apparent ambivalence.

"I can't go."

"Come again?"

"I can't go. S'not right."

"Oh is that it? Mate, I've told you not to worry about it. Once I had me accident there was no way I was going to be able to go – I wouldn't be able to get in Stan's minibus down to that London, let alone get through the turnstiles – and there's nobody that I'd rather have it than you."

Declan looks at his friend, who is now grinning, happy in the knowledge he has bestowed upon him the greatest gift one man can ever bequeath to another – a ticket to the European Cup Final. Instead of explaining to him, he takes another ticket from the inside of his jacket, this one less glossy, less professionally manufactured than the one already on the table, which Declan places it next to. It is Terry's turn to read:

THE WEDDING OF THE YEAR

"Ha, ha! Yer mam's printed tickets for yer reception! That's fab."

"Read on."

POSH AND DECS

"I've always thought that had a lovely ring to it," he sniggers.

"Not that, carry on."

SOFA £1 STANDING 10 BOB

Terry is now laughing, uncontrollably. "She's charging people to go to your wedding reception! This is hilarious."

"Carry on," sighs Declan.

"Oh, let me see …" This time Terry totally loses it and it is some time before he can compose himself sufficiently to read out the next bit he sees.

EUROPEAN CUP FINAL
MAN UTD –V- BENFICA
FULL COLOUR ENTERTAINMENT!
FULL BUFFET – INCLUDING VOLONVONS

"Volonvons? What are volonvons?"

"Something to do with prawns, I think. Have yer fettled it yet?"
"Yeah, mate. She's messed up on this one – the final isn't in colour, it's still in black and white!"

Declan sips his pint patiently as he waits for Terry to stop his laughing fit and dry his eyes, which have been weeping from the effort. He draws several looks from the regulars in the bar, who assume he's taken something.

Eventually, Declan risks another try.

"It's nothing to do with the colour," he says. "Apparently she's got that sorted. Think about it, you dipstick – if the match is on at my wedding reception …?" He leaves the question hanging in the air.

Terry begins to work it out. He looks closely at the two tickets, sitting side by side and notices that they have one striking similarity:

WEDNESDAY 29TH MAY 1968

"Oh, bugger."

"Exactly. Oh, bugger. I've got a ticket for the European Cup Final at Wembley, the first time an English club has made it, the Busby Babes ten years on, and they have to make it the same day as my poxy wedding."

"I don't think The FA will have done it on purpose, Decs."

"No, but I bet Róisín has."

"Don't be daft – she wouldn't know a kick-off time from a throw-in, that one."

"I suppose so, but what am I going to do? I can't miss me wedding, and I can't miss the match."

"Why is yer weddin' on a Wednesday anyway? Nobody has their weddin' on a Wednesday."

"It's another of me mam's bright ideas to save money. She knew there'd be less people able to go, 'cos they wouldn't all be able to get time off work. So … any bright ideas?"

It is two pints later before Terry comes up with his best solution.

"You could miss the wedding. Just get them to postpone it."

"I've thought about that. Do you have any idea what Róisín would do to me if I even suggested it?"

"Hmmm," replies Terry, and shifts awkwardly in his wheelchair at the thought.

"Well miss the match, then," he tries to sound positive. "Best, Law, Charlton and the new kid, Kidd – we're bound to dominate Europe for the next ten years! There'll be loads of other finals for you to go to".

"I don't know Terry, lad. I've got an inkling that things are going to change for me once that ring is on my finger. I just have the feeling that this is my one and only chance."

There is a further, two-pint silence.
"I did have one idea." It's Declan's turn to shift awkwardly in his seat.

"Go on then," slurs Terry, who is two pints ahead of Declan.

"Well …" Declan leans towards Terry and lowers his voice. "I'm a twin aren't I?"

Terry nods, but his eyes suggest that this is neither news, nor relevant to the current predicament.

"So, I asked Aiden if he'd take my place at the wedding. Just for the ceremony, like. Just until I could get back from Wembley."

"That, my friend, is a brilliant idea. Nothing could possibly go wrong with a plan like that," affirms Terry, apparently without any irony. "So, job sorted. Another pint?"

Declan is surprised that he didn't need to justify his idea with Terry, and warms to the theme.

"I know. The idea is perfect because it's just so simple. Only problem is, Aiden's having none of it."

"What? Why not? Who wouldn't want to help out his own brother? S'no skin off his nose. I'll do it for yer if yer want, Decs. Oh ... yeah," he adds as he immediately realizes the flaw in his amendment to the plan.

"How you going to get back after the match in time for ... yer know?"

"Eh?"

"Well, getting Aiden to stand in at the church is one thing, but you don't want him performing for you on your wedding night, d'yer?"

"Already thought of that. If I can get the cash together, Sidecar Steve said he'll take me there and back on his motorbike. Used to be an army dispatch rider, that one. Reckons he can be back in three hours if the Feds don't get us."

"Yeah ... but ... you 'aven't got any money, 'ave yer?"

"'Appen, but I've got a plan for that as well," says Declan, playing with the rough ticket that his mother has had made up. "Might need your help with that one, though."

Terry wheels himself over to the bar, placing a drinks tray on his lap for the return journey, and leaving Declan to stew.

"Yer see," says Terry, after having managed to retrieve two more pints with only minimal spillage, "yer've got to think 'what's in it for him?'. I mean, he's a bit of a dark horse is your Aiden. He's a long haired, bearded greaseball with questionable hygiene skills. Bit of a loner, he is – a rocker, but he doesn't seem to go around in gangs. Doesn't have the same sharp outlook or social interaction that you have, me old mucker. You've got to make it worth his while. What have you got that he would want?"

Declan considers this. He hadn't thought about bribing Declan and now that the idea has been proposed, he can't think of a single thing that he would have to offer him. The thought makes him a little down – he's about to be married, move in with his parents-in-law until they can afford their own house, and all he has to his name are some neat clothes, a

Dansette, and a belting collection of vinyl. He hasn't even paid Terry for the rusty Vespa yet.

His clothes are nice though, he reflects, and takes a self-congratulatory mouthful of Watney's Red Barrel. Aiden's clothes are manky, maybe he should offer him a new set of threads, that'd be tempting for him, wouldn't it? Probably not, he decides – the man just doesn't seem to be motivated by looking cool. If they didn't look identical, he would question whether they came from the same egg. Still, there must be something he would want.

"I don't know," Declan eventually says. Terry has forgotten what the question was, but nods in agreement anyway. His brain is now fuddled and he doubts he'll be as important a contributor to the conversation as he has been up until now.

"I'll just ask him. Ask him what he wants. There must be something." Declan adds. "Let's celebrate with a drink."

A bell rings, and last orders are called at the bar.

"'Aven't you got no 'omes to go to, you lot?!"

Everybody in the tap room laughs, knowing this is the landlord's idea of a joke. The curtains are drawn tightly to hide the lights from any passing Old Bill, and the majority order their drinks for the customary lock-in.

CHESTER ROAD MOTORS, STRETFORD
20th May, 1968

Declan, working as best he can through his hangover, keeps Aiden in his eye line all day, and leaving a tricky manifold gasket he makes time to bring a cup of tea to his brother. Aiden accepts it without a word, but shakes his head at the thinly veiled attempt to soften him up. Six cups of tea later, one brought with a Bakewell Tart from the cake shop round the corner, Aiden finally snaps.

"Look, I know what you're trying to do, and it won't work."

Declan makes no show of pretence. He is desperate to go to this match. He notices Terry, who is sat in the office, where he has been relegated following his debilitating accident, doing paperwork (mainly forging MOT passes), watching proceedings with from the corner of his eye.

"No, the cups of tea are just to say sorry for storming off last night. And the tart is for waking you up when I got back from the pub. But there must be something I can give you if you'll do this for me. There must be something you want."

Aiden picks up a rag and begins to wipe axle grease from his hands. He does it to buy thinking time, as there is more grease on rag than on him.

"You don't get it, do you? It's nothing to do with what I want. Or you. The reason I won't do it is because it's not fair on Róisín. A wedding is the most important day of anyone's life. It's the one day you'll remember forever. Even if I got away with it, it wouldn't be right. It would be a sham. And what if it got out? You'd ruin her life – all for a football match. You need to have a word with yourself, Declan. Grow up a little."

With this, Aiden returns to the solenoid he is prising out of an Austin 1100.

"But it's the final," pleads Declan, apparently unheard.

Terry returns his attention to his paperwork – even through the grime of the office window, he can tell that didn't go according to plan.

MR THISTLETWAITES CAFÉ AND TEMPERENCE BAR
CHORLTON-CUM-HARDY, MANCHESTER
21st May, 1968

"So, Gobind Livroop Ripudaman Sahib …"

"You must call me Gobind, Missus Marjorie Hughes, please. Or Gobbie, for short."

"Yes, and you must call me Marjorie, errr, Gobbie," annunciates Mrs Hughes.

"Yes, please, Marjorie," smiles Gobind Livroop Ripudaman Sahib.

"Now, you're sure your daughters' group are very ... colourful?"

"Oh yes, Missus Marjorie," his head wobbling, rather than nodding an affirmative. "They are the most colourful dancing girls in the whole of Manchester. Their Kameez and Salwaar are the most very vibrant and rich colours. They spend many nights dyeing their clothes in the traditional way and then they adorn their beautiful bodies with dupatta, jhumka and tikka."

"I'll look after the food, Gobind," affirms Mrs Hughes, straightening her rather plain housecoat, "but if your girls are going to dance at the wedding reception they must be the most colourful they've ever been."

"Oh yes, Missus Marjorie, they will add both colour and excitement to this most prestigious event. Thank you for giving us this opportunity. But tell me, why don't you put the name of the group on your tickets – surely 'Bhangra From Burnage' would be a most attractive addition to the night's entertainment?"

"Don't you worry about that, Gobbie. People will realise that 'full colour entertainment' is bound to be an Indian dance routine, and besides," she looks about to make sure that nobody else in the little café in Chorlton that she'd chosen to have this clandestine meeting is listening, then leans forward conspiratorially, "some people still have a problem with ... you know ..." Mrs Hughes is embarrassed and hopes Gobind will help her out. She nods at him in a 'you people' kind of way, but he fails to take the hint, continuing to smile, and waiting respectfully for her to finish her sentence. Eventually, she continues "You know ... people from Burnage. It's bandit country, isn't it? I mean, nothing against you, Gobind, but it's full of City fans."

ELTON STREET, STRETFORD
24th May 1968

Declan is sat at the dining table; to his left is his mother, to his right his intended. They are both speaking, seemingly at the same time. To Declan, it is just a wash of noise, but although he has tuned them out, he manages to nod and throw in phrases such as 'Oh, yes, definitely' and 'I'm happy to go along with that' from time to time. It appears to satisfy them. On the table in front of them is a list of guests, next to which appears an amount of money, signifying that they have paid for their reception ticket. One or two names, lacking this contribution to Mrs Hughes' raison-d'etre, have already been crossed out. Others, those of a more prominent position in the Stretford hierarchy, have the acronym 'VIP' next to their name, and are not expected to pay. The list is currently at fifty-five names.

"Well, if we are to let Father O'Leary in for free then he shouldn't be getting a place on the settee. That's all I'm saying."

"I hear you, Róisín, I hear you ... but he is a man of God, and it does mean we could get away without a Parish contribution at the end of the service. What about if we give him the footstool? What do you think, Declan?"

Declan has let his mind slip further, and misses his cue. The nearer the final is, the more devastated he feels about the prospect of missing it. He has spoken to Aiden on two further occasions, but his twin is adamant that he won't switch places. Inseparable during their formative years, they haven't got on since they hit puberty. It showed in their appearance, their taste in music and their social lives – Declan, polished and smart, one of the boys, always up for fun, always looking for a gig to go to: watching The Magic Lanterns at the Oasis Club or Pete Maclaine and The Clan at the Willows; and always, always at the match with his mates on a Saturday afternoon. And Aiden, mean and moody in his grease impregnated biker gear, meticulously tidy, a thinker, a loner ... nobody is sure where he goes on a Saturday afternoon, or at any other time, come to think of it.

"Oi! Cloth ears!" Mrs Hughes shakes her docile son's shoulder. "Shall we put the Priest on a stool?"

"Eh? Why what's he done wrong?"

"Oh, he's no use whatsoever," chips in Róisín. "You need to buck your ideas up. Take a bit more responsibility in your life."

The two women ignore him and continue talking at each other. They weren't actually interested in his opinion, but he was there so that he understood that he had to be a part of this wedding, not an innocent bystander. Declan went back to his mope, but was brought back to the surface by the report from the new television, which had been on all day, or at least until the closedown, every day since its installation. North At Six was broadcasting a live link from Wembley Stadium.

"Here we see the Benfica team surveying the luxurious Wembley turf, ahead of the game on Wednesday evening. Many of these names will not be known to the people of Manchester – Torres, Graça, Santos or their Brazilian manager, Otto Glória. But they are all European superstars in their own right. One man that needs no introduction to anybody, however, is their centre forward Eusébio da Silva Ferreira. But don't worry," chuckles the sports reporter, "you can just call him Eusébio."

Mrs Hughes scowls at the television. She will never forgive the Beeb for not showing the final in colour. The reporter continues.

"Eusébio, also known as 'The Black Panther', lit up the 1966 World Cup and was top scorer in the tournament." The camera cuts to an athletic looking black man, walking the length of the pitch, dressed in a smart blue suit. A cheeky groundsman rolls a ball to him and he playfully passes it back.

"Uh-huh! Good pass, Eusébio, sir, but you'll have to do better than that on Wednesday night!" mocks the reporter, who apparently thinks he's said something funny. "Just remember, you may have been top scorer at the World Cup, but it was our boys who won the trophy, and will no doubt continue to do so for many tournaments to come!"

"He's got that right," affirms Mrs Hughes.

"So join us here, live only on the BBC, for what promises to be one of the most exciting matches of a lifetime. Eusébio sharing a pitch with George Best? You'd be mad to miss it."

The presenter hands back to the studio with his last words burrowing deep inside Declan's cerebrum.

LEVENSHULME, MANCHESTER
23rd May, 1968

Terry gulped as he wheeled his chair towards the 10-10 Café in Levenshulme: a notorious bikers' hangout. Three young skinheads had been brave enough to tootle past on their underpowered Lambrettas and Vespas, drawing rowdy threats from the café's clientele, many of whom had raced to the pavement in order to hurl abuse. He navigated his way past the Nortons, Triumphs and BSAs that lined up outside, and backed himself in through the door, drawing snorts of derision from some of the bikers as he entered.

"You need a fucking sidecar for that, son?" quipped one, to the merriment of his friends.

Terry smiled back, hoping to convey the impression that he was a harmless simpleton and wasn't looking for any trouble. The Rock-Ola jukebox was belting out a Gene Vincent hit that he doesn't know the name of. 'Get with the decade', he thinks, but says nothing as he scans the café, looking for his mark. Eventually, his eyes settle on Aiden, who is sat on his own at a small corner table. As he closes in, he is surprised to see that Aiden is reading a book, Orwell's 1984.

"Mind if I join you?"

"It's a free country," replies Aiden. He then glances momentarily at his book before adding, "Well, for now."

Terry wheels himself as close as he can to the table.

"How did you get all the way down here like that?" Aiden is genuinely perplexed.

"Tommy the Painter put me in the back of his van. He's finishing off some window frames round the corner."

"Still. Can't have been an easy journey. How can I help you? As if I can't guess."

"Look, mate." The word 'mate' sits uneasily on Terry's tongue – it's not that they've ever been unfriendly to each other; despite them working together, and he being his twin brother's best friend, they don't really know each other at all. "I know it's asking a lot. I mean, pretending to be the groom at a wedding and that, but you must know what this means to Declan. And it will be a bit of fun. Think of it as your wedding present to him."

Terry has spewed out all his arguments in one go, and realises he has nothing left. Aiden picks up a cigarette from the packet next to him, lightsit and takes a deep puff. He returns his lighter to his black leather jacket without offering one to Terry.

"You married, Terry?" He knows he's not, and Terry shakes his head. "Nah, and when you do, you'll probably treat it like Declan is doing now. He's making a mockery of the whole thing. Think about it. Take yourself out of Declan's winklepickers for a moment and walk a mile in Róisín's shoes." He takes a second to smoke, then nods at Terry's wheelchair and adds, "Metaphorically speaking.

"Think about how she would feel if she found out later what had happened. How devastated she would be if she uncovered the truth – that her marriage was a sham; in fact, that she wasn't even married to Declan. She didn't get that nickname of 'Posh' at school for nothing, you know. And her family – they're more Catholic than the Pope. Imagine if they found out. I don't care about Declan missing a football match. He needs to think about what he wants out of life. If he wants to go to that match more than he wants to get married to a beautiful, intelligent creature like Róisín then he should man up and tell her. Leave her for someone who's going to give her the life she deserves – not be off scoring over-cut drugs or fighting at the football on a Saturday afternoon."

Terry hadn't thought of it that way. Oh well, at least he'd tried. He would have to go back to Declan and tell him the bad news but, to be honest, Aiden did have a very good point. It was only when he got to the café door, grateful that the waitress had opened it for him, that it dawned on him: Aiden was sweet on Róisín. That's why he wouldn't do it.

THE PRINCESS CLUB
BARLOW MOOR ROAD, CHORLTON
28th May 1968

"Well, Decs, me old mate, yer can't say yer r'aven't 'ad a bloody good stag do, lad. Can yer? I mean … bloody good!"

Johnny Sideburns is pissed. He is not the only one. Declan's Stag Party at The Princess Club has been a night to remember. The compere has dazzled, the band were the business, the comedians have had them rolling with laughter, and the strippers have taken their clothes off.

"I think I'm in with one of them strippers," adds Johnny, confidently. "Lovely pair of thre'penny bits on 'er as well." He crumples back into his chair and begins to dribble.

A waiter, after elegantly negotiating the minute gaps between tables whilst balancing nine pints of dimple glassed froth on a tray, places the drinks on their table – each drink, whether Guinness, Mild or Bitter, is set in front of the corresponding drunkard, as he rattles off the charge.

"My shout this Decs, lad," yells Terry from across the table, then struggles with the cast on his arm as he attempts to find the right change and a tip. The waiter is suitably rewarded for his dexterity, memory and ability to pre-assess their need for more alcohol, and scoots off to another table, like a fairground gypsy riding the Waltzer.

"Come on, Decs – get it down yer! And cheer up – it might never happen!" Fat Barry, another of the mechanics, howls to the groom to be. Declan forces a smile and takes a gulp of his beer. "Wassermadder? 'Avin' second thoughts are yer?"

"Nah, Barry. Just thinking about the match, that's all. Half the lads on me stag do are going to it instead of me wedding."

"Ah, I see," says Barry – which is not entirely accurate given that most things are currently a blur to him. "You're annoyed at them for missing your wedding. S'understandable. Them lads should show a bit of respect to you, mate. Like me good self."

"Eh? Nah, it's not that. I'm just jealous of them, Barry. It should be me in that minibus tomorrow, watchin' t'lads down at Wembley. I've not missed a home game all season, you know."

"Yeah, well ..." A thought suddenly breaks through the mist of drunkenness and slaps him in the face. He takes a second to make sure that nobody is listening, then leans closer to Declan. "Listen, I'll take that spare ticket off your hands if you want. Drink in it for you."

"Hang on a sec. What happened to you tipping up to my wedding? 'Loyalty', you just said."

"Yeah, well. You wouldn't deny me a chance to see the final, would you? Chance of a lifetime, that is. Go on, like I say – there's a drink in it for you."

Declan takes a sip from his pint and assesses the three others that sit waiting in front of him.

"Nah, yer all right, Barry."

The stage is pushed back, revealing a large dance floor, and the Stags waste no time in using it. This is where they hope to trap tonight. They leave Declan and Terry at the table, the latter cursing his injuries. Declan slides around the table to join him.

"Not dancing, Terry?"

"Very funny. What's your excuse? Last night of freedom, int it?"

A cloud appears on Declan's horizon and begins to rain profusely on his parade.

"Ooh, dear," says Terry in mock theatrics, noticing the grim look on his pal's phizzog. "Is there trouble at t'mill?"

"Not really. Just miffed about missing the match, that's all."

"Not really? What do you mean 'not really'? It's your big day tomorrow, mate. Love of your life and all that. Surely there's not trouble in paradise."

"Make your mind up: is there trouble at the mill or in paradise?"

Terry takes a long sip of his pint and then returns it purposefully to the table. He looks his friend in the eye and lets his joviality drop.

"You tell me Declan, lad. You tell me."

Declan looks away – he can't hold Terry's gaze, but he's not letting it drop.

"Declan, if you're not sure about this …"

"I don't know," Declan has turned back to the table. In truth he has wanted to talk to someone about this for a long time. "I mean I do love Posh ... er, Róisín; I'm not supposed to call her Posh anymore ... we've been together since we were eleven. Always meant to be, weren't it? Me and 'er. School discos, youth club, down The Blue Note club ... it's just expected, isn't it? That one day we'd get married."

"Well, yeah. We all expected it, Decs ... but you've got to be sure. You are sure?"
Declan just shrugs and sips his pint.

"Oh, fuck," says Terry.

RAILWAY ROAD, STRETFORD
Wednesday 29th May 1968

"Oh you look stunning, our Róisín. Very posh!"

"Mam!"

"Oh I know, love. I'm not supposed to call you Posh. But look at yourself, m'dear. Like you've walked out of one of those magazines. Pretty as a picture."

Róisín relents as she catches herself in the mirror, and a wide smile breaks through her lips, bright enough to light up the hazy Stretford morning.

"Aw, thanks, mam. I just hope he appreciates it."

"Oh, he will, love, he will. He's not a bad lad, that Declan. It's just his mates leading him astray sometimes. Yer dad were like that once, but soon as he started getting his tea on the table for when he got home from work, well ... let's just say he knew what side his bread were buttered on."

Róisín smiles again. She is radiant. She has waited her whole life for today, and is desperate for it to go to plan. And tonight, finally, she won't be a virgin anymore. At least if she can keep Declan off the ale for a while.

Meanwhile, three streets away, Declan is sitting on his brother's bed. He wouldn't consider doing this normally, but these are far from normal times. In front of him are his wedding clothes, laid neatly on his own bed by his mother. He takes the match ticket out of his jacket pocket and lays it on the bed, next to his suit. He sits and looks at both, and is still doing so twenty minutes later. He hasn't moved an inch.

Suddenly he leaps up. He takes a piece of card that has been used to tack a photograph to and writes a few short sentences on it before putting it on Aiden's pillow. Grabbing the ticket, his red and white bar scarf and his jacket he leaves the room, closing the door as quietly as he can. He needn't have bothered. Downstairs, as preparations are being made for tonight's joint reception and match showing, there is chaos. A noise resembling a cross between an excitable zoo and a war zone rumbles up the stairs, punctuated by his mother's over-bearing directions.

"If I'd have wanted it there, I'd 'ave put it there meself, yer daft apeth. And if I'd ... what are you doing, buggerlugs?! No you! Come 'ere! Aarrggghh! Put them blue roses down there. No, there! Them blue roses are to show we're supportin' the Reds today. Who left that there an all? If I had a penny for ..."

The outburst strengthens Declan's resolve and he moves into the bathroom. From there he squeezes through the window and onto the kitchen roof, where he can safely shin down the drainpipe – the reverse of the route he took so many times as a teenager, coming home late from a dance. It's 8.30am in the morning; Sidecar Steve reckons they can be back by about 1.00am if they leave on the final whistle. Whatever happens in Stretford in the meantime, he will be at Wembley Stadium.

Aiden opens the door to the house in Elton Street and is immediately hit by a course mixture of sights, sounds and smells. Gobind Livroop Ripudaman Sahib has several pans bubbling away in the kitchen, rich spices filling the air. Mr Hughes has retained his position in his armchair, possibly because of concerns that they are now one and the same, but he has been relegated to the side of the room – he continues to watch the television through all the mayhem, and is the only person in the house who has a hot brew. The window cleaner is working diligently on the inside. Reggie and Ronnie, the decorators, have been roped in to erect a small stage area, which fills the whole side of one wall. All the other furniture has been arranged in rows, facing the television. There is a space at the back of the room, which Aiden assumes is a standing area. Mrs Hughes is stood on the settee, which is now plumb centre, and is directing proceedings like a traffic policeman in the middle of Bombay rush hour.

"Make sure you sand those boards, you two. I don't want them girls getting splinters in their arses. And that chair goes th … Gobind, turn that bloody music down, I can't hear myself think 'ere … and where do you think you're going with that Eccles Cake? Put! It! Back! And you can arrange those custard creams in an interesting fashion whilst yer at it. You've missed a bit! I want them sparkling. Put that over there, you. No – over there! Oh, and if it isn't the prodigal son, Aiden Finbar Hughes, don't you be sliding past to go and put yer feet up. Get up there and get yer brother out of that bathroom – it's hours since I heard him go in. It might be his wedding day, but he's worse than any woman, that one. Gobind! Music! I'm sure you've turned that up, not down. No, I don't want a cup of tea, our Vera – yer dad'll have one, mind. Careful of that cake! I spent all night …"

Not my circus, not my monkeys, thinks Aiden and makes for the stairs. He'd normally avoid any contact with Declan, but this time he's grateful that the job he's been given will take him away from the living room performance. He's not concerned when he finds the bathroom empty, nor when he enters his bedroom to find Declan not there either – it's still a good few hours before the wedding. His mam just frets too much, he thinks, as he takes his one suit out of the wardrobe. It's only when he sees the roughly scrawled note that has been left on his pillow that a lead weight drops from his throat and lands with a sickening thump in the very pit of his stomach. He looks at it for several long seconds before he picks it up and reads it.

Aiden

Look, I know you don't want to do this, so I won't beg. But I've gone to the match. If you want to tell everyone what I've done, that's fine – I'll understand. But if you would stand in for me for a few hours I'll make it up to you. I don't know how, we'll have to sort it out later. But whatever you want, yeah? I'll be back about 1.00am. Keep her dancing until then and we'll do a switch. No harm done, all a good laugh.

Leave it with you, ar kid. Decs.

Anger sweeps through Aiden's veins and he slings his suit into the corner of the small bedroom.

"Blood and sand! How could he do this to her?" he shouts, throwing himself onto the bed. When he finally pulls his head out of his hands his eyes settle on the suit opposite him. He makes his way over and holds the trousers alongside his leg, trying them for size. Looking first towards the mirror, he takes a moment to consider a photograph of the happy couple on Declan's bedside cabinet. He stares a while at the image of Róisín, then at his belligerent brother. Picking up a pair of scissors, he begins to cut his hair.

"Whatever I want, yeah?" He mimics Declan's voice, always a shade sharper than his own. "How about some common decency and respect, ar kid?"

An hour later Aiden is looking in the mirror again. The biggest change is the absence of his beard, and he doesn't recognise himself at all. He does recognise the image that's reflected back at him though – it's Declan. From a looks point of view he has no doubt that he'll pull this off. But his anger has subsided now. Does he really want to put himself through this? It's a big gamble, but as he catches sight, again, of the picture of Róisín, he knows it's worth the risk. Forgetting anything else, he couldn't see her stood up at the altar. It might be down to Declan, but the whole Hughes family would never live it down. His mam would have kittens.

From downstairs the music Gobind has been playing suddenly takes a leap upwards in volume. He's only heard music like that before at the Gulam Sweet Centre – an Indian restaurant down Wilmslow Road. It's accompanied by some serious shouting and banging – as good a time as any for him to make his entrance. He forgets himself as he reaches the bottom of the stairs and sees, on the makeshift stage, four Indian girls, dressed to the absolute nines. They are dancing along to the music, their beautiful braided hair flowing in the wake of their sensual, energetic moves. Their make-up is stunning, accentuating wide Asian eyes, and their jewels sparkle as they catch the light through freshly polished windows. But it is their clothes that capture the imagination. So many different colours; each colour more vibrant than the last. Even the new, gaudy red and white striped wallpaper looks grim in comparison. The whole room has stopped to take them in, Mrs Hughes' arms are still mid-threat, but even she is quiet as she appreciates the spectacle in front of her.

The song finishes and there is silence. As a crowd in a Coliseum look to the Emperor to see if a Gladiator will live, or not, the whole room have turned towards Mrs Hughes. None more so than Gobind Livroop Ripudaman Sahib, although there is a look of quiet confidence about him.

"You'll do for me, lasses, I say you'll do for me!" she beams. "Right, you lot – the show's over until tonight, so get back to yer … Oooooh … our Declan. Look at you there in your wedding suit. Yer look lovely … lovely. Look at him everybody. Dunt he look smart!"
The room turns from Mrs Hughes to the handsome young man stood at the foot of the stairs. Aiden almost looked around when he heard Declan's name, but checked himself in time. It's him they were all looking at. He clears his throat.
"Hh-hem. I look all right then?" he tries.

"Look all right? Look all right? Ooh, she's landed on her feet with you that Róisín Malone. Landed on her feet, I tell you. Bloody gorgeous you look. Now come here and give yer mam a hug."

There is a tear in Mrs Hughes' eye. Not something that has been seen in many a decade, and she squeezes her son to the point of near asphyxiation. Aiden doesn't mind. It may save him a lot of trouble if he was to pass out now. He's got past the first test though – if he looks and sounds like Declan to his own mother, he must have half a chance with Róisín.

"'Ang on … what 'av you done to your hair?"

Oh. Not quite in the clear yet.

"Well, I …errr…"

"It looks far better like that. Proper short back and sides instead of that namby pamby effort you had. Róisín will be made up. She always said it made you look like a girl before. Oh, I'm so proud!" She continues to hug the life out of him until she fears they'll be late for the wedding.

An hour later, the combined flock of the Hughes family is making its way to the church. They are on foot, a further savings measure implemented by Mrs Hughes. It's a twenty minute walk along the main Chester Road to St Ann's and, in their best bib and tucker, the neighbours haven't seen anything like it since last Sunday's Whit Procession. Mr Hughes has been given a lift, on account of his distrust of zebra crossings, and is now waiting patiently at the church, sipping illicitly from a hip flask and reading Saturday's copy of The Racing Post. Jeanie and Ethel take up the rear of the procession: they are not missing this for all the tea in the Co-op. Up front, proud as punch, is Mrs Marjorie Hughes, her arm interlinked with her son's. Best Man Terry is being propelled in his wheel chair, but at this brisk pace he feels every crack in the pavement.

"Bloody Nora! I knew I should have got some suspension put on this thing!"

"'Ere!" shouts Mrs Hughes. "I'll have none of that foul language on my son's wedding day. Shut yer trap, or you'll feel the back of me hand!"

"No swearing, but mindless violence is okay," says Terry, carefully lowering his voice. "Sorry, Mrs Hughes," he adds, rather more loudly.

Reaching St Ann's without further incident requiring physical threat, the family and friends sit themselves to the right of church. Mrs Hughes and Aiden take pride of place on the front row, next to the waiting Mr Hughes who, sensing the magnitude of the occasion, and the restrained forbearance of his wife, circles the name of a horse in The Post and puts the paper away.

The organist plays softly, almost in tune. He is playing, or at least trying to play, Glory, Glory Hallelujah, but all today's hymns have been carefully chosen because of their football chant equivalents and the congregation, respectfully silent, are mouthing the words 'and the Reds go marching on, on, on!'. Every single one of them is thinking of the game to be played later that day. One of them, Mr Gregson – a man so portly he that he has struggled to get into the narrow pew – furtively takes a ticket out of his pocket and reads the words again: 'European Champions' Cup Final ... full colour entertainment'. Worth ten bob of anyone's money to see the game in colour, he thinks.

Mrs Hughes pins a dark blue rose to Aiden's lapel and he is left to silently ponder what the hell he thinks he is doing. He spots the door to the vestry and it crosses his mind that he can still get away scot free –

any indiscretion will be blamed on Declan. In fact, he could punch the priest, drop his trousers in front of the altar and proclaim his future loyalty to Martin Luther, the UVF and Liverpool Football Club – it would be Declan who did it, not him. As his mind raced away with further retaliatory strikes he could pile upon his absent brother, the organ volume raises a decibel or two and the tune switches to the traditional Bridal Chorus. He looks round to see Róisín walking towards him. The biggest smile he has ever seen breaks across her face when their eyes meet. For a moment, she is the only person in the room to him. He sees nobody else, he hears nothing; his senses are acute, but are filled to the brim with the beauty he sees in front of him. As she reaches him, Róisín leans over and breaks the spell.

"I love what you've done to your hair, Declan," she says, tenderly, the smile never leaving her lips. She lets out a sigh of contentment and turns towards the waiting Father Fergal, keen to get on with her childhood dream. She has waited for this moment for nearly twenty years – it has taken that long to break Declan down, she thinks. But he's here now and, she can see it in his eyes: he is as in love with her as she is with him. She had always had this nagging concern that he was going along for the ride, being with her because it was expected, because he'd always been with her. But now as he stands next to her and starts to read his wedding vows from the small card in front of him (his voice sounds a little odd … probably nerves, she thinks) she knows everything is going to be all right.

At that very moment, Declan is in the George and Dragon – a pub within spitting distance of Wembley stadium. Around him, the packed punters sing terrace chants and complain about the quality and price of the beer they are drinking, before happily ordering more. They have befriended a small group of Portuguese, who had entered looking for a coffee and now have a table of complimentary pints in front of them – 'courtesy of the Red Army' says a large Scotsman as he sets several more whiskys down.

"Mind you, if we lose and you spoil Matt's birthday, Jimmy – I'll be looking fae yee after the game!" he threatens.

The Portuguese smile, none the wiser, and wonder how they can get out of the pub without causing offence.

There are a couple of acoustic guitars being passed around, mostly just abused by wanna be Manc pop stars. It seems that everybody knows two or three chords, and has played out of tune, string deficient instruments exclusively in their bedrooms; and whilst the alcohol emboldens any apprehension they may have of playing in public, it also turns their fingers into thick-skinned sausages. That is until one of the Portuguese picks one up and starts strumming. Declan recognises the song and picks up the other, effortlessly playing some tricky arpeggios over the top, re-tuning as he goes along. The guitars sound stunning together and the impromptu duo get through three widely appreciated numbers before the general ambience of the bar, two or three football chants competing for dominance, makes the guitars inaudible.

"Cristiano," says the Portuguese, shaking Declan's hand. "That was fantastic", he says in a heavy accent. "If you ever come to my home town, Albufiera, you need to visit my bar. It's called Bitoque. You can play guitar for me there. If you play like that, you will never be short of friends."

"Declan, mate. And I'd love to," he laughs, as he puts the guitar behind his chair. "Unfortunately I'm getting married today."

Cristiano looks confused. "Today? At what time?"

"Oh," says Declan, looking at the clock behind the bar. "Around about now, actually."

An hour later, Declan is alone in the crowd. Now that he is here, now that the time of the wedding has come, he is suddenly hit by a huge sense of loss and guilt. He is usually leading the singing, buying the drinks, having a good time, but it all seems wrong. He looks at his pint, then at the bar's clock as it hits a quarter to six.

"Ah well, too late now," he says in an unsuccessful attempt to convince himself, and takes a drink. "My old man said be a city fan, and I said ..." he sings, and the rest of the pub join in enthusiastically.

Mrs Hughes has relented on the cost of a car to carry the happy couple back to Elton Street, but she insists on playing gooseberry and hitching a ride in the sleek black Ford, ordinarily used for funerals.

"What were all that kerfuffle about signing the register, our Declan?" asks his mother.

"Just a bit of nerves. I messed me signature up."

"How can you mess your signature up? Yours is always a bloody mess anyway. It's our Aiden who has the neat signature – yours looks like a drunken spider's had a fit in an inkwell. What happened to Aiden, anyway? I'll hang for that lad, I will. I mean, I know you two don't get on these days, but he's normally the reliable one; it's usually you that lets the side down, Declan ... no offence ... but to miss your own brother's wedding? Well ... after all I've done to make it a success an' all!"

"I'm sure Aiden must have had a good reason, mam," says Aiden, immediately regretting it as his mother narrows her eyes and throws him a suspicious look. Declan is not known for defending his brother. Or anyone else, come to that. His mother lets it go, but Aiden feels he's had a warning and vows to become more 'Declan like'.

"Hmmph!" She adds, as the car turns the corner into Elton Street. "B ... bloody ... B ... b ... b ... bloody Nora!" she stutters as she sees the line of people queuing up outside her house. "Where have all that lot come from?"

Forming the length of the street, and disappearing around the corner, is an orderly queue of men, women and children. Without exception, all of them have a red and white scarf, rosette or shirt. As kick-off approaches, they are anxiously looking at their watches. A cheer goes up as they see Mrs H stepping out of the wedding car, her mouth agape, like a startled goldfish.

"What's going on here? I say, what's going on here?!"
"Come to watch the match, Missus H," says one brave soul, cheerfully. "Busby Babes in colour, it says on the tickets. Can't wait! Getting close to kick off time though, Marjorie – you'd best be getting yer skates on."

"Yer bloody cheeky monkey! I don't remember selling you a ticket. Or you, or you ..." she says to the first few people she lays eyes on.

"Aye, I know. It were your Declan that sorted it all out for me. Alright, Declan, lad?" he offers, as the man in question gets out of the car. "Tell yer mam I paid yer good money for this." He proffers a scrap of paper, Declan's scrawl is instantly recognizable and although the words are hard to make out, it's not difficult to guess that he's copied the details from his mother's tickets. Looking along the queue, he's done it quite a few times.

"By, 'eck. There must be a hundred people! It's not Noah's Ark, you know!" shouts an understandably anxious Mrs Hughes.

"I'm very interested in those volvo vons, Mrs H," interrupts George, the window cleaner, who is holding up his own scrap of paper with the same misplaced confidence that Neville Chamberlain once did. "Never had one of those before. Something to do with prawns, aren't they? Never had one of those, either. Is it like a cockle?"

"What the bloody hell did you think you were doing, Declan!" she shouts again, turning on her son, who stutters out an unconvincing reply.

"Whaaa ...? It wasn't me! Must have been our D ... Aiden."

"Oh, no. It were definitely you, Declan. And yon fella, of course." George nods at Terry, who had arrived on the scene and, realising that they may have gone a little too far, was in the process of reversing his wheelchair in the opposite direction.

"Whoooaa ...! Hold yer horses, you. Nobody's going anywhere until we've got this sorted out!" Mrs H has the bit between her teeth. "And you lot," she directs to the queue. "There's not enough room for everyone – yer'll have to bugger off home and watch it!"

"But we haven't got colour tellies, Mrs H," say the decorators, Reggie and Ronnie, almost simultaneously – murderous looks in their eyes.

"It dun't bloody matter – it's not in colour anyway!" There is an eerie silence before a great roar of objection rises up, bouncing off the small terrace houses of Elton Street.

"Waddaya mean? 'Full Colour Entertainment' it says here!" Reggie points to the ticket. In actual fact, it could say just about anything, but Mrs H realises the game is up. She knew this point was coming, but hoped her audience would have had a few more drinks inside them first. However, she doesn't miss a beat:

"Well, yes of course. And there is 'Full Colour Entertainment'. I'm a woman of my word, everybody knows that. Gobind Livroop Ripudaman

Sahib's daughters are putting on a show – Bhangra From Burnage. Bobby Dazzlers they are – in full colour!"

"That's racist!" shouts someone in the queue, careful that they remain hidden from Mrs H.

"It most certainly is not racialist!" she retorts, affronted. "I'm talking about their clothes – every colour of the rainbow they are. The most colourful entertainment you will ever see this side of Salford Docks, I'll have you know. And who said that!?"

The queue visibly cower as one.

"Well, if we're not coming in, we'll be wanting our money back then."

"See our Declan f' yer money back!" she snaps. "But yer can mek it tomorrow. Yer not bloody spoiling his wedding day – daft apeth that he is!" She cuffs her son round the back of the head with some considerable force and launches him through the front door.

"And you Terrence McAllister – I'm going to wait until your bones are fully mended before I break them again. Get in 'ere an' all!"

Terry speeds towards the door, but in an attempt to get inside without feeling the wrath of Mrs Hughes's back hand his wheelchair collides with the front step and he goes hurtling through the air into the living room, the chair rebounding weakly back into the street. Mrs Hughes picks it up and pushes it through the doorway, colliding with the now prostrate Terry, who had not yet got over his crash landing before being run over by his own wheelchair.

"And stop yer skriking!"

At this very moment, Declan is stood with 92,000 other people, having made his way into the majestic, iconic, Wembley Empire Stadium. The late spring evening was unusually warm and, mixed with his earlier alcohol consumption, he allows himself to drift on the emotion of the occasion, all thoughts of what might be happening at home fade to the back of his mind. The Babes run out in blue, Benfica in white, and he smiles at the thought of his mother's brash red and white wallpaper. Matt Busby's entrance is greeted with the loudest roar Declan has ever heard – twice given the last rites ten years ago, his obsessive dream is in touching distance. Charlton leads his team to the centre circle and Bill Foulkes, a second survivor of the crash that killed eight of their team mates, seems a giant amongst men as he considers the impudence of the Benfica team who have dared to challenge this destiny. This is their moment. This is their fate. It is their European Cup. And here is the man to make it happen. Here is Georgie Best.

And at that exact second, as the Northern Irishman warms up by juggling the ball from knee to knee, Declan knows that he's made the right decision. He is here, and he has never been surer of anything in his life.

Meanwhile, back in Stretford, Aiden is sure that this is the biggest mistake he has ever made in his life. The Hughes' residence, two houses knocked through though they may be, is packed to the rafters. There is pandemonium. There is chaos. There is uproar. There is also cake and dancing Bhangra girls. There is music and there are vol-au-vents. There is a colour television, which is currently showing black and white pictures of George Best, as he juggles the ball in the warm up. There have been complaints and bitter squabbles. There have been threats of legal action over the wording of Mrs Hughes' tickets – 'full colour entertainment' has been a phrase of much debate. There have also been threats of violence, partially carried out by Mrs Hughes against a protesting Aiden – a sheep in wolf's clothes. But finally, finally … the attention turns away from the chaos and the vol-au-vents and all eyes turn to the television. Lacking in the expected colour revolution it may be, but it is still brand new, state of the art technology, and it is showing the team from around the corner playing against Benfica in the European Cup Final. It is a very good picture, it has to be said; diminished only slightly by the wafts of Capstan Full Strength cigarette smoke that hang heavy in the heaving room. An excited hush descends across the viewers, punctuated occasionally by a shout of complaint from the other side of the impressively clean windows, where there are still three or four people attempting to get into the house, each frantically waiving one of Declan's counterfeit tickets in the vague direction of Mrs Hughes. As the match kicks off even these stalwarts capitulate and disappear, looking for other opportunities to see the game.

Aiden notices that Róisín isn't in the room. He makes his way to the kitchen, squeezing past a dozen or more motionless men, each with a Pale Ale in one hand and a Capstan or an Embassy in the other, each oblivious to the worried groom as he makes his way through. Save for Róisín, the kitchen is empty. She sits silently, her head bowed over a table that carries the crumbs of a thousand sausage rolls.

"Róisín, I'm so sorry. I've left you here like Piffy on a Rock Bun. This ... this mayhem. It was never supposed to be like this. Your wedding day it's ... well, it's probably not how you thought it would be. Please don't cry, please don't be mad ..."

As Aiden stutters his consolations, Róisín looks up and, although her eyes are wet, he sees only happiness shining through them. There have been tears, but they've been tears of joy. She smiles. It is the most wonderful smile he has ever seen, and it melts him to the core. He forgets who he is. He forgets everything other than the beautiful vision in front of him.

"Declan, don't be an eejit," she says, using the pronunciation of the word idiot that her parents have never lost, and bringing Aiden back to earth at the mention of his brother's name. "You're right; it's not how I dreamt my wedding day would be when I was a little girl. But you know what? I couldn't be happier. This is just one day, one night, and I've got the rest of my life with you. And there's something else ... you're different ..."

Aiden tries to hide a look of alarm.

"I dunno what it is. You look the same, apart from the hair, but you're different. There's a warmth shining from you that I've never seen before. The way you look at me, I feel ..." she pauses to consider her words, " ... special ... important ... loved. You've said those words to me many times, but it's only today that I've actually felt them from you. It must be because we're married, I suppose, but as soon as I saw you in that church, I've just been floating on cloud nine."

Aiden has gone red. "Oh. But what if I'm different tomorrow? What if I go back to being the old Declan then?"

Róisín laughs. "I've uncovered the real Declan now," she says. "And you can never go back."

She leans over and kisses him. It is Aiden's turn to reach Cloud Nine, and he begins to increase the intensity of the kiss, his hands moving gently to her waist. She pulls away, but with another of those devastating smiles.

"Plenty of time for that, Declan Hughes. But look at you now, not even watching the football – that's something I would never have thought possible. The biggest game of your life and you come to find me." She pauses for a minute to consider the magnitude of what she's just said. "I told you you were different. Now get back in there and cheer on t'lads – I'll be there in a minute, once I've fixed me face."

Aiden is about to protest, but then realises she's right. Declan wouldn't have thought twice about the whereabouts of his new wife if United were playing – even if it was their wedding day. And he remembers his role; he remembers that he is only a character in a huge charade. A pantomime. A farce. He forces a smile and returns to the sitting room to lose himself in the mass.

Declan's stomach is in knots. As the game nears the end of normal time, the score is one-one and the calming, emboldening effect of the alcohol has worn off. Eusabio, Benfica's Black Pearl is clean through on goal and must surely score to win the game. Declan holds his breath – could they have come this far for nothing? But the keeper makes a fantastic save, so good that the opposing player can only stand and clap, replicating the crowd. The relief that Declan feels is short lived. The referee blows the final whistle and it is only then that he realises that there will now be extra time. That's another half an hour before he can get back to Manchester and assume his role of groom.

Husband.

His stomach takes an extra turn at the thought.

The assembled, crushed masses in Mrs Hughes' sitting room are, conversely, delighted at the prospect of extra time. This is another half an hour to drink! Aiden is not so thrilled, but surely Declan will take the opportunity to come home now? He won't stay and watch the extra time, will he? He'll take the opportunity to get back whilst the crowds are all inside, make a quick getaway and relieve him of this impossible situation.

Who's he trying to kid, he thinks.

To be fair to Declan, as soon as the referee signals the end of the match, he grabs Steve and, after some initial argument, he agrees to miss the celebrations and get Declan back to Manchester.

"I 'ope you remember what a big favour I'm doing for you 'ere, Decs lad!"

Yeah, nothing to do with the obscene amount of money I've bribed you with, Stevie, he thinks, but is wise enough to keep the thought to himself. He attaches himself to the back of the powerful motorbike, the inside of his thighs already smarting from the journey down, and hangs on for dear life. And dear wife.

Back in Elton Street, everybody has left the tight confines of the Hughes household and has spilled out onto the streets to celebrate. They've done it. 4-1 after extra time – and what a goal by Georgie Best. They dance now, in the street, as Best had danced around the goalkeeper on the Wembley turf! Other houses spill their guests, pub doors burst open. Nobody wants to be inside. The evening is still warm and there is an abundance of energy that has been pressurising over the tense first ninety minutes. The street's other twins, the Parishs, have dragged their record player and enormous speakers into the street, setting up an impromptu discothèque. They cheekily put a cap down in front of it and throw a few starter coins in before igniting the party with some Tamla Motown. Everybody has work tomorrow. Nobody cares. This is their night, their victory – they know it may never come around again and they are determined to drag it out for as long as they possibly can. The dancing begins.

Aiden and Róisín are left in the wake of the mass exodus. Mrs Hughes is orchestrating the dancing in the middle of the street. The Bhangra girls are doing a routine on the pavement – even Mr Hughes has moved a chair to the front step and sits watching the merriment, armed with a Woodbine and a heavily rum-laced glass of Guinness.

"Shall we join them?" says Róisín, her voice quiet in the silence of the living room.

"You don't mind?" says Aiden, who is desperate for the sanctity of the crowd after the early fraudulent, close and intimate encounter in the kitchen.

"Of course not. Let's enjoy the moment. Actually, I feel quite special that this should happen on my wedding day. Look at everyone. They couldn't be happier, and that's what's important in life, isn't it? Being happy?"

Aiden answers with a smile and leads his counterfeit bride out into the street, a pulse of electricity flowing through his whole body as soon as he takes hold of her hand. Outside, the party is in full swing and they join a dance near the record player, lost in each other's eyes and the intoxicating atmosphere.

It is 2.00am before Sidecar Steve drops Declan off, right outside Old Trafford. A great crowd has gathered there in front of the dark, tiny windows of the ticket office. He stops only briefly to witness the festivities, more fervent than any he has seen there before, then hurriedly jogs the short distance to Elton Street. He stops at the corner, aware of the street party from the noise of the twins' speakers, and the shrieks of laughter and celebration. He conceals himself against the cool stonework of the Victorian terrace and inches forward his face and hands to view the length of Elton Street: like a Chad cartoon … 'Wot? No City fans?'.

There must be two hundred people on the tiny street, but he sees Aiden and Róisín immediately, dancing to Sam and Dave's 'Soul Man'. One of the Parish twins (he's not sure which, Jeff or Stu, he can never tell them apart) is inciting the crowd with his own wild dance routine, but though the song is rousing, the newlyweds seem to be dancing to a song of their own – a slower, more intimate number. Declan is incensed. That's his girlfriend out there! His wife, in fact. He makes to confront them, but then realises he can't yet make himself known – he needs to wait for an opportunity to switch clothes with Aiden, and no doubt take some serious abuse for dropping him in it like that. Still, it looks like the plan has worked … Róisín is smiling, seemingly oblivious to the duplicity. Actually, he's never seen her like this before. She seems to be almost floating with happiness. Like he is after five pints and a last minute winner. He watches, patiently, awaiting his chance.

Terry sits in his wheelchair, somewhat peeved. His best man speech was largely overlooked, due to audience anxiety as the impending match loomed, teamed with the wrath of Mrs Hughes for his contribution to the ticket fiasco. He had had a ticket for Wembley and couldn't go and now, following the win, he can't join in the celebrations. He itches to be out of his plaster, but can only watch. Perhaps because of his inactivity, he spots the covert figure, lurking furtively at the corner, and recognises Declan immediately. He slowly rolls his wheelchair backwards towards his friend.

"'Bout bloody time!" he half shouts, half whispers, trying, like a poor ventriloquist, to keep his mouth from moving. He needn't have bothered – nobody is paying him any attention. Declan, standing around the corner, back to the wall, ignores the jibe.

"How's it going? Do you think she's on to it?"

"Whaa? Nah, not a bit of it. I don't know what you said to your Aiden, but he's carried it off to a T."

"I didn't say anything. I just left him a note and hoped for the best."

"Really?" Terry is amazed. "Well, he's thrown himself into the role – look at him now!"

Declan peers cautiously around the corner again, catching his twin in a rather tender embrace with Róisín. Caught by the rays of an orange street light, her face confuses him. He dismisses the thought, but it stays at the back of his mind, burning: is that the first time he's ever seen her … happy?

"You need to get a message to Aiden. Tell him I'm here and we need to swap clothes; swap round again."

"Good luck with that," says Terry. "They haven't been apart long enough for me to speak to either of them on their own since the match ended. It's like they're attached to each other – s'not natural."

The conversation stalls as they watch the couple end their embrace. Aiden has clearly whispered something funny in her ear, as Róisín's head falls back in laughter. She kisses him lightly on the bridge of his nose and they hug.

"She's never kissed me lightly on the bridge of my nose!" complains Declan.

One of the Parish twins, knowing when they have the audience vibe, changes the disc to 'Hold On, I'm Coming' and the small street fills with

Soul. Róisín and Aiden move from hug to dance – naturally, seamlessly. They look good together. Very good.

"You know, Terry – maybe I should leave them to it."

"Whu …whu … what are you talking about?"

"I've never seen Róisín like that. She looks so happy with him, far happier than she's ever been with me. And Aiden too – just look at him – when did you ever see that grumpy grease ball look so happy? Or so smart, come to think of it."

"You can't just leave them! Aiden would just come clean, drop you in it. And even if he didn't, it would be a wedding based on a lie – you couldn't let that happen."

"Why not?" Declan pauses to consider his words. He's known this for some time, perhaps since he and Róisín first held hands, back at Fat Tommy Duckworth's ninth birthday party. But he's never before been brave enough to say them. "If it was me and Róisín that were married, that would be a lie."

"Eh?" which is the limit of Terry's vocabulary at the moment.

"Terry, I love Róisín. Love her to bits. But, well I know it's a cliché, something they might use in a hippy song lyric or something, but … I'm not in love with her. I love her like I love you."

"Uh …eh?" says Terry, which is an improvement on his last contribution to the conversation, if only in that he has managed to double to number of syllables that he's used.

"I mean I love her like a best mate. Like brother and sister. Like someone I enjoy hanging out with. I'd do anything for her if she asked – lend her money, watch her back, be there for her when she's ill … so when she talked about marriage, it was just like she assumed that's what I wanted and … if I'm honest … I just didn't like to say no."

"Blummin' good job I've never asked you to marry me then!" Terry is recovering, but still can't believe the situation. "You couldn't write this!" he adds.

They watch Aiden and Róisín for a few moments in silence. There is a bond, a current between them. Anyone could see it, even the two half-wits who had manufactured this lunatic liaison.

"I think I'd be doing all three of us a favour," says Declan. "I'm going to sneak back into our house and get me stuff. There's some Portuguese lads I'm going to catch up with."

"And what am I supposed to tell them?"

"Don't tell them anything. It worked last time. It looks to me that Aiden will be pretty chuffed with the outcome."

Terry looks at Declan's twin. It's true that he's never seen him like this before. The gruff, bearded, moody cynic is like a child, dancing and laughing, clean shaven and smart-suited, the energy of a ten year old on Sherbet Dip.

"Yeah, well yer not leavin' me t' deal with yer mess, this time, Decs. I mean, bleeding Nora! Yer can't just run out on yer wedding day. You can't just …"

But Terry is talking to himself. Declan has gone to climb the back drainpipe and enter the house through the bathroom window, leaving his friend to complain on his own.

"Well, thanks a lot!"

Aiden and Róisín are staring into each other's eyes. It's 3.00am and even the most ardent revellers have decided they'd better call it a night – although some have to be dragged off by the ear by long suffering spouses. Jeff and Stu have packed away their record player and are counting up the money left in their hat, their minds already anticipating a trip to The Spin Inn at weekend – an opportunity to increase their ever-growing vinyl collection.

"Well, I think it's time for bed," says Róisín, she raises an eyebrow and smiles suggestively. "I know it's only at me mam's until we get ourselves a flat but, well, at least they've left us alone tonight. We've got the house to ourselves. Our first time … 'special' … like you said."

For Aiden, this breaks the spell he's been under for the last few hours. During this time he had almost forgotten that he was playing a role, that Declan was coming back to take over. If signing his brother's name on a wedding register wasn't enough, if defrauding this wonderful woman wasn't going to leave him feeling ashamed for the rest of his life, well … he couldn't take her wedding night as well. She's saved herself for this night, but for Declan, not for him. He just wouldn't be able to live with himself.

"Róisín, I have to tell you something. You have to know …"

"Shush," she says. "Not another word. I'll go and get me things from yer house and we'll walk over to mine … ours." She smiles again and is gone, leaving Aiden alone in the street, but with the trouble of the world on his shoulders.

Not quite alone. From the shadows, silently slides the less than ambulant Terry McAllister. He brings his chair to a halt next to Aiden, who doesn't even notice he's there until he coughs, awkwardly.

"Well, you got what you wanted, Terry. Where's the boy wonder?"

"What made you change your mind, Aiden? That day when I came to see you in the café – you even had me convinced it was a bad idea."

"Well, I was blummin' right about that, wasn't I? Worst idea I've ever had."

Terry waits for Aiden to answer his question. When it's clear he's drifted off into his own thoughts, he prompts him again.

"Well?"

"Oh … well … I couldn't just let her wait at the altar whilst Golden Balls swans around London watching the football. I know her. It would have destroyed her. Now I've spent these few hours with her, it's going to be me who's destroyed."

"You love her, don't you?"

If Terry was expecting a denial, he would have been wrong. If he thought the hardened, cynical rocker, Aiden Hughes, would laugh off the question and tell him not to be so daft, well ... he had another think coming.

"More than I ever thought possible," he said, simply and plainly.

They looked at each other for a moment before Terry decided to tell him the latest.

"Declan's not coming back."

"Say that again. Say it again, slowly, and explain to me why."

"He's gone, Aiden. Or going ..."

At that exact second they could hear the put-put-atta-put of the Vespa, and looked up as it passed the top of the street. A blue blur, they were able to make out the hunched figure of Declan, trade mark fishtail Parka coat, the warm breeze disturbing his otherwise immaculate hair, guitar strapped to his back, a roll of clothes tied to the rear pannier.

"Portugal, apparently."

"Oh, brilliant. So how do I explain this one to Róisín?" Aiden's anger is up now. "What does he expect me to tell her? She'll kill both of us now."

"He saw you two together, mate. I think he knew he couldn't compete with that. I don't think he wants you to tell her."

"Tell me what?"

"Oh ... Róisín ..." spluttered Terry.

"Yes: Róisín! Tell me what?"

But Aiden is calm. He wants to tell her. He needs to get this off his chest, and whatever his part was in the charade, he still feels he did it for the right reasons.

"Róisín, please don't be mad, but ... I'm not Declan ... I'm Aiden."

"Oh, I know that – is that it?"

"You know?"

"Realised when we were chatting in the kitchen earlier. I knew something was up when you came in there whilst the match was on. And when you went back in I realised you walk differently than Declan. You know Declan practices his walk, don't you? He tries to copy that Carnaby Street swagger, but he ends up looking like a gorilla that's dyeing for a shite. So what now? Do I have to give you back, or do I get to keep you?"

Aiden is too shocked to respond. He is struggling to take in this interesting turn of events. Terry too is gobsmacked.

"Okay, so you've both lost the power of speech. Not a totally disagreeable quality. I would like to know where the little gobshite is though, and what he has to say for himself."

Terry recovers first. "He's gone off with some Benfica fans, apparently ... Portugal, but ... he said it was because he saw you two together, he said he wanted you to be happy."

"Ah, Terry, loyal to the end ... defending a bloke who leaves his bride at the altar and emotionally blackmails his twin brother into taking his place. And thank the Lord Jesus and all the Saints that you did, Aiden – otherwise I'd have been waiting there like you said earlier: like Piffy on a Rock Bun."

"But, how did you know ...?"

"I found the note he left you when I went into the house to get some things. I'd left a brush in your bedroom and saw it when I went back for it. I had to hide on the landing though, you know ... when I heard Declan climbing through the bathroom window. I didn't want to bump into him," she said in a matter of fact way. "I didn't want him to change his mind about going."

Aiden still can't speak.

"Well," she smiled. "Are we going?" She holds out her hand to Aiden, who looks at it for a moment, like it's the most amazing thing he has ever seen, before returning her smile and grabbing hold of it. As the sun starts to rise, threatening another uncharacteristically warm Manchester day, they walk towards Railway Road. Pausing at the corner, Aiden looks over his shoulder to the lone, lonely figure of Terry McAllister, sat dejectedly in his wheel chair, watching them disappear. He has lost his best friend tonight. Although some best friend – he will now have to face all those people who will want their money back after their ill-fated ticket scam on his own.

"And you, Terry," threatens Aiden, seemingly having recovered his voice without any noticeable aftereffects. "I should be having words with you about your part in all of this!" But his tone and his face softens. "Still, perhaps I should be thanking you for the way it's turned out. We should catch up for a pint together, my round …" He looks at Róisín. "In a day or two, maybe …"

They turn the corner and they're gone, leaving Elton Street empty, save for a solitary wheel-chaired figure who spins his wheels and begins to whistle as he bumps slowly over the cobbled street back to his home.

Sombreros for Goalposts

European Cup Winners' Cup Final

Camp Nou, Barcelona, 24th May 1972

This wasn't supposed to happen.

You've got to understand that I come from a very small village. Some of the things I've seen today have scarred me for life – of that I'm sure. I know I'll never be the same again. And to think I was excited because I was going to see a football game. Not just any game. A little different from the ones we played as children in the village; with no shoes, no kits, sombreros for goalposts. What am I talking about? At sixteen I'm still a child now, though I feel much older. I am watching the European Cup Winners' Cup Final. Or at least I was; what I'm seeing in front of me now could only be described as war.

I'd joined the Policía Armada for one reason only: I was made to. I'd thought at first it may have had its merits, at least I'd be leaving the family home. It's not that I don't love my family, it's just that when there are thirteen of you living in a three room house it can get very difficult. Now I live in a dormitory with 19 men, all of different size, shape and degrees of personal hygiene. At least, where I lived, we washed ourselves in the stream occasionally. In my parents' house, just twenty kilometres from Madrid, but in a village that could not afford its own donkey, food was scarce. If we had an orange we would have to keep quiet about it, for fear of jealousy from our neighbours. It would be split into segments and shared. I've never seen an orange with thirteen segments though, so it rarely got to me.

My name is Jesús Sanchis Vargas. I suppose there was always going to be a Jesús in my family with my mother being called Inmaculada and my father being a carpenter. You can see why I am a little disappointed with my current role in life – the only miracle I have seen so far is the one time my friend Rafael did not try to steal the chorizo from my plate when he thought I was not looking. Actually, my father is a builder's labourer, but a carpenter makes for a better story.

I thought I'd be fed better in the police, but it is not so different. At least there is one less mouth to feed at home, and from time to time Generalissimo Francisco Franco pays us just enough of our wages to stop a revolt. (Talk of revolt is nonsense, of course. As a young Brigadier he once executed 200 miners after he quashed their strike). Nobody talks of such things above a careful whisper – my colleagues see themselves as brave, but not stupid. We are so brave, we patrol in pairs with submachine guns, in towns that could not buy a bullet between them, let alone a gun). Because of our uniforms they call us los grises – 'the greys' – and they also call us 'el legado nazi' – the Nazi legacy. Do you know how this makes me feel? It is like an Atlético supporter having to wear a Real Madrid shirt every day. It is torture.

I was made to come to this match, but I would have volunteered and I would have done it for free. We had a radio in the village, and we would always gather around it to listen to the football. It didn't matter who was playing, or where they were from. In our minds, the commentators would bring the game to life – I had never even seen a television until this year, but I could still enjoy Best dancing down the wing, Eusabio, Puskas and Muller. I laughed out loud as I listened to that old radio we had built ourselves, savouring the commentary as the words painted pictures in my mind: Garrincha beating his man then waiting for him to recover so that he could beat him again. Well, there was little else to brighten our young lives.

This was how I learnt English, listening to the football commentators on the BBC World Service, then talking to the old men in the village; those that we knew had fought alongside the English against Franco in the thirties. They would tell me the meanings of those words: swerve, dink, chip, studs-up. They would tell you the meaning of those words, but they would not admit how they came to learn them. Even now, it would still be dangerous to say that you were not on the side of the Right.

The build up to the game was very nervous: we expected trouble. One of the teams was Dynamo Moscow – as a boy, I would probably have been jailed just for listening to their commentary on the radio. Communists, you see, and in Franco's España there isn't anything worse than a Communist. You would have thought that near starvation and a brutal, oppressive right-wing regime may be up there, but no – there is nothing worse than Communism; they told us that from being very small children. So we expected trouble and we were out in force. We had felt like an invading foreign army all day – we were Madrileños in Barcelona, the capital of Catalan, after all. Franco's Police: brutal, vicious thugs who struck fear into the very bones of malnourished farmers and bent-double old ladies. There were very few Moscow fans there to hate us, but that didn't matter – the whole of Barcelona had turned out to hate us on their behalf. Very thoughtful of them.

But in the end, it was neither the Soviets nor the Catalans we had to worry about. I had heard the phrase 'Tartan Army', but I didn't realize the fans of the other team, Glasgow Rangers, were a real army. They weren't dressed like any army I'd heard about, although I have to admit that I was terrified when I first saw them. The stories we had heard of food being plentiful in other countries had to be true after all, because although most of them had drawn, pasty-faces, they had enormous stomachs. You will laugh when I tell you this, but I actually thought many of them were pregnant. Pregnant men – I told you I came from a small village. My friend, Rafael, explains that it is because they drink so much … something called 'Heavy' … that their stomachs bloat like a woman in her third trimester. Some of them wore skirts with handbags tied to the front, so you can understand my confusion. Many wore scarves and hats, despite the warm weather. And they must not sell shorts in Scotland – having seen the legs of those that stripped to their large, white underwear to dance in the fountains, I can understand why. You can imagine how I felt: thousands of loud, pregnant, rickets victims, over-dressed and adorned like Chieftains in their flags and tartan, chanting aggressively and puffing asthmatically into strange octopus-like pipes that made a sound that could only have come from the very depths of hell, as they marched down Las Ramblas demanding more alcohol. I was terrified – and that was before I heard them speak! Madre Mia! What sort of language is that? My English was no help to me at all. They speak words I have never heard before, and in an accent that is a cross between a bad tempered goose and a wasp with a hangover. I preferred the noise of the bagpipes.

What a wondrous place this Scotland must be – plentiful food and drink, and where nobody cares how you look, what you dress like or how ridiculous you sound. They have so much money that they wear extra clothes in warm weather, they have an unlimited supply of cigarettes and they are drunk from the early morning until … well, the next early morning. They are laughing all the time and they play like they are school children in the park. What a fabulous place Glasgow must be to live: truly, the streets must be paved with gold.

The game went well for them. If this is what happens when they win, thank all the Saints that they didn't lose. It was a great match to watch, and I was completely enthralled in everything that happened on the pitch. I forgot where I was for those ninety minutes; I forgot about my worries: my hunger was replaced by their hunger for the ball, my fear forgotten amid their fearsome tackles, my persecution put aside as I watched, open-mouthed, at the way those blue-shirted warriors went three goals to nil up. At half time the Tartan Army partied like they had already won.

But it was then the turn of the Moscow team. A double substitution and they got a goal back – the game turned, and Rangers had to defend wave after wave of attack. With four minutes to go, just after a second Soviet goal, the ball was kicked into the crowd and was not returned to the pitch. Instead, a pitch invasion from the Scots! ¿Qué carajo es esto?! This surely broke the rhythm of the Moscow team; and when the referee blows the whistle in injury time again, the Tartans decide that another invasion is necessary. I do not know if it was the final whistle, but the teams disappear and do not come out again. Rangers have won!

I see these strange Scottish people. They may wear skirts or ridiculous bell-bottomed trousers, and make torturous sounds, but they are mainly good people. I have heard reports of their hooliganism in other towns today, how they spray their gang names on every wall, but in Barcalona they have been laughing with the Guàrdia and the Catalans on Las Ramblas all day. They are friendly individuals, even feeding stray dogs and tramp-pigeons. They are surely just enjoying this moment and partying. If I was the chief of police, that sycophantic Franco puppet, I would have let the Scots have their party. Instead, he sends us to stop them. To batter their heads with our batons and show them they do not mess with the might of El Generalissimo. I find it better to hide near the dugout and watch. I have no stomach for mindless brutality. I'm glad I did, for it is now that we find out why these Tartans are called an Army. I watch as they first defend themselves from the sticks of my compadres (unheard of) and then, I still cannot believe I am seeing this, they fight back! They fight back and they begin to win. Maybe the Policía should have drunk more, if this is how you can fight when you have all that beer in you. It is carnage out there. It is the first time Franco has been beaten since the start of the Civil War, more than thirty-five years ago. He will not be impressed and, as usual, it will be his own people that suffer.

I stifle a small laugh as I hear the Catalans that are watching from the neutral section – they are cheering on the Rangers fans as they beat the Policía at their own game. Catholics cheering Protestants – what else will I see tonight!?

And then, from nowhere, I fear I am in trouble. One of these Tartan rascals, a fat man with wild red hair and an even wilder beard, is running towards me. His arms are high and threatening, his shriek comes from the battles we learn about at school, of Bannockburn and Falkirk, and aimed at me. His weapon of choice: a bottle of whisky. I realise, a little too late, that he means me no harm. He is celebrating. He is drunk, but he is happy; he meant to hug me, to dance with me – I could see the confusion in his eyes, the split second before my baton crashed against his forehead.

I am sorry. I am sorry for what I did and I am ashamed. However, looking at this unconscious, drunk foreigner, his bottle of whisky still clasped to his hand despite both his predicament and his level of inebriation, gives me an idea.

It is an idea that I am even more ashamed of, but I will do it anyway.

I take the man's clothes and leave him in his contaminated underwear. I am worried that they won't fit me – they don't, but I can get away with the skirt thing by wrapping it around me a few more times. The jacket is both too large and too short at the same time, the sombrero (I learn later they call it, absurdly, a tam o'shanter) is too large, which makes it fall, fortuitously, over half of my face. I have drunk small amounts of wine before, so I take several long slugs of the remaining whisky. It is full of fire and burns from the inside. Dear God! How can they drink that stuff? I translate the label on the bottle and see that it is thirty years old and that it is only a single malt – no wonder it tastes so bad! I douse myself in the remaining liquid, leaving a centimetre in the bottom for effect, then look for a passed-out drunken Scotsman to lie next to.

I don't have to look far, and I have plenty of choice. I can't think I can possibly get away with this, but I can try.

~~~

Half an hour or so later, the pitch has been cleared and the stadium is virtually empty. The Tartan Army had decided on a strategic retreat when the Policía unclipped their guns. From the one eye that I half open every now and again, I can see the Guàrdia Urbana helping the drunken and the injured out of the stadium. These are the local Barcelona police, they are not like us, and when they approach the small group of human debris that I have joined, they do not use their batons or unkind words to move us. I think I can sense their embarrassment at the brutality that the Policía Armada showed these guests in our country. I shuffle along with this group out of the stadium, trying from time to time to replicate their ancestral grunts, but mostly just keeping quiet, keeping my head down, keeping that fiery liquid from making me be sick.

Outside, the group I am with begin to break up and go their separate ways. I stick with three tartans that seem the worst for wear and hold my breath as I follow them onto a shabby bus. I expect to be challenged, for someone to ask for a ticket perhaps, but nothing happens. The men collapse into seats and are soon joining their countrymen in a chorus of growling snores. The stink on this bus is abnormal. It reminds me of our Dormitory back in Madrid, and with the effects of the whisky wearing me down, I find a vacant seat and close my eyes.

A man shakes me rudely awake. "Passeport s'il vous plait, pourri chien!"

I don't know any French, but recognise 'Pasaporte'. In the fug of my sleep, almost without thinking, I hold up the passport that was in the jacket I had borrowed from the unfortunate red-bearded Scotsman. He takes it and grunts, then tosses it back to me. Before I even have time to be nervous, he has already moved onto the next passenger. The sombrero covering most of my face must have helped and maybe he thought I had shaved my beard, but as I watch him wake each person on the bus, receiving either confusion or abuse from each dishevelled collection of rags that he can rouse, I realize the poor man just wants to get his job done and get off this stinking char-à-banc. He is not looking too closely at the documentation.

I cross the border into France. I have escaped El Generalissimo and España – that beautiful country, full of hate and recrimination, lacking in food and clothing, medicine and hope. I am a secret refugee. For the first time I am excited for my future – it is 1972 and little Jesús is going to live in Glasgow!

You Only Singh When You're Winning

A John is for life; not just for the transfer window

John Sourbutts was a man that took after his own name. Sourbutts, not John. Despite being an American slang word for a toilet, nobody ever takes after the name John. Nobody ever looks at a newly born child and thinks 'he looks like a John – we'll call him John'. You just get called it and you become a John.

This John wore almost permanently the sour expression of a man who had inadvertently sat on something wet and cold, but was silently suffering the discomfort because he didn't want anyone to know he had placed his butt in such an uncomfortably damp situation. His face would have contorted to this expression if, for example, someone had uttered an American word where a perfectly good British one would have sufficed. Like using 'butt' instead of 'arse' or 'backside', for instance. John certainly wouldn't have been happy about that. John didn't like change, and saw the Americanisation of the English language as a personal slight.

Harry Singh, in a very roundabout way, also took after his own name. Singh; not Harry. It would be hard to look at someone and say 'oh, yes, you can see why they called him Harry – he's most certainly Harry-like'. But Harry wasn't Harry's real name. It was just the name he'd gone by when his family fled Bangladesh in the mid-seventies and ended up on the outskirts of the suburban sprawl of a large Northern city. Surrounded by untrusting eyes and trying desperately to fit in with his suspicious new class mates he'd called himself Harry rather than Harshit, following the fortunate intervention and advice of the school nurse who had checked out his somewhat undernourished body prior to releasing him into the wilds of the schoolyard. Forty years later he still went by Harry – he even had many close friends who were unaware his name was anything else. But Harry liked to sing. From those first desperate days in the classroom where his refugee status, charity shop clothes, poor English and laughable accent had made him a source of ridicule for his fellow eight-year-olds, to his current position as CEO of his own shipping company,

Harry had always sung. He was known for it. When he learnt that he'd been accepted into Cambridge University, for example, he stood on his desk and sang. Later, whenever he closed a big boardroom deal, adding a few more 000s to his growing fortune, he would break into song. Harry Singh sang when he won. And he was always winning.

John and Harry's paths had not crossed for many years. John still remembered Harry turning up in his class halfway through spring term. He wasn't one of those who poked fun at the unfortunate, unwilling migrant, but he hadn't exactly run to his defence either. If pushed, he might have remembered his father helping the Singh family clean up their house after it was firebombed by some out-of-town National Front thugs, or his mother helping Mrs Singh with any official paperwork that she had to deal with. Later, as Harry excelled in his studies, John was more interested in sport and fixing old motor bikes. They were just different people, very little in common. When Harry went off to the sixth form and John began his carpentry apprenticeship, neither would have thought they would meet again – had either of them given it any thought. Which they hadn't.

So John grew up, oblivious to the success of his classmate. He became a very good carpenter and was much sought after – not just because of the quality of his work, excellent though it was, but because he was fair. Firm, but fair. He would refuse to cut corners (unless he was making something that required him to cut corners, of course). He would never botch a job, use cheaper material or rush to finish, but he would always charge a fair price. Sometimes, when he could see a customer was struggling, he would even undercharge. John, unlike Harry, was never going to be a millionaire. And although he worked hard, he always had Saturday afternoons off to support his team. Rubbish though they were, he would always stand and support them. He would swear and curse at them for ninety minutes, but would not hear a bad word said about them by anyone else.

Middleton Town were his club. He didn't give a toss about darts, snooker, or this new-fangled karaoke malarkey that they all had down at the Trades Club. He did an honest week's graft, and then he went to watch his team. End of. And when they were really struggling, the first time they were in danger of going out of business, he was one of the few that stepped in and saved them. Not with money, because none of them had that, but with a bit more honest graft. He and about twenty others pitched up at the ground and did their bit. They cut the grass; they painted the lines; they fixed the toilets, they repaired the corner flags. One of them, a vocally gifted used car salesman who had called himself 'Rusty' for reasons that he would never discuss, not only persuaded the nearby pie manufacturer to extend the Club credit, but convinced them that a Middleton Town Pasty was worth a production line of its own, with 10% of the proceeds going directly to the Club's highly overdrawn bank account.

John Sourbutts had, amongst various other tasks, almost single-handedly built the Club's Executive lounge: possibly the most under-used area of the ground, but a triumph of building on a budget nonetheless. John lived for that Club. Every spare minute was spent in the upkeep of the ground, and although the threat of bankruptcy was always looming, his efforts, and those of a few other hard core veterans, made sure that they stayed one step ahead of the liquidator.

Perhaps half a step. And closing.

He would turn up every week, every Saturday and Wednesday night when there was a game on, and support his team. He would shout, swear, scream and spit his opinions across the stadium that he had help to build, maintain and develop and, let's face it, would probably not even be there if it wasn't for him. Quite rightly, he felt he was a little bit more entitled to his opinion than the thousand or so other supporters that would bother to brave a cold weekday evening to watch a drab nil-nil draw against a team that few had even heard of. It wasn't a venue for the football tourist. Or purist.

One-nil down to Mingston United in the FA Cup first round, John sang out with the Middleton Town Ultras:

'We shall not, we shall not be moved
We shall not, we shall not be moved
From a team that's going to pay the tax man soon
We shall not be moved'

He didn't care too much that they were losing, that they were going out of the FA Cup. The couple of hundred faithful that stood behind the goal had been on fire tonight. A large bass drum had been the backbeat to their songs: vicious, sarcastic and ridiculous; and they'd danced, pogoed along for the last 84 minutes, daring the opposition supporters to keep up with them.

Mingston scored again, and at last they heard a noise from the hundred or so opposition supporters who had made the trip.

'Three-two, we're going to win three-two', retorted the Middleton fans.

Middleton scored immediately from the kick off. Two-one down with two minutes to go it would seem to be only a consolation goal, but John and the rest of the zealots behind the goals went fucking mental.

'Let's go fucking mental,' they sang and bopped and boogied, ludicrously. To a man they were all going to work the next morning, so they were going to enjoy this.

"Heard the latest?" Bernie the Bevvie, the Middleton Free Press's sports journalist and gardening columnist nudged John and shouted in his ear.

"Rah, rah, rah, have you heard the latest? Rah, rah, rah: Middleton are the greatest!" sang John, who mistook the question for a prompt to a song. Nobody joined in, and John's face went sour. He always joined in if someone started a song near to him.

"No," said Bernie. "I mean, have you heard the latest news? Apparently the Club's been bought."

"Don't be daft. Who's going to buy this Club?" John's eyes were on the game as he talked, but a thought smacked him right between the eyes in much the same way that Mingston's centre back was just doing to Middleton's forward on the pitch. "Hang on … it's not a building company or a property investor, is it? They've talked about buying the ground to put houses on here before!"

Penalty to Middleton and Mingston are down to ten men.

"It's not what I heard," said Bernie, whose demeanour had turned to that of a man who had a sure fire tip on a bent race at Belle Vue Dog Track and doesn't want anyone else to know. "Someone who wants to put money into the Club, and ..." he looked around sheepishly, "it may surprise you to know that it's an old class mate of yours. Tell you what – buy me a bevvie in The Crown after the game and I'll let you in on the secret."

John's face scowled again. How many times had he heard that line from Bernie before? But Middleton had put the penalty past the keeper and John was washed away on a raging sea of delirious supporters. After the melee had calmed he tried to work his way back to Bernie, but a last second Middleton winner sent the Ultras into pandemonium and he lost any chance of getting the answer out of the reporter this side of a double whiskey in The Crown.

A Bern in the hand is worth two in the Black Bush

"So what's this about an old classmate?" John pushed the large whiskey, a Black Bush no less, across the table in The Crown's snug and took a sip of his Spitfire Ale. He didn't like to drink on a weeknight, not with a customer waiting for a new staircase the next morning. However, anything to do with the Club, and he had to know about it.

Bernie took his own sip and savoured the taste on his tongue before allowing the golden liquid to slide down his throat. He waited for the burn to subside before he spoke.

"Who do you think could afford to buy the Club that you went to school with? There's only one person who ever made it big in this town." Bernie allowed himself a small smirk – John could have worked it out for himself and saved himself the price of a large malt. He hadn't though.

"Eh? Anyone could have. Even that bloke who searches the bins on the High Street could have afforded it – it's been on sale for a quid for as long as I can remember."

Bernie sighed. Clearly high finance wasn't John's strong point. Or even low finance, if there is such a thing.

"The Club is a quid, of course it is. But you're buying the debt, aren't you? And the wages, the tax liability." Bernie took another sip and for a few seconds his mind wandered from the excited bustle of the post-match boozer to the quiet Antrim village of Bushmills, where the drink was distilled. John, impatiently, prompted him. "And all your general running costs as well. A set of new nets sets you back a few hundred quid, and if that pitch doesn't get re-laid this summer you may as well plant potatoes in it."

John looked at the last of the amber liquid as it disappeared from the glass and was licked, rather sensuously, from Bernie's lips. That's five quid he would never see again and, worse, he could have worked it out for himself.

"Harry Singh."

"Bingo," said Bernie and, knowing he wouldn't be getting anything else out of John Sourbutts tonight, went off to find another victim.

Tomorrow's Chip Paper

John's anguish at spending an unwarranted five pounds was heightened the next day when he bought the local newspaper, the Middleton Free Press, and read the whole story. Although not before scowling at the lazy alliteration.

BUSINESSMAN BUYS BELEAGUERED BLUES

Bernard Bolte – Sports Correspondent

Middleton Town FC has a new owner. Multi-millionaire businessman Harry Singh, who grew up in the town, has bailed out the football club in a surprising buyout. Mr Singh, originally from Bangladesh, went to Middleton Comprehensive and Sixth Form College before he left for University and business superstardom. But he has never forgotten growing up here and this is not the first time he has been generous with his cash. Four years ago he paid for the restoration of the large pie factory chimney which had come to dominate the town's skyline for nearly a hundred years. And only last August he donated a sizeable sum when local schoolboy Barry Wiggins needed life-saving surgery in the United States.

"When I read that my local football club was facing administration, I thought it was time to step in," said the entrepreneur, who is currently based in New York. "I've been looking for a project outside the business world, and this is exactly the type of thing I would like to throw myself into."

Mr Singh has never been afraid of the limelight, and was recently the subject of a fly-on-the-wall documentary series, with cameras following him from the boardroom to the bedroom as we saw how the other half live.

"And don't think I'm going to stop at paying off the debts," finished Mr Singh in a short press release originating from his Manhattan head office. "I want to put Middleton on the footballing map!"

Don't miss Bernard's gardening column, 'Beautiful Brilliant Begonias', on page 5.

Whilst he had to admit this was a much better proposition than Administration, John had a bad feeling about it. For one thing there was that word: 'project'. And although paying the debts off, securing the Club's future, was great too, he just hoped Harry Singh would understand he might own the Club, but it would never belong to him.

Trick or Beat

Nothing was very different on Saturday, when John returned to the ground. He needed to attend to two of the doors in the Gents' toilets that were in danger of falling off their hinges. After that, the small caravan that served burgers by the touchline needed some roof repairs after Brenda, who had cooked and sold them for over twenty years without a penny in wages, had complained that rainwater was getting into her chip oil. Town were away later that afternoon, so everything was quiet. He didn't know what he might have been expecting, but there was nothing that might suggest one of the world's richest men was anywhere in the vicinity. The toilet in stall three still needed unblocking, for example.

There was nothing different in the afternoon either, as Town surrendered a one-nil half time lead to eventually be beaten four-two. The euphoria surrounding the uncharacteristic success of Wednesday night's cup win had already begun to fade. There were a few early songs sung by the Middleton Town Ultras which joked about their new owner and how they were going to conquer Europe, but these soon faded along with the performance on the pitch.

The following Wednesday, John finished his work early and went straight to the ground. This time there were a few reporters in evidence, buzzing around, looking for evidence of Singh's millions. Like the home supporters, they left the evening's match disappointed, having got nothing from their visit. John reflected that it wasn't all bad news – he'd at last been able to fix the showers in the referee's changing room. They worked perfectly now, but he would still be able to switch the water from hot to icy cold if the Official had had a shocker.

It was a little different at the next home game though. John arrived late by his standards – just four hours before kick-off. He still wasn't confident about the blocked toilet although, despite the miserably overcast day, there was little sign of any rain to test Brenda's caravan roof. His mind was deliberating on whether he had time to give the touchlines a quick going over. The first thing that he noticed was different was when an eighteen stone bald American gentleman in a dark suit told him to 'go fuck himself up the asshole' as he threw him out of the entrance reserved for players and officials. That's very odd, thought John – why's he wearing sunglasses in the middle of November in northern England? Further protestations just brought more sexually related abuse, so John tried the Staff and VIP entrances, both of which were met with equally forceful ejections by equally mountainous Americans, each of whom wore sunglasses and had a predilection for sexual slander. Undeterred, John slid in through a hidden gap in the wall where he knew some of the kids used to get in for free. It was a tight squeeze, and he was grateful that he hadn't followed the diet choices of the Americans that he had just met.

Inside the ground, he noticed there was rather more activity than he usually found at 11.00am, even on a match day. For a start, there was a team of, he guessed, twenty workmen busying themselves around what passed for the directors' box. He doubted that they were volunteers like him – they all wore the same logo-adorned uniform and, to a man, the same cap. They didn't stop to laugh or swear at each other or have a cup of tea either, so he doubted they were British. Rows of shiny new seats were just getting their finishing touches. Padded seats, he noticed. Who'd have thought? Seats with padding at a football match. It was clear there was work going on behind the directors' box as well. How had they managed to rebuild what was once the directors' bar so quickly? That hadn't been used for years. On the pitch, he could see that brand new posts and nets had been erected and a man was sitting on a machine which was repainting the touchlines with a meticulousness that even John found disconcerting. He probably wouldn't need his little home-made, hand-rolled contraption today. Everything seemed to be in order – he'd just take one more look at that blocked toilet in trap three and then read the paper until Brenda got here with her baps.

John had never been very interested in Rugby. He couldn't even work out the difference between the two codes. So when two enormous Americans flung him to the floor and suggested he do something very unsavoury with his mother, he wouldn't have been able to tell you whether the rugby tackle that pinned him to the turf was within the laws of that strange, odd-balled game, or he'd just been flattened by a steamroller. It would normally have taken him several moments to get up from the ground, and fortunately he'd landed on the part of the pitch that was always boggy, even in August, but the two Americans assisted him in this rather more quickly than he would have liked. Seemingly on his way back out of the ground, the steroid-pumped security guards were halted by a diminutive although clearly authoritative figure.

"Guys! What did I say about being careful with the natives? What's he done anyway?"

"Trespassing, Mr Singh."

John adjusted his eye line as best as he could, given the headlock that he was currently failing to escape from, so that he could get a better look at his former classmate. Singh had changed somewhat. He was now a distinctly rotund figure, almost spherical, so that with the shine of what was clearly an impressively expensive suit and his matching pink tie and pocket square, John thought he resembled a Christmas Tree bauble. This was a man who didn't miss too many meals.

"Trespassing? Is that all? That's really no excuse for beating him up, you know. You're not in America now – it's frowned upon here."

"Can't be too careful, Mr Singh. You know we've had problems with loonies, and he certainly looks the sort."

"Well, he's trying to say something. Why don't you release him from that headlock so that he can speak, but keep a firm grip – just in case?"

"As you wish, Mr Singh."

John took several large gulps of air before he felt confident enough to speak.

"Thank you," he begrudgingly started with, but then needed a few more seconds to recover his oxygen debt.

"Oh, you're very welcome. Take your time. Sorry about all the manhandling, by the way, but you really shouldn't be trespassing. Marvin here has shot people for less, you know."

"I wasn't trespassing. I work here. Well, I work here for nowt. I'm one of the volunteers that have kept this place going for the last twenty years. I was just off to check the blocked toilet before I was assaulted by these two." John tried to put emphasis on the word 'assaulted', in the hope that it would infer the threat of legal action. His windpipe had clearly taken some of the impact though, because he realised he sounded like a character from The Simpsons and therefore not really in a position to threaten anybody.

"Well, that sounds a perfectly reasonable explanation, but how do we know that? Have you any identification, any papers proving this? I mean, you sound a decent enough chap and all that … you don't look like a lunatic … although who can tell, these days? … but you'd be surprised how much opposition I get to my investments. I can't be too careful. Threats have been made, you know."

"Identification? Papers? No I have not! I've been coming here for over forty years. The last twenty I've half built what you can see around you now. I've given up all my free time and never asked for a penny in return. You should be showing me your papers!"

"Hmmm ... well, if that's true, then I suppose a 'sorry' and a 'thank you' are in order. Tell you what, as you've no ID I'll let the boys here carry on with throwing you out of the ground and you can come in later with the rest of the fans. But come and see me this week – if you can make the trip to my hotel in Manchester – we'll sit down and have a proper chat. After you've been properly searched and everything. As Marvin says – we can't be too careful."

Marvin, or the other one, John wasn't sure which was which, began to move him in the direction of the exit.

"Hang on a second!" John wasn't going to give in. He never gave in. "You don't need identification from me – you know me!"

"Do I? I don't recognise you, but I do know a lot of people. Did you used to work on the yacht?"

"No Harshit," John decided to put a lot of emphasis on Harry's real name – just like the bullies had done in school. John wasn't a bully. Hated them. And he'd forgotten all about the time that the class had inadvertently found out Harry's real name and taunted him with it until the threat of detention from the teacher had quelled the children's delight in their new-found cruelty. But the mind knows best how to defend the body, and from somewhere that memory had sprung to the surface. "I did not work on your yacht. I did once see you wet yourself before you were made to sit in the corridor until the school managed to get your mam down with a clean pair of pants though."

Marvin, or the other one, stopped his ejection of the trespasser. He'd worked for Singh for six years and he'd never heard anyone speak to his boss in that tone, never mind reveal that he'd once wet himself at school. He'd been asked to carry out several reprisal beatings by Mr

Singh in his tenure with his company, a task he always enjoyed, and was fairly confident that there was another one coming.

Harry Singh wore an expression that neither of his security men had ever seen on him before. It was a mixture of anger, incredulity and surprise. With possibly a small measure of murderous intent thrown in. Be fair to Harry though, you don't rank with the world's business elite unless you can recover quickly and take advantage of a situation.

"Okay, let's cut there," he said, and it was only then that John realised a film crew was on hand. "You wipe that last part and we re-run it my way. Got it? My way."

A man who John assumed was the director, and clearly knew not to bite the hand that feeds, nodded furiously and started making notes on a clipboard.

"Right, if you stand him here, we can go from the point where the gentlemen released him and he started talking like Kermit the Frog. Got it?" Harry had recovered his composure and was looking to move from damage limitation to positive outcome.

Marvin, he assumed, dragged him back three feet, thought about how he had stood beforehand, and arranged John in the hold he had previously been in. Clearly, Marvin had done this before. Harry too didn't miss a beat.

"Hang on a second!" he said, in what John thought was the worst ham acting since the batteries died in the TV remote and Eastenders came on. "I know you, don't I? Didn't we used to go to school together?" Harry was laughing now, turning to the camera with a 'who would have thought it?' expression on his face, his arms open wide. "Well, let him go then, Marvin! This is an old friend of mine. But I'm sorry, I never forget a face, but ... I can't seem to remember your name. It has been thirty years or so!" This last bit too he said to the camera, a broad, politician-like smile across his face.

"It's John," said John, a broad, John-like scowl across his own face. "John Sourbutts."

"John Sourbutts, of course. John Sourbutts!" The smile never left Harry's face, but John knew he hadn't a clue who he was. "Well this is great, John. John Sourbutts. Tell you what, why don't you watch the match with me today? We can catch up on old times – all the fun we had at school."

John didn't remember too much fun at school, and if he remembered correctly, Harry had had even less. Especially once they'd found out his real name. He didn't really want to watch the game sat down next to Harry, either. He wanted to be behind the goal, stood up with the rest of the Ultras, singing songs that he would never repeat in front of polite company. However, he would like to know about Harry's plans for the club, so …

"Sure. Why not?"

"Why not indeed, John! In fact we have one or two esteemed guests with us today and I'm sure you'd be interested in meeting them. Great to see you again, old pal. Now Marvin will take you to the bar, where they'll look after you until nearer kick-off. I've got a few things to attend to, but I can't wait to have a laugh about all the tricks we used to get up to."

This surprised John, because he couldn't remember getting up to too many tricks at school either, and none at all with Harry. It didn't surprise him as much as what happened next though, as Harry embraced him in a bear hug. John had never coped with physical contact very well.

"Great to see you again, John. Great to see you, John Sourbutts. Right – cut it there, but I want to see the rushes of that later. Got it?" he finished with a pointed look at the director.

And with enough word repetition done to help him remember the name John Sourbutts for the next few hours at least, Harry was off.

"This way please, sir." Marvin, or the other one, said, his tone remarkably different from before the encounter with Harry, and with less threat of physical, emotional and psychological, sexually motivated violence.

John followed; the 'other' security officer kept two steps behind, watching suspiciously.

The camera crew had stopped filming, so they didn't catch the sour expression on John's equally suspicious face.

Hitting the Bar

John sat in the newly refurbished Directors' Bar. In fact newly built would be more apt. It had been a no-go area of the ground for some time now, condemned by the building inspector and ignored by the fans. There were only two directors of the club anyway, both of whom were unpaid, so it would have been a pretty lonely bar to be in most of the time. Not today though. As John grimaced at the work ethic of whoever had attached the foot rail to the bottom of the bar, his pre-match drinks, on the house, were augmented by some very interesting people watching. As kick-off drew closer, John recognised various celebrities, accompanied by very glamorous and good looking hangers-on, make their way into the bar. They ignored John and he ignored them. He wasn't dressed for the occasion, and he wasn't one for dribbling over celebrity, not even the ex-players that he recognised amongst the TV presenters and pop stars. That was until he saw Lucio Bandiera. John despised the culture of what he saw as the vastly overrated, overpaid, over-sensitive elite of world football, but he knew a good player when he saw one. And Lucio Bandiera was one of those. An Italian world cup winner, he'd stayed loyal to Milan, the home town team he joined aged 8, until he was forced out at the age of 35 when a board room coup gave a new manager the go-ahead to clear out the old guard. John had read that he'd signed for an American team for a big, last payday. He sidled up to him, speaking clearly and slowly despite the many lagers he'd consumed. He wasn't sure how good Lucio's English was, but felt that the bottle of Peroni he was holding would somehow enamour himself to the Italian.

"Errr … Signor Bandiera … welcome to Middleton. It's fantastic to see such a great player as yourself at our humble ground," John stuttered, in awe.

"Ah, thank you, my friend. It is good to be recognised and I am very happy to be here." Perfect English, heavy accent.

"Yes. I've always loved the way you bossed the midfield, and your range of passing was the best in Europe for ten years."

"It is very kind of you to say so."

"So tell me, why do you spoil all that natural skill and talent by kicking, nipping, diving, rolling around and generally cheating when things aren't going your way?"

He hadn't meant it to come out like that, but it was a genuine question and concern for John.

The Italian hard-man's face froze for a second. Many players, through the years, had seen that same icy stare and feared for their safety, but then Lucio just burst out laughing.

"You English with your sense of irony. So funny!"

John, several Peronis to the good, or bad, wondered if he'd misunderstood his question and was just about to press the point when they were interrupted by Harry Singh.

"Lucio, John Sourbutts, I see you've met each other ... and you seem to be getting on, too. Remarkable." He turned to John. "Well, that's my first surprise to you blown. Has Lucio told you he's our new player-coach?"

It was John's turn to laugh now. And the thought of Lucio Bandiera, two-time European Cup winner, turning out for Middleton Town deserved a laugh. Before he could say anything though, they were joined by another instantly recognisable Galactico of the game. Edson Bragado was a World Cup winner; but apart from doing it twice as a player, the big Brazilian had also won it as a coach before going on to manage around Europe, winning the Portuguese, German, Spanish and English leagues. He'd been Chelsea's manager until the summer when, after what was a disappointing third place finish, he'd been sacked on the basis that he'd managed to bring the club into disrepute more times in a season than Patrick Vieira had been sent off in his lifetime. And that's a lot.

"And Edson, this is John Sourbutts. I've been doing a bit of research and it turns out John is considered our number one fan. Not only does he go to every game, but he also spends his spare time working for the Club. And get this – he was in my class at school! John, meet our new manager, Edson Bragado."

Edson shook John's hand. John allowed it to be shook and dribbled.

"It is people like you that make the game what it is," said Bragado, plainly and sincerely. John couldn't speak.

"Well, let's take our seats then, gentlemen. You two need to understand what work's in front of you and you, John, need to sit next to me and tell me what you think." He leaned in closer, out of the others' earshot, and John noticed the TV camera filming on the periphery. "And I do remember you now. I had my team do some research on you since our meeting this morning. I still didn't remember you until they sent me some pictures of you as a boy, then it came flooding back. Your parents were good to my mum – she never forgot their kindness and neither did I. I'd really appreciate it if you'd help me with the Club – you know, sort of an advisory role. Think about it. But now let's enjoy the match!"

It was twenty-seven minutes into the game before John felt his dizziness finally dissolve and he was able to function again. By this time Town were 2-0 down, disappointing the biggest crowd in several seasons.

Sour Grapes

Questions in the after match press conference virtually ignored the five-nil score line: nobody was really interested in today's game. John sat at the back, avoiding the limelight, but enthralled by the proceedings. On the top table sat Harry, Edson and Lucio but, despite the gravitas of the football glitterati, it was the businessman who commanded the attention. Harry was in full flow, he amazed the assorted media, some from countries John couldn't even pronounce, with his introduction of his new manager and player-coach, but his future plans stunned even the most hard-faced hack. Harry still believed that Town could be promoted to the Football League proper this season and the Club's fortuitous FA Cup run, he believed, would continue for several more rounds to come. How was this achievable by a team currently languishing fourteenth and who had just been battered at home by a team four places below them?

Because Harry had announced plans to flood the team with out of contract professionals before signing hand-picked superstars in the January transfer window.

"You've got to believe me," he enthused. "You've got to beee-leeeveee!" he shouted before standing on the table in front of him and singing at the top of his voice:

"For now you've got to believe me! We're going to win the league!"

Everyone clapped and cheered. The cameras zoomed in on the charismatic businessman, the hacks scribbled furiously, smiling – the drab post-match conferences they attended, even in the Premier League, had just been smashed from their memory. They were going to have fun with this one, they thought (until it all came crashing down, which it inevitably would, and they'd be there to write 'told you so' headlines about it).

John didn't join in the adulation and sycophancy. Nobody had thought to ask about the outgoing manager, local lad Mick Maddox, who had played for Town for ten years before an injury forced him into the expenses-only Manager's role four seasons ago. And nobody asked about the current players, many of whom had given up their wages, such as they were, to keep the Club afloat this year. John felt uncomfortable about this new 'advisor' role, and although he hoped that he might be able to do some good with it, his semi-permanent scowl returned to his face.

The Bean Machine

His contract for his Club advisor role arrived at 7.00am on the Monday morning. He signed for the envelope, delivered by a very smart young man who drove a very smart new car, and put it to one side as he rushed to Mrs Philpott's to give her kitchen worktops some attention. He started to read it on Monday evening, but got as far as page two before he lost interest and picked up the Middleton Free Press instead. Amongst the eight page special on the weekend game, dominated by the editorial aftermath of the press conference, John noticed a couple of column inches on how many of the gentlemen supporters had been 'caught short' following a rather unpleasant smelling flood in the main toilet block. The blockage in trap three, thought John.

First thing on Tuesday he dropped the contract off at the Car Showroom, where Rusty had promised to pass it onto the firm's accountant who apparently knew about these things; contracts and whatnot.

"Let me give it to the bean counter," he said whilst putting an overfamiliar arm around John's shoulders. "Here, take a look at this Focus Estate ... would be perfect for you in your game."

John managed to get away from Rusty's grip around twenty minutes later, although not without promising to look at the figures on the Focus later in the week – the Johnsons needed a new garage door and he'd told them he'd be there at 9.30am prompt. He ignored several calls from Rusty's mobile number until he knocked off for lunch in the early afternoon and eventually picked up.

"Whoaa! John, my main man," came the enthusiastic and rather shrill voice of the car salesman through John's antique Nokia. "Did you read how much they want to pay you for talking about football? You can forget that Focus, partner, it's a Mondeo for you!"

"It's a good contract then?"

"Listen, I talk shit all day and make a decent wage out of it, but if I could bang on about football and get that kind of money I'd even consider giving this lark up. Anyway, Mr Bean says to come round and he'll talk you through the restrictive covenants."

"Restrictive what-a-ments? What are they?"

"I don't know, do I? I just say things and I sound knowledgeable – it's how I make a living. Bean will tell you. Here, what do accountants use for contraception? Their personalities!! See you later, gator!"

John heard Rusty collapse into a laughing fit and pressed the large red 'Off' button. He forgot about the conversation during the afternoon as Mrs Johnson had wondered whether he could plain a couple of millimetres off her kitchen door in with the price, but the Nokia offered its shrill signature tune as he was putting away his tools and he agreed to meet Rowan, Rusty's accountant, on his way home.

"You've landed on your feet," said Rowan as John walked into his modest office, not failing to notice that the shelves could do with realigning. "If you play this advisory malarkey right, you're going to need an accountant yourself – not that bookkeeper you deal with now."

"Pauline does a good job, and she charges a fair price."

"Hey, don't be so defensive! I'm just saying that this could put you in a different league, that's all."

"So there's money involved?"

Rowan gave John a sideways look, unable to tell whether he was being sarcastic or not. He wasn't. John hadn't expected to be paid. He took an offered seat and waited for Rowan to tell him.

"Okay, so the basic fee is £1,000.00, but that's per meeting. It says that if you have two in a day, then your fee doubles, and so on. On top of that you're entitled to all reasonable expenses. This includes flights and hotels, and it says that these will be booked for you by Singh's people and, get this, it will always be first class and five star. And you get paid another grand for every travelling day to compensate for loss of income. How about that? A grand a day!"

"Why would I need a flight and a hotel to meet at the Club?"

"Eh? Oh no – don't be daft. Singh won't be based at the Club, he could be anywhere in the world. You just fly out, tell him how the Supporters would feel about his decisions ... like a one man fans' forum ... and pocket the cash. Easy money."

"Isn't the purpose of a fans' forum to hear lots of different views and come to a balanced decision?"

"I don't know – I prefer tennis."

John couldn't disguise his disdain.

"Rusty said something about constricted governments."

"Restrictive covenants, yes. It's the usual stuff, although they're very firm. You know, everything you say is confidential, not allowed to speak to the media about anything that's discussed, or anyone actually ... clearance before television and radio interviews ... let me see, what else ..."

"It's okay, Rowan – you've told me enough, thank you."

"What? Oh yes, well, no brainer really. Here's your contract back, and don't forget what I told you about upgrading your accountant now. If this Singh fellow does half of what he's parping on about in the papers, you could have yourself a nice little earner!"

Straight Black Coffee From The Horse's Mouth

As it happened, the first meeting was at the Club. Harry was standing in the middle of the pitch, talking to three people, two of whom were wearing yellow hard hats. John doubted that anything would fall on them there, but he appreciated their dedication to health and safety procedures. A large paper was being pored over, and there was a lot of pointing going on. John stood patiently to one side and waited. Marvin and his fellow security guard also stood and waited, less patiently and with a fixed, distrusting sneer pointed in John's direction. John smiled and blew them a kiss, which they pretended not to notice. Harry took a glance at an expensive looking watch and wrapped the meeting up.

"John! Bang on time. I love people who are punctual."

"It doesn't pay to be late. I know that in my game. Time is money."

"Excellent! I wish everybody was of the same opinion," said Harry, with a thinly disguised look of disapproval at the now departing workmen, who were scuttling away with a look of guilt etched across their faces. "Come on, let's grab a coffee and we'll begin our first meeting. How exciting!"

John followed Harry across the pitch and towards the Executive Lounge. As the two security guys dropped in behind them, each of them scanning the immediate area for any potential threat, John turned and smiled at them.

"Come on, Marvin. Keep up!" Neither responded, and John leaned in closer to Harry. "Which one is Marvin, by the way?"

"Eh? Oh, I don't know. Both? Neither, I guess. It's just a name I call the security guys. They seem to respond and they don't seem to mind."

"Right. You don't think that that's because you're paying them and they quite like keeping their jobs?"

"Probably. Pastry? The lattes are very nice?" he offered as they reached the bar; a little out of breath from walking up the steep terrace.

"Straight black, extra shot," shouted John above the din of the espresso machine, immediately regretting both his choice of words and the kiss he'd previously blown 'Marvin', who he'd just noticed was carrying a gun under his arm. "Are guns entirely necessary?" he asked Harry

"Oh, yes. Like we told you, we get a lot of weirdoes on our tails."

Harry sat at one of the tables, facing the pitch, took a sip of a frothy coffee together with a large bite of a cream cake he'd taken from a refrigerated buffet. He sighed contentedly. The Marvins stood at each end of the room, each with their hands held together in front of them, as if they were protecting their crown jewels in a defensive wall. John sat opposite Harry. He enjoyed the strength and bitterness of the coffee as he waited for the meeting to begin, not knowing what to expect. After a few moments, Harry seemed to snap out of a dream and smiled broadly at John.

"Okay, so … first things first. Did you sign the contract? Where is it?"

"Oh, no. I mean, I thought about it, but in the end I just thought I'd do it for free and then there wouldn't need to be a contract."

He said it so matter of fact, so calmly, that Harry, not one to lose the initiative in any meeting, was momentarily flummoxed. And there are very few people who are authentically flummoxed these days.

"It's not just about the money, John. I'm prepared to share my biggest secrets with you. Who we're going to buy, for example. That sort of knowledge is highly confidential – in the wrong hands it could be very dangerous, affect share prices ... we have to have a confidentiality clause."

"Oh. Can't you just trust me? Most people do. It's like, if I do a job for someone and I give them a bit of extra discount, we agree to keep it between ourselves. Not tell the neighbours who might have paid a bit more."

"John, we're not talking about a new garden gate, here. If I do a deal with Ronaldo's agent and it gets out, it could blow the whole thing."

"Are you doing a deal for Ronaldo?"

"John, we're not even in the football league yet – I was just making a point." He wiped the remains of the cream cake from his lips – it had lost its taste, he thought.

"The thing is, Harry, I'm a fan. Now, I know a lot of fans would love to know what players are coming into the Club, but to be honest half the fun for me is guessing who we might be in for and then arguing about them with my friends. I'd hate for that to be taken away. It's best you just don't tell me things like that."

"Okay, but what about the wages. I can't have you blabbing what the new players are going to be on. It would cause dressing room unrest."

"Don't tell me then. I thought you just wanted to know what the fans would think of some of your plans and that maybe you'd take those views on board and make changes. I thought I could arrange a Supporters' Meeting in The Crown, so that I can tell everyone and then feedback in our next meeting. I think that's the right word, 'feedback.'"

"How much did the contract say I'd pay you per meeting?"

"A grand."

"And you don't want a grand?"

"I'm just happy to have an insight into what you're doing, so that I can tell the others who've been coming here since we were both at school together. Some of them before. This Club has been one of the few constants throughout their whole lives. Some of them have changed their wives, their religion, their politics – Nathan Greenhalgh has even changed his sexuality, got rid of his bits, the lot – but none of them have changed their team, and they've been here every week to prove it. I owe it to them to tell them what's going on, and I don't want to have to check a contract every time I want to say something to them." He took a sip of coffee whilst he moved his foot to hide a clump of sawdust that had fallen from his boot onto the newly laid carpet.

"Let me show you something," said Harry, and stood in front of the large windows that looked over the stand and the pitch below. He raised his arms to signify the whole stadium, like an angler bragging about catching the largest fish. "Look at it all," he said.

"I know, wonderful, isn't it?"

"You think so? The whole of one side of the ground hasn't been used in three years. Condemned by the council. And the bits that we can use are falling apart. The changing rooms are a joke. Not even the toilets work properly. Matchday catering is done from a caravan at the side of the pitch, and some of the players we have look like they've sampled too many of the burgers they sell from there."

"They're good them burgers. And the pies."

"I think it all creates the wrong atmosphere, John. Some of the language I heard on Saturday was appalling. I think we need a fans' charter, code of conduct or something. There was a chant at the poor referee during the second half that was entirely inappropriate to say the least. Maybe drink had something to do with it – perhaps we need an alcohol ban in the ground? Now, those guys I was with earlier – if I decide not to sack them for being late – they're going to build a new stadium over in Lowerton for us. Forty thousand capacity, all seater, state of the art everything. There's room for car parks, fan zones, the lot."

"Move from here? What are you thinking of?" stammered John.

"Don't worry – perhaps this will become our training facility ... or perhaps you will be able to buy a house here one day! Imagine that: your kitchen could be right where you have stood all these years. But we have to move, John – this place will never fit 40,000 people in it whatever we were to do to it. We'll attract the best players in the world and they will have the best that money can buy for them."

"Forty thousand? I'm not very good at maths, but I think that's nearly forty times what we get now. And Lowerton? We're Middleton – I know it's only a mile and a half down the road, but still ... how can we be called Middleton Town if we play in Lowerton?"

"If we build the facilities, if we bring in the players, we will get forty thousand every week, with more locked outside!" Harry was on a roll. "And don't worry about geography. Newton Heath moved to Trafford, and look at them now! And Bolton didn't change their name to Horwich Wanderers when they moved ground ..."

"Well they should have," said John, remembering a bitter tap room argument that he'd lost at the time.

"John, you are my trusted advisor on this. Go away and think about it. But don't be sentimental. In business I've learnt not to be sentimental. Do not dwell on the past – think of the future! Think of watching the best footballers in the world, every week. Think of winning cup finals, trophies. Think of the glory, John, think of the glory."

John was mortified. He couldn't stutter a single syllable. Harry took this as a good sign and went in for the kill.

"I can't tell you any more, John, until you've signed the contract. But as a gesture of good faith I will make sure that you get the payment for this meeting. Imagine, John – no more fitting kitchens in council flats any more, you're part of the football aristocracy now. Oh, and errr ... I'm sure that we can rely on you to be a good advocate for the Club. You know, change the hearts and minds of the fans, that sort of thing. In fact, that's a good idea – why don't I make you an official ambassador? How does that sound? John Sourbutts: Middleton Town Club Ambassador? I'll get the lawyers working on changing that contract straight away. Let me think about your salary and bonuses – they should be fitting a Premier

League Club, because that's where we're going, John, that's where we're going!"

With that Harry left the room, failing to catch John's last incredulous question.

"All-seater? Did you say all-seater? … Christ on a bike!"

A Room With A Brew

Twelve people sat in front of John, each with a steaming plastic cup of vending machine coffee. He had hastily convened an emergency meeting of the snappily titled 'Love Middleton, Hate Harry; Stand Up For Direct Action Committee'. It was their first ever meeting, and most wondered what they were there for. John had called all those supporters who had both volunteered to help at the ground over the last few years and were members of the fearsome Ultras; and, with the exception of a few that were on holiday, they had all attended: eager to hear what John had gleaned from his meetings with the new owner. The upstairs of the car garage, which was usually only used to train sales people how to become their customers' best friend within thirty seconds of meeting them, had been commandeered for the cause. This would normally have been Rusty's domain, but all eyes and ears were on a ponderous John. Unused to being the centre of attention, he shuffled his notes.

"So," he said. "Thank you for attending the first ever meeting of the 'Love Middleton, Hate Harry' Stand Up For Direct Action Committee."

"Who thought that one up?" interrupted Tony.

"I did, what's wrong with it?"

"Well, it's a bit of a mouthful, isn't it? How am I going to remember that?"

John stared at Tony Two Shirts for a second – so called because he only ever wore one of two shirts: a home one or an away one. "Tony – two things," John sighed. "First of all, I've heard you sing all thirty-eight verses of 'Mingston Are A Massive Club' without getting one word out of place, even on dubious quantities of even more dubious 'pub's own' ale. And secondly, if you keep interrupting we'll not have time to deal with this very clear and present danger to our Club."

John read the last few words from his notes. He had watched clips from several films the night before, hoping to find inspiration, and he had foregone his first idea of replicating Mel Gibson's Braveheart speech in favour of a few Harrison Ford understatements.

"Fair enough," said Tony Two Shirts, with a smile.

"As I was saying, welcome to the first meeting of … well, welcome to the meeting. I have grave news from my time with Mr Singh."

"Bloody lucky bugger you are, getting that gig with Harry. I hear you met that Bandiera and Bragado as well, you lucky …"

"Tony."

"Sorry."

"… Grave news, indeed. First of all, Singh doesn't plan to redevelop our proud ground …" Here John paused for dramatic effect. "He plans to knock it down and build one elsewhere – in Lowerton!"

Silence. John took this to be a stunned silence, until Nasty Noel piped up.

"Well that sounds good."

"Yes. A nice new stadium. Makes sense really, if we're going to be attracting top players," added Sausage.

"Pointless rebuilding the old one – you'd struggle to sort that pitch out anyway," chipped in Jesus Tattersall.

A general chatter of approval bubbled around the small room, much to John's consternation.

"But St Peter's is our spiritual home!" he interrupted, the room quietening again at the anger and disbelief in his voice. "We've been there since 1907 … through thick and thin."

"Mainly thin." A quiet, anonymous heckle from the back, which John ignored.

"Think of the days we've had there! The goals, the glory – even the cold, wet, sleet-strewn, mind-numbing defeats – they've all been part of our make-up, our DNA. We shouldn't throw away all that tradition. Our feet find their own way there on a Saturday afternoon – we don't want to be going down to Lowerton. It's a different town, for goodness sake!"

"It's not really, is it? I mean, it's just like Manchester and Salford – they've just blended into one. Actually, it's nearer for me ..."

"It'll be on that old gas works site. Eyesore that – about time someone did something with it. Might even put our house prices up."

"Be good to have a roof that doesn't leak on you and a proper food place. Maybe they'll get some decent beer in ..."

Again, the conversation rumbled in favour of the move.

"It's going to be all-seater," said John, evenly, which brought the discussion to an abrupt halt. "And Singh's thinking of an alcohol ban."

"Well, why didn't you say so?" said Nasty Noel. "What do you want us to do to stop it? It's an outrage!"

Direct Action against the Club was agreed unanimously.

The Other Side of the Fifty Pound Note

The next morning, two things happened. John checked his bank account, making sure that he had enough to pre-order a loft hatch and boarding for John and Sally at number 3, and noticed that £1,000 had been deposited by a company he'd never heard of. Then, there was a return visit from the smart young man in a smart new car, delivering a smart new contract. John wedged the contract behind the clock on the mantelpiece, unopened, finished his coffee, and went off to replace the stair rods for old Jack Mullaney.

By the time Saturday came around, the contract hadn't moved, but old Jack was made up with his new staircase. John dressed in his usual match day attire and, picking up a large banner that had been delivered the night before, he made his way to the ground. He'd been fretful all morning. He'd been accustomed to getting there early to do some maintenance, but those skills weren't required anymore, and he hadn't been summoned to any more 'meetings'. It wasn't the lack of activity that was affecting his mood: he was about to lead the first ever demonstration against the Club that he loved, and it just didn't sit right. His pace to the ground was slow. The banner seemed heavy, but it was his trepidation that made his feet drag. They met at The Crown, of course – fifty diehards, each with at least a share in a banner similar to the one that John had. The slogans were many:

'Love Town, Hate Harry'

'Don't Throw 109 Years Away'

'We're Middleton, Aren't We?'

'Pies Not Prawns'

'We Don't Need No Code of Conduct. We Don't Need No Fan Control'

'Reclaim Our Game'

'No Sitting – We're Not Knitting'

'Stand Against Modern Football'

and

'Middleton Town Motor Company'

The latter was part of the deal Rusty had negotiated with his employers – they had paid for all the banners providing that one with their own company name and logo was featured prominently in any media coverage. The football world was intrigued with Harry's aims for the Club, and a live spot on Football Focus had been arranged for the day. Indeed, John's Ultras, most balancing cans of strong Belgian lager along with their banners, were standing right next to the large BBC satellite van that dominated the pub car park. The TV crew were excitedly arranging their cameras to capture the demonstration – a bonus they hadn't expected.

After a few words, the banners were held higher, and the Ultras began their march to the ground, singing as they went.

'Thank you Harry for buying the Town
If it wasn't for you, they could have shut us down
But don't take us anywhere
And don't tell us not to fucking swear'

As the cameras followed, the Football Focus presenter started interviewing the fans.

"So what's this all about, I would have thought that the Middleton fans would have been happy to see investment in the Club?"

"Investment, yes. But this Club has been part of the town for over a hundred years – why would we want to move to a sanitised, all-seater stadium in another town?" Sausage had thought his argument through.

"Errr … so that the Club can progress? So that it can attract better players and move up the league?"

"You don't need a new Stadium to do that. We could rebuild the old one and achieve the same thing." Tony Two Shirts chipped in.

"But Mr Singh has bailed you out of debt – you could have gone under. Surely you should support the plans of the man who has saved you?"

"Ask John," said a star-struck Nasty Noel, nodding to the person next to him. By this time, as fans joined in en-route, the demonstration had more than doubled. The songs were louder, the spectacle greater – the TV crew loved it.

"Hang on a second," said the presenter. "We're now live with the Studio … in three, two … Well you join me here at Middleton Town's St Peter's Stadium where we expected to do a report on a good news story in the lower leagues, but instead we've walked into what is fast becoming quite a significant demonstration against the owner and his proposed move to a brand new forty thousand seat stadium in nearby Lowerton. I'm just about to speak to their leader, who I believe is called John."

A camera and a microphone were pushed in front of John's face, and he was live on national television.

"So, John, Harry Singh, who grew up in this town, has rescued the Club from almost certain extinction, brought in better players and is now investing in a brand new stadium to replace one that's falling down. What's this all about?"

"Well, some of the people behind me have been supporting this club for over sixty years. I do appreciate that Mr Singh's heart is in the right place, but to come in here and wipe out our team, lads who have given everything for the Club, despite holding down day jobs, sack a manager who worked for free when his playing days with us came to an end and, worst of all, take us away from our beloved St Peter's to a sanitized, plastic version in another town where we have to sit down and behave ourselves? What's the point? What's the point of football if we all become customers rather than fans? If we're not allowed to stand and jump and sing and shout?"

"Well, the Premier League has been all seater for decades now, and it's the most successful League in the world."

"How do you measure that success? In ticket prices? TV Revenue? The grounds are full, but they could be fuller, and for how much longer? The cost and the lack of atmosphere has priced the kids out, the sixteen or twenty year olds who don't have rich parents, and they're being replaced by football tourists who go once or twice a year – exactly what the clubs want, of course, because they're the ones that will spend fortunes on merchandise and food. Much better than the fan who tips up at five to three, full of Stella, and spends nothing – even if he's been ploughing money into his team for the last thirty years. Even if he's one of the ones that are going to help make any sort of atmosphere. When I go to a ground I want to stand with all my friends, not just the one or two I've managed to get my season ticket next to."

"Well, strong words there. But surely you must be thrilled with the players that Harry is bringing in? And the manager and coach too? That must be exciting, surely?"

"It is, and it will be great to see some of those players in a Middleton shirt. We've had the odd former superstar here over the years, trying to extend their playing days, and it's been amazing to see their skills next to our part-time lads. Now I don't want to be accused of being grumpy," said John, ignoring a burst of laughter from those around him, "but there's a difference between that and flooding the team with out-of-contract Gallacticos. How fair is that on the teams that we play, for example? And anyway, bringing in players should go alongside developing our own lads – I don't see that on the manifesto."

"And do you intend to stage a walk out or miss the game?"

"You're joking aren't you? Fifteen quid my ticket costs me – I'm not missing a single minute."

At which point a team of security guards fired tear gas into the protesting crowd, causing a mixture of mayhem and incredulity, and resulting in the camera crew being half-trampled as the dispersing fans ran for clear air. It made great television.

The game, which attracted a modern day record attendance of over 4,000, was a six-nil canter for Middleton. Six of their players, all making their debuts, had all played for their country at one time, and had showboated their way to victory. Two of the opposition players, tempers simmering throughout the match, had eventually had enough of being made to look ridiculous and had been sent off for 'intent to cause serious injury'. Not that they'd got within two feet of their intended targets, but the intent, most definitely, was there.

John had watched from his usual spot behind the goal, more quietly than usual. He thought the game had a feeling of an exhibition match about it. He was grateful that an attempted Mexican wave had failed miserably, but understood the crowd were trying to make their own entertainment – the result was in the bag from twenty minutes in. He just hoped nobody would bring a bloody vuvuzela next week.

A buzz on his mobile midway through the second half told him that Harry would like to see him after the game, and could he present himself at the VIP entrance? He didn't know that there was a VIP entrance, and certainly didn't remember building one himself, but he found it easily enough. He expected to be refused entry by the Marvins on the door, but they seemed to be expecting him and ushered him inside. A young lady in a meticulously tailored suit led him up some stairs that hadn't been there a week ago, along a corridor that smelled of drying plaster and through a door that he noticed jammed slightly against the architrave. He found he was in the bar where he'd first met Bragado and Bandiera. Harry saw him immediately, but put a solitary finger up to signify he'd be just one minute, his eyes moving to the bar to suggest to John he should get himself a drink, all the time continuing to engage a small group of celebrities in what, eventually, they were to find a most amusing anecdote.

"John," said Harry when he'd eventually managed to get away from his entourage. It was only one word, but it seemed to convey a tone of disappointment that is usually reserved for a small child who has been caught crayoning on the new wallpaper.

"I see there's no alcohol ban in here then," said John in response. Harry ignored it.

"What was all that about on television? The demonstration? I thought we had an understanding, that you were an Ambassador to the Club? We can't have Ambassadors to the Club leading demonstrations against us. It would be like Kofi Annan leading a demonstration against the United Nations."

"Is that why you tear-gassed us?"

"Yes, that was very regrettable," said Harry with a look of genuine concern. "Bad publicity." He frowned, clearly thinking of the potential ramifications, wondering whether Fox News would get hold of the footage. "Sorry about that, by the way," he mumbled, in what a few people would have mistaken for an apology. Very few.

"Oh, that's all right," replied John, apparently oblivious to the lack of sincerity. "I'd always seen those pictures of fans getting tear gassed and wondered what it felt like. I never thought I'd get the opportunity to find out unless I went to the Milan derby, or maybe Argentina or somewhere like that. Now I've experienced it in Middleton. Every day you learn something new – I'm quite grateful, really. It was ... exciting."

Harry gave him a quizzical look, but decided not to pursue John's thought process. "Look, John, I've been thinking ... what's that?" John was pushing a brown envelope, clearly full of cash into Harry's hands.

"Oh, that's the thousand pound consultancy fee – I thought you should have it back. I mean, I didn't earn it, and in fairness I've probably done what you didn't want me to do. It's like when I put that shed up for Mrs Foggarty ..."

"John, you're giving me a brown envelope full of cash in front of a room full of people, some of whom are journalists. Don't you think that might look a bit odd for both of us, given the current ... shall we say 'hostilities' between us?"

"Hostilities? Oh no, I've never been called hostile. Grumpy, bitter, irritable, moody ... but never hostile. We just have different points of view, that's all. I don't want to fall out about it. You use your money to get what you want, and I have to use other things ... like a reasoned argument, for example. Is it because it's in cash? It's just Rusty wanted a Summer House building for his hot tub ... God knows what he'll get up to in there ... anyway, I prefer a cheque myself, keeps it all nice and clean with the tax man, but I think Rusty gets paid cash for some of the trade deals he does and he insisted I take it."

"John, you've just led a demonstration of several hundred people against me. It went out live on the BBC and has been seen all around the world – it's even made the business news on CNN, just to further embarrass me – and you don't think that's hostile?"

"We were just making a point."

"Well, couldn't you have just come and had a word with me about it all?"

"Would you have changed your mind?"

"Well, I would have taken your views on board, and perhaps modified the errr ... plans ... to errr ... accommodate the interests of the paying supporters, the lifeblood of any club ... to ... errr ..."

"Okay, so now you're aware of the depth of feeling, can we look at redeveloping St Peter's? We could look at a reduced price membership to bring younger supporters in, or even free ... I'm one of the youngest that goes now, and I'm nearly fifty. We could have one of those safe standing sections, so you don't get your health and safety in a pickle. We could re-lay the pitch and rebuild the North Stand. Barry the Builder reckons that if you did it right, you could increase the ground to 25,000 capacity, no problem. And, okay, I know you don't like swearing, but come on … that's a step too far. Let's look at having a positive policy instead – let's promote social inclusion within the community, equal rights for joiners, that sort of thing."

"John, I'm not going to …"

"And recruiting all these Harlem Globetrotter players. You can see that totally ruined today's game, can't you? The odd hammering here and there is fantastic – makes up for the one-nil defeats on a wet Wednesday in November – but we're going to do that to teams every week in this league. That's just boring. I want to turn up to a game not knowing if we're going to win, lose or draw, otherwise what's the point?"

Harry was mute. He'd never considered this, and he found the idea difficult to deal with. He did what he always did when faced with a point he didn't want to consider and ignored it.

"Anyway, as I was saying … I was thinking that this paid advisor role isn't good enough for the profile of the Club. I need to announce that the demonstration today was a misunderstanding, and that I will always do what is best for the fans. What better way, John, could I demonstrate that than having a Supporters Interest Director on the Board? And what better way of playing down this whole debacle today than by announcing that the leader of the demonstration, John Sourbutts, has agreed to be that Director? What do you think of that, John? John Sourbutts: a director of Middleton Town Football Club!"

"Harry what do I know about running a football club?"

"What does anyone know, John? Why do think the game is run so poorly from the top down? There are clubs at the very height of success, of world fame, and they are run from the board room as if they were a chip shop in Oldham. And not a very good chip shop either. There's corruption, nepotism, incompetency and a self-serving arrogance that wouldn't last five minutes in the real world."

John said nothing. He just blinked and looked at him.

"What?" said Harry after an uncomfortable silence. "You think that I'm like this?"

John said nothing.

"I'm different. I know what I'm doing. I'm not like all the rest."

John said nothing. Perhaps he raised an eyebrow, almost imperceptibly. You would have needed a slow motion replay to be sure.

"You certainly couldn't accuse me of corruption," he said, ignoring the wad of cash he was holding.

"And yes, I have given jobs to lots of people I know, but that's not the same. I have always been right in business and I will be right now!"

Again, John said nothing, but he firmly held Harry's gaze – something that he rarely saw in any of his business negotiations, not even from oligarchs, petro-billionaires or even the hard-bitten gangster types that he sometimes had to deal with to protect his shipping routes.

"Tell you what," said John, eventually, relieving a little of the pressure that had built up. "I know nothing about running a football team, and you know nothing about being a supporter. I'll sit on the board with you, but only if you stand with me, behind the goal, on Monday night."

It was Harry's turn to be silent, although it was more to do with him not quite comprehending what was being asked of him. John could have asked him to stand waist deep in effluent, catching sardines in his mouth for the amusement of Japanese tourists, and he would have been no less confused. John continued.

"Monday will be good because, despite it being a ludicrous night to play football on, it's the FA Cup against Wigan; three leagues above us and we're only slight underdogs because of our team of footballing mercenaries. Go in disguise – incognihendo I think they call it. Come and see what it's like to really be part of a football club, not just to own one like other people own a nice car or a fancy yacht. Come and listen to what's being said, sung and shouted. Be part of it, then go back to the board room and make your decisions."

"Monday is my big night, John. I don't want to be squashed in with the rank and file, pretending I'm one of them, like that cockney-geordie fellow. We're on television. I want to sit on the half way line in the directors' box with the cameras panning over to me, like they used to do with my friend Elton John at Watford."

And so John had his trump card.

"Hmmm … you could do that, I suppose. Like every other megalomaniac chairman that ever bought a football club. Or, and this is just a thought, imagine the material your film crew could get of you sneaking into the Irwell End in a black CP Company coat and Stone Island jeans … hidden microphone and camera. It would make the news. Imagine the publicity – you would be seen as a footballing hero, one of the fans, trying to do the best for them."

Harry knew a good business move when he saw one. "I'm in!" he said, and a huge grin spread across his face.

"Not so fast," said John. "We still need to get you a ticket."

The Corridor of Uncertainty

The little stadium crackled with an electrical excitement not felt there for a very long time. The crisp, cold December air drew soft clouds of warm breath from the eleven thousand capacity crowd, though not one of them felt the winter chill against the burning expectation of the game. Wigan Athletic, not long out of the Premier League and with their own charismatic chairman (who once broke his leg in a cup final, so he will tell you, from time to time), brought a quality of football not seen in the memory of even the oldest Middleton Town supporter. And this was matched by Middleton – the silky skills of the paid-by-the-week superstars mixing well with the grit and determination of their amateur team mates. Harry felt surreal. He was used to drinking fine spirits and expensive wines, rather than the rough, earthy textures of the real ale that John had bought him in The Crown. Like most things he'd done in his life, Harry had thrown himself into what he saw as an adventure, as well as what he appreciated was good television. He was unused to the hooligan clothing brands he was wearing, although less so than the silicon mask that he was using to hide his true identity. Nobody had recognised him – the place was packed and everyone was at least one drink the wrong side of a hangover. John had still insisted on going to the bar every time though, primarily to avoid him being recognised, but he was also worried that if Harry went he may ask for something more exotic, or at the very least more expensive, than the stuff normally drunk in a small northern working town.

The two hours Harry had spent in The Crown had proved a good apprenticeship, and now the songs he had learnt were tripping off his tongue. Beautifully crafted lyrics danced alongside rhythmic, almost mesmeric percussion of the supporters' clapping, as he joined the thousands around him in a chorus of hard-edged melodies, floating sweetly above the ground towards the pocket of away supporters:

'You're going to get your fucking heads kicked in.'

The game itself pulsed, reacting to the fervour of the crowd, and Harry was washed away within a sea of spectators behind the goal, several times losing sight of John. For a split second he hoped the hidden cameras wouldn't lose him in the crush, but he dismissed the thought immediately – he was enjoying this and, in that moment, nothing else but the game on the pitch mattered.

Middleton scored and it was like he'd been placed in a tumble dryer. Several times he thought he would lose his balance and fall, but there always seemed to be a hand or an arm to keep him upright.

The songs kept coming, the crowd kept singing. He couldn't believe that half-time came so quickly, and was disappointed when the referee blew. John shared a flask of coffee with him, augmented by several nips of Brandy, and Harry was only momentarily concerned about how such behaviour would impact on the official alcohol sales. He was breathless, excitedly chunnering about the exhilaration of the first forty five minutes, almost unable to contain himself.

"It's only one-nil though," said John, failing to curb Harry's enthusiasm. "Long way to go yet."

Wigan came out fighting in the second half and quickly went two-one up. If anything, the volume of the Middleton supporters increased and Harry

Singh, for once, sang harder when he was losing than when he was winning.

It was as if the crowd, he observed later, willed the ball into the net for the 85th minute equalizer, and as the last few seconds of injury time ticked away, he was convinced that he and the thousands around him had sucked the ball goalwards for the winner themselves. Pandemonium ensued, and Harry Singh was a changed man.

Beyond the halfway line of doubt

Twelve months later, John Sourbutts stood chatting to the worker who was trying to flush the drains again. Trap three had overflown at the weekend, despite his pre-match attention to it, and it was clear that they had needed professional help to get it fixed once and for all. They could do that now though: spend a little money on upkeep here and there, rather than rely on volunteers all the time. He looked up at the Harry Singh Stand and spent a moment in reverie. He and Harry had become friends after that Wigan match. They'd spent hours together planning the redevelopment of the ground, with every little detail approved by the Supporters' Trust that they'd set up. Community Schemes were launched, school children were given free tickets, a junior academy was set up, and over the summer, alongside the demolition and rebuilding of the dilapidated old stand, a brand new pitch was laid. Ten per cent of the ownership was given to the season ticket holders. Just like that.

The cup run had lasted two more games and, together with their play-off place promotion, had put the Middleton Town fairy tale at the very front of media interest at home and abroad. That had faded now, of course. Now, we are just another Club that once had its day in the limelight, he thought.

"The sun shines on a lazy dog's arse at least once a day," he said quietly.

"Eh?" replied the drain man.

"Oh, doesn't matter ... I hadn't realised I'd said that out loud." John returned to his own thoughts. The new season in a better league had brought more possibilities for Harry's self-promotion, but it wasn't his driving force anymore. Harry had kept a couple of the older professionals he'd paid stupid amounts of money to join his project, but only to help the younger talent that he'd started to bring in from their newly set up academy and scouting team. The second season under Harry's stewardship had started well, but not too well – they didn't win every game, and most games were close enough that you were never sure of the outcome until the referee blew his final whistle.

Still, they were in third place in the league and looking good when Harry died.

John looked up to the big letters on the Stand above him, which spelt out his friend's name. Harry had never seen that Stand completed, and John doubted he would have named it after himself if he had.

They'd been lucky. After his death Harry's wife wanted nothing to do with the Club. You couldn't blame her really, she was only twenty-six and her country of birth, Cuba, had never really been big on football. The easiest way out for the Estate Managers was to sell the lot to the property developer who had put in an offer before Harry had even gone cold. The Ultras owed Rusty for getting them out of that one. Without the slightest thought for himself, he'd tracked down Estelita to her Florida villa and persuaded her that the Club should be turned over to the Supporters Trust as a fitting long term memory to her former husband. Rusty told us he'd been sharing a bed with her for six days before he got her to agree to it. His end of the bargain was that he acquiesced to marry the beautiful, athletic, dusky, sensual millionairess and live with her in whichever of her seven mansions she happened to be in at any one time. The things we do to support our Club, eh? Like I said, always thinking of others, that Rusty.

In the end, Harry was undone by his past. I'd always thought he was being over-cautious with two Marvins forever covering his back, but it turned out that two weren't enough. Not that it was the crazed lunatic (or aggrieved, concerned victim, depending on which way you looked at it) that did for Harry in the end. Okay, so him bursting out of a gaggle of journalists at a post-match press briefing and firing a gun at him didn't help. But the gun was loaded with paint pellets, designed to embarrass the man who had closed down and asset stripped a foundry he'd bought, not to kill him. It was the ensuing heart attack that killed him. Or more accurately the lifestyle of alcohol, tobacco, rich foods, over-work, stress, and little or no exercise that had preceded it.

The drain man was putting his pipes and hoses back onto his van.

"Well, it's blown all the shit away, but I can't guarantee it won't all be back again in the future," he said. "Depends how you treat it, I suppose."

"Very true," replied John. "Very true."

Hitting the Bar

It's not quite seven-thirty in the morning and already I'm on my second pint: Guinness of course – it's the nearest thing I'm going to get to breakfast by the looks of things. That's what you do at airports though, innit? Straight into the bar, whatever the time. Some of the boys had a couple of cans on the way down here as well. Mappits! They'll be mullered by the time we take off, and we've got all day and all night ahead of us. Fackin' too right! Football Tone gets a round of Sambuca in ("Fack that fackin' Oozo, that's shite," he says). I don't really want one, but it goes down in one. Has to, really. After all, this is my Stag do.

We call him Football Tone 'cos he's into football and his name's Tony. Not that complicated, really. I mean, obviously we're all into football, but Tony is the only one who still actually plays the game. Not a bad player either, as Sunday League goes. The rest of us? Well, we just love to watch it. Season Ticket holders at The 'Ammers – that's West Ham United to you. Not that I can go as often as I used to though. See, I've been saving for me wedding, and fack me it's nearly here – just four more days! I tell you, I could hardly believe it when I copped with Zoë – diamond girl she is. Two years down the line and I pops the question – you should have seen me: down on one knee, the lot. Shakin' like a geezer with Parkinson's I was. Proudest man on the manor when she said 'yes', I can tell you. And this is me Stag do, see. I've had to cut down a bit on watching the footie so we could raise the money for a flat, but when The 'Ammers get drawn in Europe, first qualifying round of the Europa League, week before the wedding – well, me and the lads had to 'ave one last blast together. Before I settle down, you understand.

Football Tone's chatting up some posh looking bint, but she's 'avin none of it. Looks like she's on her way to some business meeting or sammin'. He should stick to his own kind, realise his level. Wingnut and Jamie are playing pool, but they're the ones who were drinking in the van on the way up, so they're playing like a right pair of tossers! Still, bad as each other, I suppose. And Stinson, he's our leader really, well he just sits there smoking a fat cigar and looking like he owns the place. The cigar's not lit, of course – he just thinks it looks cool and he likes the opportunity for aggro if some jobsworth comes and tells him to put it out. He's alright, really, Stinson. I suppose. Insists we call him by his last name for some reason. I think it's because it sounds harder than Justin, his first name, and Stinson likes to sound hard. Oh yeah – if there's any trouble about, Stinson's usually in the middle of it! Nutter. Not that we look for any Barney Rubble, though. I don't want you to get the wrong impression. We're just after a bit of a lark, that's all. A bit of the old laughing gas.

We get a final call for our boarding, 'Will the last passengers for Easijet Flight EZY2001 to Athens please board immediately.' We're fackin' famous! I'm glad of the excuse to leave my third pint as we run through Luton Airport, half-worried, half laughing, and we get a right offensive stare from the old boiler at the Gate. She's like 'I was just about to close the Gate – you are very, very fortunate,' and we're like 'we're very, very sorry, but Mister Stinson here is diabetic and we was just giving him his medicine,' and she doesn't know whether we're taking the piss or not, so she just checks our Passports and lets us on without another word. Result! We're on the plane: The 'Ammers against AEK Athens and my Stag do all in one. Football Tone orders a round of drinks, but the air hostess tells us we have to wait until the plane is in the air, so we all 'boo' together. Fair play to her though – she just laughs and tells us to put on our seat belts. Bit of a darlin' too.

Not that I'd cheat on my Zoë though. No chance. I know how lucky I am. Today's Tuesday, tomorrow's the match, and on Saturday I get married. What a week! Don't know what these chancers have got in store for me on this trip, but I'm gonna keep myself out of trouble.

'Ave a laugh though, oh yeah! 'Av some quality giggles.

Jamie is chatting up the stewardess, and seems to be having more luck than Football Tone did earlier. He's the boy though, Jamie – good looking fucker and can talk the knickers off a nun that one. None of us have had problems in that department though. That's probably why we get on so well together, I suppose: we were always down the Ikon Club on a Saturday night, after the match; trappin' off with the Minge, taking the piss out of each other if we got shot down. Those were the days. That's where I met my Zoë. There she was, legs up to her armpits, long blonde hair, everybody in the club staring at her, and Stinson says 'Go on my son, get in there.' Then he starts laughin', the cant, like she's so far out of my league, like she's fackin' top of the Premier and I'm chained to the bottom of the Unibond Reserves. He was right of course, but I thought 'Fack 'im, why not?' You should have seen his face when I'm still talking to her half an hour later and she gives me her phone number! Back of the net!

Jamie is explaining to the air hostess that it's my Stag do and will she sit on my knee for a photo. She's not having it, but she's laughing and serving us some cold Kronenburgs.

"Leave it out," I say, doing my best Eliza Doolittle, "I'm a good boy, I am."

That gets 'em laughin', though they tell me they'll get me later. Wingnut orders another round even though we've only just started on these. "You've got to get them in," he says. "They don't carry much stock on these trips. Anyway, we can afford to 'av a few drinks after all the money I saved us on this flight."

He's bragging, but he's right. Wingnut took the day off work when they made the draw, then he sits on his computer and books us the cheapest flights before anyone else cottons on. Eighty notes to Athens and back – you can't argue with that. Well, Zoë did argue, at least at first. Fack me – you should have seen the old boat race. It wasn't the money, really, it's just she doesn't really have a high opinion of me mates. But she was alright in the end, bless 'er. I mean, you can't give up your mates just because you're getting married can you? Thick and thin, these boys, thick and thin.

I must have fallen asleep because the plane is beginning its descent into Athens Airport. The boys are quiet and I sense something's wrong. After a minute I put my hand to my face and they burst out laughin'. Only covered me in fackin' toothpaste, the Mappits! And because the seatbelt sign is on I can't go to the toilet and wash it off. After a minute or two the stewardess comes past and gives me some wipes. The lads all boo, then burst out laughing again. We sing 'I'm Forever Blowing Bubbles', the West Ham anthem, as the plane lands. A few of the other passengers look put out, but there's couple of little kids smiling and joining in with us, so fack 'em!

Only hand luggage, so it's straight outside for a fast cab to the Hotel. Bit of pissing around 'cos there's five of us, but we get one of them people carriers in the end and it's fine. Wingnut has bought some more cans from a little café in the Arrivals Lounge – we share them out, but the driver won't take one, even for later. "Come on, Granddad," I say. "You aff to av a drink with the famous 'Ammers!" But he pretends not to understand the Queen's, so we leave 'im alone and try and guess who's farted. It's Wingnut, of course, so we take turns to slap 'im. Meanwhile the fackin' driver's going like Jenson Button, and even Stinson puts his seatbelt on.

Into the two star Hotel Atalos, booked courtesy of Mister Wingnut via the Internet. "Wot-a-loss', more like!" We laugh 'cos the rooms are a bit like the cells in Porridge, and I wind up Stinson by saying 'Leave it out, Fletcher,' but he takes it as an insult, 'im being a bit older than the rest of us an all. I'm sharing with Stinson in the better room, and Wingnut, Jamie and Football Tone have the room next door. Wingnut draws the short straw and has to sleep on a pull-out cot, and we take the Michael 'cos he's never going to score with a bird on that thing. Me and Wingnut went to school together, and that's where he got his nickname. He had a short haircut and big sticky out ears. When he was twenty he had 'em pinned back, and at the same time had his teeth whitened, his eyes lasered and highlights put in hair. He went from a fackin' spanna' to God's gift overnight. Least he did when he got rid of his orange complexion caused by some cheap fake tan he put on. It was his twenty-fifth birthday last month and his family had this bash for him down at the British Legion. Fack me, did we laugh when we saw those old pictures of him his old man 'ad pinned all around the room! Took it well though, Wingnut. Best mate a man could have, that one. Shame I got landed with Stinson, really, but it's best to let him have the better room. There's a bit of an edge to Stinson if he doesn't get his own way.

We're not bothered about the rooms because we don't intend to spend much time in them anyway – we just want to dump our bags and get straight into Athens – but Jamie says he needs to shower first, in case he pulls later. We complain, but the rest of the lads agree 'cos they're all thinking the same thing. I'm glad of half an hour off the booze but whilst I'm having mine, Football Tone does a reccy outside and comes back with some cans and a bottle of Vodka from the corner shop. What a team this is! Drinking for Queen and country we are! We ask the geezer in reception where the best place to drink is and he tells us the Plaka or summink. He gives us directions, but we just wander around for a bit. Football Tone is getting restless 'cos he aint 'ad a drink for five fackin' minutes, but the rest of us are chilled, just taking in the scene. After a bit we find a fackin' Hard Rock Café place and we dive in – we're all a bit famished and we can get a drink in there anyway.

We gets inside and realise that it's not a real Hard Rock Café, but just one that some Greek geezer has tried to copy. This is even better, 'cos it's really just a cheap drinking den that serves a bit of Pub Grub. Lovely jubbly: we're set for the afternoon in here! We orders five pints and five shots, and this Mappit at the end of the bar comes over. He's about fackin' ninety years old, but still has this long hair trailing down his back, and he's dressed head to toe in black leathers. Looks like Keith

Richards' dad or summink. Anyway, it turns out it's his bar and he obviously likes our company 'cos he offers us all one on the house, which we politely accept. You can't be rude to these foreign slags, can you? The place starts off quiet, but busies up and we even get a few more West 'Am fans joining us for a bit of an old sing-song. After 'Blowin' Bubbles' has been done to death, Keith fackin' Richards sticks on some Bon Jovi and we all sing along to 'Livin' on a Prayer'! Football Tone stands on one of the tables and does this incredible air guitar act. Now in the Eagle and Child back home he would have been thrown out straight away, no messin', but the bar staff here think it's hilarious and even join in a bit. I'd be happy here all night, but Stinson wants to see a bit of Athens, by which he means some other Athens pubs. Fair enough. We get up to go and Keith Richards does this 'oh you're not leaving now, boys, are you?', but he's had enough of our money so we make our exit. He follows us outside and offers to wave down a couple of Joe Baxis for us, explaining that in Greece people share taxis that are going in the same direction. Sounds a bit of a liberty to me, but when in Rome …

Me and Football Tone jump into the backseat of the first one, and this bloke in the front seat says something in Foreign to the driver then turns to us.

"You over for the match?" He says in this weird accent, and when we says that we are he smiles and says that he is too. Turns out the geezer's called Jason and comes from Clapham! Moved over here twenty years ago after he trapped off with this Greek bird on holiday. He now lives on one of the islands, and has worked as a waiter in her old fellah's restaurant ever since! Anyway, he says he's got West 'Am running through his blood and he just had to come into Athens when he heard they were playing – managed to get here the night before for a bit of R&R, he says winking at us. Football Tone smiles – he likes the sound of this and asks him what he's got in mind. He smiles again when Jason tells him he's going to take in a few strip joints and then see where the night leads to. Tone gets straight on the blower to the others and they're easily talked into letting Jason be our tour guide for the night. I laugh along with them – Zoë wouldn't be too pleased, but I'm only looking, ain't I?

So the two taxis pull up outside this Strip and we bundle out. Jason asks us to hang on a second and goes over to one of those street traders. He only goes and buys a claret and blue West Ham fackin' beach towel! Comes back saying that Greece is too hot for a scarf, but he'll get some use out of the towel after the match. He's got a point I suppose, but it seems a barmy time to buy it. Wingnut laughs and asks him what he's going to use it for in the titty bar.

We introduce Jason to the others and pile into this place, full of neon lights and chrome poles. There's nothing much happening, but Jason says it's early. He talks to the barman in Foreign and we get our beers cheaper than the other mugs in the place - still ten Euros a throw though. We grab a table in good view of the stage and Jason and Wingnut need to find the lav. We've only just sat down when this darlin' Russian bird comes over and says how good looking we all are. Stinson falls for it big time, but Jason tells him she works here and her job is just to get you to buy her forty quid cocktails, which are really just orange juice anyway. Most punters fall for it because they think they're in for a shag, and when they get their credit card bill through a month later it's too late to do anything about it. Most of 'em won't even ring the credit company because they don't like to query a transaction that says 'Erotic Sex Bar, Athens'. Too busy hiding the statement from the missus anyway. Stinson is pissed off with this, 'cos he likes to think that he's the streetwise one, so he decides to complain that there's nobody dancing. This big geezer comes up and tells us there'll be plenty of girls on in five minutes and we'd better get another drink before they start. We stump up another fifty Euros for five Heinekens, and sit back ready to enjoy the show. An hour and another hundred Euros later there's still no dancing, so Football Tone gets up on stage and starts swinging round the pole like he's some ballet bird or sammin', and it gets a big round of applause from all the sad old geezers sat at the bar. Fack me – there must 'av been seven or eight bouncers arrived from nowhere and Football Tone is soon on his way out the front door. We rush out after 'im, 'cos it's all for one and one for all, and for a few minutes there's a bit of a standoff, but then they just tell us to fuck off and they go back inside. Stinson tries to get us to rush back in after them, but none of us are up for it, and he doesn't try too hard to talk us into it. Big blokes those, and you don't know what sort of hardware they might have in there.

And anyway: I'm getting married on Saturday – last thing I want to do is get banged up for the night!

We follow Jason, who seems to know where he's going, and Wingnut and Jamie are deep in conversation with him. I can't hear what's being said because I have to listen to Stinson telling us about what he would have done to the bouncers if we'd have backed him up. Night has set in now. I'm not wearing a watch, but I check my moby and it says it's seven 'o clock, which I think means it's about eleven over here. My head's down a bit, and I'm feeling a bit ropey from all the boozing and Stinson banging on about drop-kicks and forearm smashes. We follow Jason through this door, and I wonder where we're going. It's a bit like someone's house. A bit shabby too. Down a corridor, everything's dark and there's this old hag of a woman sat there watching telly and smoking a fag. There's a smell I can't place, but it reminds me of a cheap deodorant or old pot pourri. We sit down in these plastic garden chairs, and I wonder where we are and what we're doing. The only light in the room comes from the telly and this weird blue lamp in the corner; the only noise is from this daft whiney music that I didn't hear at first because the old gal had the volume up on Greek Eastenders or whatever. Jason talks in Foreign to her, going ten to the dozen, then turns to us and says that there are only two girls on tonight. I still haven't sussed what's happening, even when these two, and I'm not over-exaggerating here, minging, fucking mooses in the dirtiest fucking underwear you have ever seen, walk out from the next room and start parading up and down in front of us. I mean, excuse my language, but fack me! Jason looks and sounds embarrassed as he says, "Okay. Do any of you want to fuck them?"

I can't believe he's serious. There's a silence, I think because no one can believe he's serious either, then eventually Jamie manages to say, "Er ... no," with just the right mixture of amazement and sarcasm. Jason doesn't look offended. I think he knows he's onto a real loser here. "Okay then," he says. "We'd better go." Jason says something that sounds like an apology to the old woman (well, they're all fucking old, so I should say the oldest), and we go back down the corridor. Outside, for a moment, nobody says anything. Then, a bit bashful, Jason apologizes and says that it's usually quite good in there. We burst out laughing and Jason smiles, looking relieved. We take the piss for the next twenty minutes as we find some food. Fair play to Jason – this time he comes up trumps. We think he's thrown us another spanner as we walk into this deserted fish market. Oh, the smell! It was nearly as bad as back in the brothel (I still can't believe I've been in a brothel – I don't say anything, but I'm scared stiff Zoë will find out). In the middle the deserted market is a little café. He tells us that when they start delivering the fish, in a couple of hours, the place will be choc full, but at this time you get the best Souvlaki in town for four Euros and no queues. It looks a bit dirty, but the food was really tasty, and they served big bottles of Amstel too.

We finish a couple of bottles each and I think that it's time to get back to the hotel: big day tomorrow, football to think about. When I suggest this, the lads just laugh – no way were we stopping now. Jason says he wants to make it up to us by taking us to this really great disco bar he knew. Wall to wall strumpet – couldn't fail to score. I try explaining, again, that I'm getting married on Saturday, but they tell me not to spoil the fun for everyone. And anyway, Jason has already ordered the taxis. We leave the café with the lads on the second round of 'Get Me To The Church On Time.'

There are flashing lights, loud music … there's a girl, she's smiling and we're dancing … then there's fresh air, I'm running … I'm not running very fast because I'm laughing too much … I think I'm laughing because I don't know why I'm running … or why I'm laughing … I'm very drunk … maybe something else, but I don't remember taking anything …

… I wake up. Sort of. I half open my eye and the briefest of squints at the room confirm that it looks even more like a prison cell in the half-dark of morning. I close the eye again – I can 'feel' someone else in the room with me, rather than see them, so Stinson must have made it back too. Good – I need to sleep this off. I was hoping to sit in the sun today, top up my East London paleness in time for the wedding; but that's not important now. Sleeping off this humungous fackin' headache is.

I can't drift back off though. What is that fackin' smell? It's rank, whatever it is. I start to think that one of us didn't make the toilet in time. I bury my head under a brittle, inflexible blanket, but it doesn't seem to stop that smell permeating through my whole system.

There is more than one other person in here; again, I feel this. Shit! That means Stinson's brought some girl back. Or worse! Fuck, no! Don't tell me I've brought someone back – I could never forgive myself, not just a few days before the wedding. The boys were all joking that what 'appens in Athens, stays in Athens. I know they mean it too – they'd never let me down those boys – but it's about what I feel. I couldn't forgive myself. I remember the face of the girl in the club, swimming in front of me. Well, I remember there was a girl. Her face, like everything else from last night, is a blur. And now I'm thinking that Stinson might not keep what happens in Athens in Athens. He loves being the centre of attention, he does. My mind reels as the worst case scenario forces itself into my head: Stinson choosing his moment to let it slip about how Zoë is a much classier bint that the girl I fucked on my first night in Athens, or summink. When would he do it? At the reception? As she walks down the aisle? He'd make it sound like it was supposed to be a private comment to someone next to him, but just loud enough for everyone around to hear. The whispers would grow and someone would tell Zoë just before or just after she marries me. The thought rips at my stomach. I have already made my mind up to tell her myself when I think I'd better verify the situation first.

And what is that fackin' smell?

I slowly pull the blanket away from my face. Eyes blink several times before I can face opening them onto the greys of the room. It's cold, that's the first thing I notice as the shadows become shapes and my brain starts to process the information in front of me, making the shapes recognizable and, at the same time, trying to tell me what they mean.

I am not in my hotel room.

I am not in any hotel room.

I am in a fucking prison cell.

Though it's not very big, there are six or seven people in here. Most are bunched up and asleep. Four on the floor, one, like me, on some sort of shelf-bed, and one who just stands there, leaning against the cell wall and staring straight at me. I can't make out the other shapes, but the one looking at me is most definitely a man. A big, ugly, mean and moody looking man. My earlier concern that I might have brought a girl back to my hotel room jumps back to the forefront of my mind and mocks me – 'if you're going to have sex on this holiday,' the thought says, 'it ain't going to be with a girl, me old china!' Even now, as the guy pulls himself from the comfort of the wall and takes a step towards me it runs through my mind that at least I won't have to tell Zoë I slept with another girl on my Stag party. I may not be able to tell her anything, as the guy picks me up by my shirt lapels and slams me against the wall.

I think that I scream, but all I can hear, in the dark confines of that small, cement room, is a frightened yelp. Simultaneously, as the terrified squeak escapes my lips, I realize that I have no pants on. I am fucking petrified.

The man barks some Foreign at me. To be honest, if he was speaking perfect Radio Four I don't think I would have understood him. I felt nothing when he hit me against the wall, anesthetized by my own adrenaline probably, but now I feel a sharp pain spreading across the back of my head, and a warm, thick mucus trickles down the back of my neck. I feel the oncoming of concussion and pray for a blackness to swallow me.

It doesn't, but he stops shouting and moves away, back to his spot against the wall. As the Tsunami in my head subsides I realize that my hearing, dulled from the crack to my skull, is now returning. All I can hear is the startled panting of a coward. The coward is me. I have a moment of shame. I am a West Ham fan. I have seen action on many occasions. I have battered and been battered, but I have never run – not even when the odds were stacked. It was never me, the fighting – I'm not actually the type of person who likes to hurt anyone, if I'm honest. But if you turn a corner and come across an ambush, maybe a rabble of ugly Mancs, Scousers or, worst of all, Millwall, then you stand and you fight. You certainly never let them see that you're scared. You are Michael Caine in Zulu; you are Jason Statham in everything.

Like I said, I am fucking scared now though. There is nowhere to escape in here. Would someone come to help if I shouted? I don't know, but I get the feeling they wouldn't.

The action, brief as it was, has woken the other occupants of the cell: the grey, sleeping shapes and shadows. Faces peer at me and my attacker, and then look away. I desperately look at each of them, hoping to see Stinson, Tony, Jamie or Wingnut. They're not amongst them, and my heart sinks. I'm on my own. With no trousers. Shit.

Just as I think I've got my breathing under control, one of the shapes from the floor gets up and starts to make his way over to me. I feel panic rising for a moment, but he doesn't look all that. Wiry fella with glasses. Nah, he ain't all that – the sort that looks like he reads books, probably. I brace myself anyway, but he sorts of puts his hands up as if to say 'easy, tiger'. I'm cautious, but I nod for him to continue.

"Are you all right? I didn't see what happened, but I heard most of it."

I look at the big geezer in the corner: he's still staring at me, but the trickle of blood running down the back of my neck seems to have stopped.

"I'm fine."

"Okay, young man. I was merely trying to help." He lifts his hands in that same 'don't mean any harm' gesture and starts to back away. He's clearly Greek; he speaks posh English, but with a heavy accent. I reconsider, quick-like, as I think I need all the help I can get.

"Wait," I say. "Sorry, geez – I could do with some help, really."

He smiles, like he knew this is what I would say, sooner or later. I don't like it, but I don't have a lot of choice at the moment.

"Why did the big geezer take me out, mister?" I ask him, trying not to look in the direction of the man-mountain in the corner. He looks confused for a minute. I just realize he probably doesn't know what I mean by 'take me out', or that he's got me confused and he thinks me and the big fella are an item, but then he seems to make sense of it and says,

"Oh, he said he's deeply offended by your government's insistence on keeping the Parthenon Marbles, stolen by the felon Elgin in 1812, and that he is now holding you personally responsible for their return."

I blinked. "Really?"

"No, not really," he smiled. "He actually said that when the food comes he's going to eat yours and if you try to stop him you'll get more of 'that'. It's just me that likes to get the dig in about the Marbles."

I wasn't really sure what he was banging on about to be honest, but he seemed okay and, like I said, I needed a friend.

"And I wouldn't worry about the food. It's so bad you won't be able to eat much of it anyway. Not for a day or two, until your stomach gets used to it – I've seen it before with people like you. I take it this is your first time in a Greek jail?"
I ignored the question … it was something else he said …

"What do you mean 'a day or two'?" I stammered. "There's a match on tonight!" It sunk in: "And I'm getting married on Saturday!"

I must have sounded like a right whopper, the state I was in: like an hysterical little girl – everybody in the cell was watching me now. I could feel the panic rising up through the dullness of my hangover. I was close to tears, close to losing it, but I didn't care. If I missed that flight home, missed that wedding, my life was over anyway.

The geezer just shrugged.

"Well, you may be lucky – you are English, after all, and therefore above the laws of most countries. Although sometimes they like to make an example of tourists – what are you in for?"

"I … I have no idea. I don't think I did anything." The absence of my trousers suggested otherwise.

A couple of the shapes, now moving sluggishly, stretching and yawning, looking slightly more like humans, chuckled at my last remark. Clearly we weren't the only people who could speak English in here.

"Okay," he said. "Maybe. Welcome to my world – I didn't do anything either. Mikolas."

I wasn't sure if that was his name or he was just clearing his throat, but he offered me his hand and gave me that eyebrow movement that says 'and you are?'. I shook it and mumbled my name. His eyebrows changed to say 'huh?', but before I could repeat it, he suddenly spat out the word "Batsos!" Again, I wondered if he had some sort of cold, but it must be their name for the Feds, as four of the bastards open the large metal door and drag me out.

They don't bother to give me anything to cover me privates, so the pain of being lugged down this corridor subsides against the embarrassment of my bollocks swinging around in front of four uniformed Gestapo-wannabees. I'm chucked into a small interview room and left.

… and left.

I don't know how long for. Seems like days, but it might be minutes. Then there's a crunch of a key in the door lock and this geezer pokes his head round. Looks like another book-worrier. He nods to the Gestapo, which I take to mean he doesn't mind coming in on his own (I probably don't look at my most threatening) and sits down opposite me, placing a small pad and pen on the unsteady table between us. The table is not the only thing that is unsteady … I am shaking like … I don't know … I regret using that Parkinson's simile earlier … seems like bad Karma.

"Okay," he says. A wave of relief washes over me. He's English and he's posh. He's here to get me out of this place, I think. He's here to get me out of here with some new trousers. I start thinking I might make the wedding. I get giddy and think I might make tonight's match. I am probably reading too much into one word.

"So, my name is Farrington-Brown, British Embassy, you are Andrew John Neill, British National of Arnold Circus in London, twenty-four years old. Correct?"

I nod.

"Is there anyone at home you'd like me to contact for you?"

"Fuck, no!" I almost shout the words. "I don't want anyone to know about this. I just want to get out of here."

He looks at me, and I get the feeling I was being over-optimistic earlier on. His attempt at a smile goes wrong … like he heard something funny and smelt something bad at exactly the same moment.

"Andrew, let me be blunt," he pauses for effect and I feel like lamping him one. "You're looking at years in prison. It's difficult to tell you how many, because of the way they work over here, but it will be years, not months."

I go into shock. He must have me mixed up with someone else. He waits, patiently, as if he's a doctor and just given me weeks to live … which is pretty close to how I feel as well. There are many questions that spin through my hung-over, alcohol washed mind, but I eventually stammer out, "Who … wh … wh … what did I do?"

He writes something down on his pad. I can't read it upside down, but I'm sure he's only doing it to wind me up, the fucker. I decide not to get mad at him though. Eventually, he looks up from the pad and says, "You don't remember anything?" He takes my silence and blank look as a 'no' and leans back on his chair – a brave move, given the state of it.

"Andrew, you were arrested in the early hours of this morning, whilst stood on a restricted part of the Acropolis where you had draped a twenty feet by twenty feet claret and blue flag bearing the legend 'Fuck the Recession, We're on a Session' emblazoned across it. You were singing a song about blowing bubbles and you were," he pauses to consider his words ... "I believe the colloquial term you use is 'mooning' to the whole of Athens whilst using a torch between your legs to ... let's say 'highlight the effect'."

There was a silence whilst I took this in. He wasn't finished, though.

"I believe your coup de grâce was to break wind loudly before shaking the oversized bottle of Amstel you were drinking and soaking the arresting officers with lager froth in the manner of a grand prix winner."

There was a bit more silence. I almost laughed. Not because what I'd done was funny, but because he must have been winding me up about his earlier 'throw away the keys' speech. What he'd described was worthy of a fine and maybe a night in the cells to calm down, which I'd already had. Nobby here doesn't look impressed though. He leans forward, the chair groaning in protestation.

"Andrew, I can tell that you do not appreciate the seriousness of this situation. You are not in England now. To start with, the Greeks are understandably very touchy about the current financial recession – many haven't been paid for months. They are going without food, never mind looking forward to an extended period of drinking alcohol in a boisterous manner and for a prolonged period of time. Add into that the charges of desecrating one of the world's most significant monuments, drunk and disorderly, exposing yourself to a female ..."

He stopped as I started at this last point.

"Oh yes, one of the arresting officers was a woman ... and an AEK Athens supporter as well, I believe. You hit the jackpot with that one. Now, where was I? Oh yes ... exposing yourself to a female – sexual offences are dealt with very severely over here – and finally assaulting two members of the Greek constabulary; albeit with the contents of a bottle of Dutch lager."

I can't speak. He can see that I had 'got it' now.

"Well, I'll see if I can get you any toothpaste, that sort of thing. I've done my bit though, so if you've nothing else to ask I'll be on my way. Depress me these places."

I know I should say something. Argue the point. Demand justice. Ask to see my lawyer. Insist on my phone call. I sit here instead, feeling hopelessly lost and knowing that I've just made the biggest mistake of my life. I don't even care about the prison sentence, but I care about losing Zoë.

I don't have a lawyer to ask for. If I had my phone call, I can't think of anyone that I would ring.

I get dragged back along the corridor, one of the guards punches me in the side of the head, without warning, although he does spit some words into my ear afterwards. I don't understand the words, but I do understand that this is just the start of it. This is what I have to get used to.

I am returned to my cell. Without ceremony and without trousers. The ferocity of the prison stench hits me as soon as I'm pushed through the door: sweat, fear and desperation. Maybe those smells were just me; or maybe I'd read too many American detective novels as a kid. There is more though. My nose had probably got used to it before, but now I can see it: a pool of liquid that can only be piss, leaking from a chemical toilet which sits in the corner of the room and is currently being sat on by a grizzly looking bloke who is clearly dealing with the effects of over-enthusiastic diarrhoea. Three of my fellow inmates are smoking, and the debris and odour of a thousand more smokers adds to the foul stench. I have braved the toilets at half time down at the Park, but they have nothing on this place. Maybe it's the temperature, rising now as the sun turns the cell into Hell's sauna. There is noise coming from the shutters, high on the far wall – they let in a small amount of light from the outside, and an even smaller amount of fresh air. There is a pigeon caught there … it must have flown into them and got caught. It is in its final death throws, making one last twist for freedom before the inevitability of joining several of its species that were already stuck there weeks and months previously. They are in various forms of decay, adding to the rank ordure of the cell. I'm not very good at similes and metaphors, as you know, but this pigeon, life fading in the reek of this squalor, seems to sum up my position.

I've lost my mattress, thin and dirty as it was, and my blanket, brittle and dirtier, to other inmates. Inmates. The very word seems unreal to me, something from a film or television, and I think of the joke I'd made about Porridge to Stinson yesterday. I sink to the floor, my back against a wall; I don't mind losing the mattress, but the blanket would have at least hidden my nakedness. I feel exposed, and those other jokes we told as children about prison sex have never seemed less funny.

Mikolas sits down next to me, and I look at him, grateful for someone that might offer me a scrap of hope, or at least advice. He sees the desperation in my eyes.

"Let me guess," he says. "Graffiti, vandalism, fighting, causing offence?"

"Yes. And the rest," I reply.

"You don't look like a thug to me. Perhaps you were drunk. But this is not England, where you can piss on a statue of a war hero and get a ticking off. This is a country that fights for its pride. We have to – it's all we have left."

"I think I was drugged."

"Maybe. Probably. It doesn't matter – whatever you did they will deal with it severely. I'm sorry. I can tell you what to expect, what it will be like in the real prisons, but I can't give you any hope. In all likelihood, your stay in Greece will be a lot longer than you thought it would be."

Zoë. All I could think about was Zoë.

Mikolas was right about the food. I try some, but I can't keep it down and I end up adding to the mixture of bodily fluids on the floor – I'd had made the toilet, but there was somebody using it at the time. In the evening I'm vaguely aware that the match is going on, not too far from here, but in another world. It's a world that isn't important to me anymore, and thoughts of the game slip from my numb and battered mind.

A break. A couple of guards saunter in. Everyone is on edge, apparently half expecting a cunning kick, or a bruise from a baton. This time they request, almost civilly, one of the inmates to join them and fire off some rapid Greek at me and Mikolas as they throw a pair of trousers in my direction. They are too big and have several holes, but I am so delighted to be wearing them that I almost forget to ask Mikolas what they'd said.

"They're transferring me to Korydallos Prison tomorrow morning," he says, pensively, when I eventually remembered. "And you're going too," he adds, looking me straight in the eye. I've seen the look he gave me before, from someone else. That time it was on a doctor giving me the news that me old nan wouldn't be surviving her operation. This time Mikolas thought the same about my own chances in Korydallos Jail.

People come and go all night. I'd say there is barely 20 minutes when there isn't some noise or the other, either from inside this dank crypt, or from out in the corridors. Screams, shouts, laughs, bangs … I doubt I would have slept anyway. Mikolas passes the time by telling me about the prison. The guards won't be the ones to worry about there, he says. He advises me to try and stay with the Greeks. The Greeks are the best, but they will all try and make me take drugs then, when I am hooked, they will make me sell them. When I get caught, which I will, then my sentence will be increased. He tells me this like it will happen, like I need to just roll with it and keep my head down, like I won't have the choice to say no.

Morning peers through the glass shutters, failing to inspire either the trapped, dead pigeons or my hopes, and it isn't long before the locks on the cell's door are again rattling open.

This time they've come for me.

There is only one guard, a big one though, and he just looks at me. He nods his head for me to get up and follow him, whilst sneering his contempt. It can't match the contempt I have for myself. Does Zoë know yet? Me mam and dad? What will they say in the Eagle and Child – will they laugh over their pints and call me a loser, or will they sip silently, knowing it could have been any one of them?

I reach the corridor and the big geezer pushes me forward. I have to sign some papers – they're not in English and there's no-one to translate them for me. It is only after I sign them that I wonder if I should have or not. I'm not thinking straight, I'm not myself. He unlocks two more doors, and he pushes me through each until we reach a larger one, a double door and bolted to mean business. But he doesn't open them. He stares at me for a while, then leans close to my ear, grabbing the back of my shirt at the same time. I just stare at the ground. His impressive moustache is complimented by the stubble on his unshaven face: both scratch me as he delivers an unintelligible threat. His spit sprays the side of my face as his words – unknown, but understood – are delivered to me. I smell his body odour, I think that his last meal consisted mainly of onions, and then, as his threat reaches a crescendo, he throws me into the wall.

I bounce off it, stunned, but somehow still upright. This gives me a tiny uplift. I stand up straighter. I raise my chin a touch, pull back my shoulders a little and look straight at him.

"What, you fackin' Millwall or summin'? I'll see you outside, my son!"

I don't know what made me say that. I am expecting a beating. He looks at me funny, but then shakes his head and starts to undo the bolts in front of us. Maybe he didn't understand. Maybe his mates will give me a kicking on the way to Korydallos. Maybe, if Mikolas is right, it's not the guards I should be worried about.

He opens the door and the bright, early morning sunshine streams in and assaults my senses. I catch sight of the prison van, just as I raise my hand to protect my eyes, which have seen nothing more invasive than a forty watt bulb for the past thirty-six hours. He pushes me forward, but I keep on my feet and I give him some more verbals, unsure where this newfound swagger is coming from, and already feel it crumbling.

"You push like a fackin' gal, you tart!' I still manage to stammer, bracing myself for another punch.

It doesn't come. Instead, I hear the door slamming behind me, its noise disguising the shouting I can hear in front of me, so that I think I can hear English, so that I think I can hear my name.

Firm hands clasp my arms – I am being propelled towards the van I had seen, and I start to despair again. It hits me that they didn't bring Mikolas with me, and I realize how much I needed him here. I start to open my eyes, still sensitive to the sun's mocking rays. Wingnut's head comes into focus in front of me. It's blurred from the sun, so I wonder at first if I'm hallucinating from lack of sleep and food.

"Fackin' legend, mate!" This Wingnut apparition seems to be saying to me. "Did you hear him to that big fucker, lads? 'You push like a girl, you tart!' Fackin' legend!"

I am bundled into the van, but it's not a prison van ... it's a minibus of sorts ... I look for the familiar sight of the taxi meter, and I'm relieved to see it up front. A fat, ugly driver, his bald head already sweating despite the early hour, is tapping the meter, which is clocking away; his moustache seems to have exploded across his enormous, wart and acne-filled face as he looks back at me. I think he is beautiful.

"C'mon. C'mon!" I realise it is Jamie who is now talking. "Vamos!" he cries, which is the international word for 'Let's get the fuck out of here!'

The driver complains loudly, throwing his arms around, but he sets off and soon has something else to complain about, rebuking the angry horns from other cars as he joins the main road. But I had heard the word 'airport', so I don't care.

"We won, mate, one-nil," Jamie is telling me. It takes a moment to realize that he is talking about the football. About the match. "Two players and our manager sent off, mind. Not bad seeing as we only got here via the Fair Play League."

The game seemed so important a couple of days ago, but now I don't care. I'm happy to let him carry on though, as he describes a tackle, a mazy run, and a crisp, low shot to the far corner. I am just so happy, so relieved to hear these voices, to be back in this normality. Then I interrupt him, as a thought hits me like a baseball bat on steroids.

"Who knows? Who knows about this back home?"

"Nobody, mate, nobody. And nobody needs to know. What 'appens in Athens, stays in Athens – remember?" Football Tone's words console me, but I am still worried.

I am still worrying airside, as we push ourselves into the queue for the plane. All through passport control we feared that some hero of officialdom would drag us into a side room and tell us we wouldn't be going anywhere. We feel like actors in The Great Escape as we shuffle forwards onto the boarding platform ... there is no Gestapo to say 'Good luck' to us and I collapse into the plane's seat. Wingnut, face screwed up to let me know how badly I smell, sprays me with a deodorant that he has removed from his hand luggage and we all laugh in relief. The relief doesn't last, as I worry again about Stinson saying something to Zoë about what's happened.

Stinson. Where is Stinson?

"Where is Stinson?" I say, and the lads stop larking about with the deodorant, which they have been pretending to spray on two kids who'd started laughing with us. Their faces go serious and a knot ties in my stomach.

"Stinson took the fall." Jamie says. The lads busy themselves getting into their seats now, the fun seems to have stopped abruptly.

"Look," he continues. "We were all off our faces that night, but you were probably the worst 'cos you've not been on it for a while. Cushty nights in with Zoë are not the same as hammering it down at the Bird and Bastard wiv yer muckers, are they? I don't know … we all took some pills that Jason had with him … we tried to talk you out of it, but you were having none of it. It didn't seem to matter at first, but then things just got out of hand. We were wired – we all went on a sightseeing tour at three in the morning, and that's when you got arrested. It was all proper funny until you threw your lager over the police. They didn't like that, especially as your strides were round your ankles at the time."

"I know all this," I say, as the air stewards begin their life jacket demonstration and we quieten our voices under the instructions one of them is banging out.

"Yeah, well … what did you think this morning? That they'd just let you go? 'Off you go, my son, on your way and we won't say no more about it'? Nah, they wanted to make an example of you – you were going down, and down for a fair stretch too, according to that Farrington-Double-Barrel-Whatsisface … Brown …"

The air stewardesses are packing away their demonstration life jackets and taking their seats for take-off. The plane is moving cautiously to the runway, and I think I've worked out what's coming next. "You met Farrington-Brown?" I prompt.

"Yeah, we went to see him, we needed to know how you were and what we could do to help … what a tosser. He couldn't have given a flying one about you, mate. He just wanted all the paperwork sorted out so that he could get back to his gin and tonic or whatever. Anyway, last night, after the game, Stinson gave him that. Told him that it was a case of mistaken identity, that it was him that was responsible for everything and they had the wrong man."

"But the police – they wouldn't have believed him, they must have known it was me?"

"Oh yeah, they had you bang to rights, son – red handed and bare arsed. But when Stinson says he'll sign a confession, in English and Greek, well … I think they just thought it would be easier. They get their drunken Brit arrest quota, and there are no complications further down the line. Go to Jail, go directly to Jail … do not pass 'Go', do not collect two hundred nicker, and especially do not launch an appeal where you say you didn't know what you were signing.

"So, we told Stinson it wasn't right. It's one thing sticking up for your mates, but a few years in a Greek Prison to get you off the hook? That's above and beyond that is. But Stinson, he just said, 'Nah – I got to see the game; he gets to marry Zoë. I think I've got the best of the deal.'"

We all tried to smile, but couldn't. That would be a line that would sound great in a Best Man's speech, but it won't be allowed to see the light of day. My mind turned to the wedding and Football Tone, as if reading my thoughts, tries to reassure me.

"Don't worry, son. Remember, what 'appens in Athens, stays in Athens."

Well, that includes Stinson, I think, as the plane finishes its ascent and the seat belt signs ping off. Staying for a lot longer than we all thought.

Post-Match Press Conference

Thanks for getting all the way to the end of 'Studs Up'. It would be great if you would like my Facebook page, here:

www.facebook.com/davidlindsayauthor

The only way that I will get more people to read this book is if you write a review for me. There are many review sites, but Amazon is the one that matters most. I'd really recommend that you do this, otherwise some people with a monkfish may visit you.

And you can also read my novel, FAT Girlfriend, found on Amazon, of course. All the proceeds go to Georgia's Children of the World Charity.

About the Author

David Lindsay was born; let's get that misconception cleared up straight away. He was bullied at school, mainly by the teachers it has to be said, and with more than a little justification. In order to save time, the phrase 'Could do better' was pre-printed against every subject on his school reports. This with the exception of Religious Education, where it would normally read 'Worrying'.

He was dumped onto the economic scrap heap of recession hit 1980s Great Britain with only seven 'O Levels' and two 'A Levels'. A child of the Thatcher dictatorship years, a repressed, guilt-laden and failed Catholic, still suffering from premature milk withdrawal, near-starving and penniless, he took the only option available to so many of that desperate, pitiful generation who had neither good looks nor quick wit to fall back on. He took the shameful and degrading step of working for NatWest Bank. His mother never forgave him; her account was with The Midland.

With rock superstardom and football mediocrity ruled out at an early age, the interminable boredom soon had him looking for a different career and, unable to find one, he instead worked in a car showroom for nine years. But the lure of a safe, boring job that paid lots of money and contributed heavily to a final salary pension was never far away – everybody has to have a dream – and he managed to wheedle his way back into the finance industry, working for a succession of large corporate lenders.

It was during this period that he started to write his novel FAT Girlfriend, eventually published in 2014. Okay, self-published. Whilst his bosses admired his long hours, presuming he was working on extrapolation of current sales figures or funding ratios*, he was actually planning his escape from the day-to-day blandness of office life. Seeing himself as a character in The Great Escape, working diligently on a book rather than a tunnel, right under the noses of the prison guards, he went to bed dreaming of what he'd say in television interviews once he'd outsold The Bible.

Today, translated into seventy three different languages**, FAT Girlfriend has made him a household name – just not in as many households as he'd like. Three, actually, and sometimes his dad gets him mixed up with one of his other brothers. He was immediately sacked from his job on publication.

The collection of short, and not so short, stories collectively known as 'Studs Up' was published in 2016. This will no doubt lead to another 'redundancy' when his bosses find out what he's really been working on.

* He still doesn't know what this means, despite being able to talk for hours about it.

** This isn't true. It hasn't even been translated into English yet.

Photo credit: AJ Ward

29957667R00118

Printed in Great
Britain
by Amazon